BECCA SWIMS ON

BECCA SWIMS ON

KATE BREITFELLER

Copyright © 2022 by Kate Breitfeller

All rights reserved.

No part of this book may be reproduced in any form or by any electronic or mechanical means, including information storage and retrieval systems, without written permission from the author, except for the use of brief quotations in a book review.

All characters and events in this publication, other than those in the clear public domain, are fictitious and any resemblance to real persons, living or dead, is purely coincidental.

ISBN: 978-1-7353048-5-4

EBook ISBN: 978-1-7353048-4-7

Cover Art: Yummy Book Covers

For All of the Dreamers—It's never too late!

1

Amelia hissed at the rooster under their table, shooing it away with her foot. Becca tucked her feet under her chair and eyed the animal, now glaring balefully at the older woman.

"If that thing attacks me because you made it mad, I'm not going to be happy." Becca arched a brow at the older woman.

"Pfft! Don't be such a baby. These chickens are more domesticated than most of the tourists round here." She kicked her foot out again. "I wish these idiots would stop feeding them though. Chickens used to just wander around and now they are worse than seagulls. Stupid tourists."

A couple, enjoying their lunch under the tropical canopy of the restaurant, shot a startled glance at the women.

"Shh. They can hear you."

Amelia shrugged and waved her hand at them. "No offense."

Becca shook her head at the couple's expressions. There was no use in chastising Amelia. Her friend meant no harm. She simply missed the days when Key West was a small town with dirt roads.

"Well, the tourists are how I pay my bills… so play nice."

But Amelia wasn't paying attention. Her focus had shifted to the man holding a guitar a dozen feet away from them. He had taken a seat on a stool under the sheet metal overhang that the restaurant used as a stage for their live music.

"He's cute. I don't think I've seen him before."

"Me, either."

The man noticed their interest and shook his shaggy, blond hair away from his face with a cocky grin. Becca gave a polite smile back, but Amelia's eyes gleamed.

Becca recognized the expression. "Don't start."

Amelia opened her eyes wide. "I didn't say anything. I just said he was cute."

"Uh huh." Becca took another bite of her fish, refusing to glance the man's way again as he strummed a chord.

"You don't think he's cute?"

Becca chewed her food, ignoring her friend.

"He looks like he could be a good time."

Becca caught the wink Amelia threw the man, and he rewarded them both by firing a finger gun, not missing a beat in his song.

Becca's cheeks heated. The couple Amelia had insulted before was now openly staring at them.

"No, thanks."

"Okay, okay. Finger guns aren't great, but he might be good for an evening or two."

"He's too young for you."

"Not for me, honey." Amelia scowled. "It wouldn't kill you to go out with some guy and have a good time."

"No, thanks." Becca repeated, keeping her tone mild. She and Amelia had had this conversation more times than Becca liked. Amelia wanted her to date, to in Amelia's words, "get back up on the horse," but Becca was done dating. She'd proven to herself over the last year that she had terrible judgment in men.

"So?" Amelia crossed her arms over her chest. "You're just going to be alone forever?"

"I'm not alone. I have you, Dana, and Rey... not to mention my son... I am perfectly happy with my life now, exactly as it is. Working for Dana has given me an incredible opportunity to not only display my paintings but to talk about art all day. Everything is perfect," she finished, adding a toothy smile for emphasis. Becca realized she may have overdone the enthusiasm, but the last thing she wanted right now was a lecture from Amelia on dating.

Amelia's face softened at the mention of Becca's son. "How *is* Owen doing? Is he getting settled in over there? Found all the closest pubs?" Amelia's belly laugh rang out drawing even more attention their way, but it didn't bother Becca.

Only two weeks ago, Becca and Rey had taken Owen to the Orlando Airport, bound for a semester abroad in London. Her son and the FBI agent had grown close over the last several months, and Becca was grateful for his support. When Rey had given Owen the standard half-hug, half-backslap thing men do, she had struggled to hold back tears. So much had changed in the last few years. In many ways for the better, but it was still hard knowing he was so far away.

After the fiasco in the Bahamas the previous August, Owen had gone back to their hometown, Sun Coast, Florida, to start his sophomore year of college and attempt to put his problems behind him. The semester had started well, and Owen seemed to adjust to being a normal twenty-year-old again.

Six months had passed and Becca's blood still boiled when she remembered how her ex-husband, Jake, and his new wife, Nicole, had used Owen as a cover for their money laundering operation. In the span of 24-hours, Owen had learned not only was he implicated in a massive fraud, but he had also become the prime murder suspect when Jake's business partner was murdered at Jake and Nicole's wedding.

Amelia's hand waved in front of her face. Becca blinked rapidly, coming back to the moment. "Sorry."

"It's fine. So?"

"Actually, this is the happiest he's been in a long time. It's only been a couple of weeks, but he has called me almost every day, which is definitely an improvement. He seems to really like his roommates and classes so far." Becca thought for a moment. "I think this fresh start is the best thing for him."

Amelia nodded, but if Becca had thought her sidebar about Owen would distract her friend, she was wrong. "So, not only is he starting his own life, he's thriving in a completely different country. Hmm, I wonder what lesson we should all take from that?"

"It's only for the semester." Becca frowned.

"You know what I mean. He's not here." She tapped her finger on the table. "And, while Dana and I both love you, we're not going to give you the same kind of attention I'm talking about." She pursed her lips. "Well, Dana might. Sometimes I think she'd jump on anything that smiled at her, but last I checked, you were strictly into men." Amelia's eyes lit up. "But if you are open, I might have some ideas…"

"Sorry to disappoint you, but still heterosexual."

"I'm not sure you can use 'sexual' as any sort of qualifier about yourself."

Becca scowled. "Why are you so hung up on me needing a man in my life? Been there, done that… and it ended horribly each time. I think if nothing else, I've learned that I'm a lot happier on my own."

She ruthlessly silenced the voice in her head that whispered, you were very happy with Harry. The happiness at the time didn't make up for the pain that came later.

Amelia smiled sadly, as if she could read Becca's thoughts. She reached out and patted her hand. "Just so you remember, you aren't on your own. You will always have me."

Becca picked up her glass and took a drink. Her appetite had disappeared. "Tell me about this friend you are taking me to meet. Mrs. Clarke?"

Amelia's eyes narrowed at the abrupt change of subject. "Miss Helen? You'll love her. They don't make them like her anymore."

"What does that mean?"

"You'll see. She's also got some pretty pictures I think you will like… might help inspire you for your event."

Becca grimaced. She and Dana were hosting an art workshop at the gallery for a charity they'd become involved with. Art for Kids, was a program aimed at exposing at-risk kids in South Florida to art. Becca was excited to host, but so far she had drawn a complete blank on what her theme should be.

"Gee, thanks for reminding me. This conversation has been *so* pleasant. Thanks again for inviting me," Becca drawled. "Let's see, we've covered my messed-up family, lack of love life, and my looming deadline."

Amelia's laugh rang out. "Anytime, honey. Anytime."

2

After leaving the restaurant, Becca was surprised that they continued down Duval Street instead of turning onto one of the side roads that led to the more residential areas of Key West.

"Where are we going? I thought we were going straight to your friend's house?"

"We are."

"Is she in one of the new condos?" It wasn't unheard of for some of the transplants to buy second homes in condo resorts, but Becca had definitely gotten the impression that this friend was someone Amelia knew from her younger days.

Amelia smiled mysteriously, catching the skirt of her purple kaftan when it billowed around her in the winter breeze. "You'll see."

Becca rolled her eyes but let it go. Amelia moved at her own pace, the result of a lifetime living on island time. They stopped in front of a beautiful, old home near Whitehead Street, and Becca's mouth dropped open.

Amelia spread her arms wide. "Ta da!"

"You're kidding, right? Your friend lives here?"

"Yep, moved in after she got married in 1946."

"1946? How old is she?" Becca was starting to worry that they were intruding on an invalid.

"She'll be ninety-five on her next birthday. I wanted to bring you here before she leaves."

"Oh." Becca's voice was subdued.

"She's not dying. Well, I mean she is... but she's moving out of the house. It's just too much for the family to maintain, and with the property market what it is, she figured she should liquidate before she goes to make it easier on the heirs. Her brain is still razor sharp. It's just her body that can't keep up anymore."

That made sense. Real estate in Key West had risen astronomically. It took almost all of Becca's savings to purchase her tiny cottage. A home of this size, so close to Duval Street, was probably worth millions. Becca was excited to see the interior of the house she had passed so many times. She had always assumed that the large, white house with the two-story wrap-around verandas was owned by the historical society like most of the other older homes on the island.

As they entered through the white picket gate, Becca ducked under the Spanish Moss dangling from a giant banyan tree taking up most of the front garden. Roots from the tree had pushed up the cement front walk, and now, up close, Becca could see that the woodwork needed a fresh coat of paint and there were telltale signs of rot on the gingerbread trim. Even while marveling at the beautiful architecture of the old home, she couldn't imagine what the upkeep on a house like this would be in the tropics.

Thankfully, the steps leading to the porch seemed solid. When they reached the front door, Becca pointed silently to the louvered windows propped open.

Amelia chuckled. "They put in central air back in the '80s, but Helen prefers to let the trade winds cool the house. She says it's quieter."

Becca made a face. She was a big fan of modern air conditioning, particularly in this climate. But on a day like today when the temperature was a nearly perfect seventy-two degrees, she could understand why Amelia's friend enjoyed the breeze.

"She's a different generation. She spent most of her life here without it." Amelia shrugged at Becca's response.

A man, slightly older than Becca, yanked the door open with a sour expression before they had a chance to knock. "Mrs. Jordan."

Becca's eyes widened in surprise. She had never heard anyone refer to Amelia by her formal surname. Everyone on the island either called her Amelia or Miss Amelia, depending on their age. However, it wasn't just his use of her name that startled Becca. It was his openly unwelcome tone of voice. Becca glanced at Amelia with a what's-going-on look. Amelia said they were invited, but it wouldn't be the first time Amelia played fast and loose with what Becca thought of as basic polite interaction.

"Hello, Robert. It's been a long time since I've seen you on the island. I'm sure Miss Helen is glad to see you." Amelia displayed an enigmatic smile, but her voice had a challenging edge.

The man shoved his hands into the pockets of his khaki pants and glared at the women. "I visit my great-aunt as often as I'm able."

"Hmm, I'm sure she's grateful you found the time… especially now, when she's getting her affairs in order and divvying up her collection."

Robert's chest puffed out underneath his pink golf shirt at Amelia's not-so-subtle implication, and his eyes narrowed to tiny slits. "She's in the solarium."

Without another word, he spun on his heel and climbed the heavy, wooden staircase to the second floor. Becca's eyes tracked him as he made his way across the open catwalk and entered a door above them.

"What the heck was that about?" Becca's eyebrows were practically in her hairline.

"I just like to prick that giant balloon of an ego he has," she said with a dismissive wave. Casting a final glance upstairs, Amelia led the way toward the back of the house.

It was obvious she had been there before as she strode confidently over the woven rush mats covering the scarred pine floor. Becca trailed her fingers over the wooden cutwork of the banister, her eyes following the pattern up until it reached a central carving depicting a sailing ship. She wished Amelia hadn't gone so quickly. She wanted to take in all the details of the foyer. Framed photos of people in fashions that spanned at least ten decades covered the wood slat walls.

"Come on, there'll be plenty of time to explore after our visit." Amelia smiled at her knowingly from where she had stopped.

Becca tore her eyes away from an antique ship-in-a-bottle. "I'm coming. This place is amazing!"

"You haven't seen anything yet."

In the solarium, they found a tiny woman seated in a high-backed rattan chair. A young male attendant wearing scrubs sat nearby, quietly reading to her. Becca was curious, particularly after walking through her time capsule of a home. All Amelia had said to her about her friend Helen was that she was a staple around Key West until age had left her almost homebound. The only other tidbits Amelia had given her on the walk over were that Helen had married into an old Key West family and that Becca would love her.

Stepping into the room, they could finally make out the young man's words. "Lavinia put a hand to her bosom. Would Rafe come for her? Her heart beat like butterflies..."

"Melie!" the older woman cried, interrupting the man's reading.

Becca bit the inside of her lip and tried to keep from laughing.

What the heck are they reading?

With a grin, Amelia stepped forward, grasping the woman's hands where they rested in her lap, before kissing her on her wrinkled cheeks. "Good afternoon, Miss Helen."

The young health care worker rose to his feet, marking their place in the book with an expression of relief. "We can pick this up tomorrow, Mrs. Clarke?"

The elderly woman's lips lifted in a mischievous smile. "Of course, Jason. I can't wait to find out if Rafe will arrive in time."

Jason's face blanched, and he murmured something about getting them some lemonade before disappearing back into the house.

"Are you torturing that boy, Miss Helen?" Amelia asked dryly.

Helen adopted a prim expression, but her eyes twinkled before she winked at Amelia and Becca. "I shouldn't, I know. But fun's hard to come by these days."

Amelia gave Helen a fond smile and picked up the book the young man had left with the cover face down. With a snort of laughter, she turned the book so that Becca could see the cover.

Becca's eyes rounded at the image of a bare-chested, muscular man dressed as a pirate with one arm around a scantily clad woman whose breasts were in danger of falling out of the dress she wore. The title *A Pirate's Booty* was emblazoned in crimson script across the top. Becca smiled appreciatively at the elderly woman, who remained unfazed by their reaction to her choice of reading material.

"You're aware, you can't make that poor boy read this out loud to you, right? There are laws against that kind of thing now."

"Don't squawk at me, girl." Helen scowled, her voice reedy but strong. "I don't make him read the good bits. My parts may not all work so well anymore, but my imagination does just fine. Besides, when I fell asleep in my chair the other day, I woke up and caught him reading ahead." She chortled at the memory.

Becca lost the battle, and a giggle leaked out. Helen's penchant for romance novels was one thing, but calling Amelia 'girl'...

"Never mind that. Who is this young woman?"

"It's been a long time since anyone has called me that, but I'll take it." Becca smiled.

"Bah, you're practically a baby." Miss Helen lifted her hand. "You two take a seat. I'm getting a crick looking up at you." Amelia and Becca took seats on the wicker settee Miss Helen indicated, as Jason returned with a pitcher of lemonade and three glasses on a tray. Amelia poured and passed the glasses to the women.

"So, you're Melie's artist friend... Betsy?"

"Becca."

Helen waved her hand again. "That's right. Thank goodness, too. Betsy is a wretched name. Never met one that wasn't a tart." Becca choked on her lemonade. "There was one here in the '50s that stalked those poor boys over at the Navy yard."

Becca's mouth fell open in delight, a grin stretching across her face.

"I told you, you'd like her." Amelia spoke quietly then repeated it louder so that Helen could hear them.

The two older women chatted for a few minutes, catching up on local gossip. When the elderly woman asked, Becca shared a bit of her own story in response to the questions. The conversation drifted toward people long gone and names Becca didn't recognize. Her eyes began to wander around the solarium. Several potted plants were scattered about the room as well as unusual knickknacks set on the Victorian-looking occasional tables. One of the decorations particularly grabbed her attention. A dark, wooden, Christian cross approximately two feet tall seemed out of place in the room. It sat on a table in the corner, but even without direct light, Becca caught the glint of what remained of the gold leaf decorating it.

"Ugly old thing, isn't it?" Miss Helen had noticed where her attention lay.

Becca nodded politely. It was hard to make out the details from where she sat, but it appeared to be a basic, wooden cross, heavy but unremarkable.

"Go on. Get a closer look at it."

Amelia nodded at her, and Becca dutifully went over to inspect it. She hadn't actually been *that* interested, but she wanted to give it an appropriate amount of attention so that she didn't hurt her host's feelings.

Becca squinted, leaning closer. "It's definitely unusual. I don't think I would call it ugly." She flashed a smile at the woman avidly watching her. "I've never seen a religious item decorated quite like it." Becca had studied art in college and she was aware that the foliage and vegetables depicted on the cross were not the norm for religious art. "Do you mind if I shine a light on it?" Becca held up her phone.

"Just bring it into the sunlight. You aren't going to hurt it. That thing's been on more adventures than any of us."

Peeking back over her shoulder to be sure the woman was serious, Becca lifted the cross—surprisingly light for its size—and carried it to where the women were seated in front of the large windows.

"My husband's family is overly attached to the thing." Miss Helen sniffed. "I've never cared for it myself, but it's one of those family heirlooms that everyone reveres, but no one knows where it came from." She chuckled. "And you feel terribly guilty for getting rid of. I've dropped it, *accidentally* of course, a few times, but the darn thing wouldn't break."

Becca listened to the story while inspecting the cross. There was nothing particularly remarkable about it. It had clearly darkened with age, but Becca suspected with careful cleaning the flecks of gold leaf along with the red and green paint she could still see might reveal a more detailed painting. Currently, all she could make out were olive green vines, what appeared to be gourds and… corn? Becca's brows drew together.

How odd.

"The way the story goes, Frank's—that's my husband—grandmother even wrapped it up in a bedspread and took it with them when they fled to higher ground during the hurricane in 1909."

Becca eyed the cross dubiously. It didn't appear to be worth risking your life for, but perhaps the grandmother had been a religious woman. "It stayed in Miami for the longest time until my mother-in-law died, and then it ended up back here. I would have been happy to get rid of it years ago, but Frank insisted it always be displayed."

"I never knew your husband was religious!" Amelia sounded surprised.

"He wasn't." Miss Helen's voice was matter of fact. "Family superstition and all that. I swear, you see this house and it's like no one ever threw anything away."

"Amelia said this was your husband's family home. It's amazing these old houses are still standing after all these years."

"Captain Clarke was originally from the Bahamas. He relocated to Key West like many of the salvagers that immigrated in the 1820s. The settlers used what they learned about living in the Caribbean combined with what they knew about ship building and built these houses to last." Miss Helen's voice was proud. "After the Captain died… that portrait in the front room is him. Looks a bit like my Frank, I think." She exchanged a knowing look with Amelia. "Key West was a lucrative place to be in those days."

When Becca looked confused, Amelia explained. "After the United States Government cracked down on the salvage companies, Key West became the richest city in America for a while."

"I've never heard that. How?"

"The shoals off our coast make this a wrecker's paradise. In the early 19th century, the Bahamian wreckers would sail over to salvage but then take their loot back to the Bahamas. Eventually, the U.S. Government wanted a taste of that tax money and so they built the Customs House. Any wreck salvaged off the Keys had to be brought through the Key West auction houses. With the auction revenue registered with the government, they knew exactly how much tax to collect." Cynicism oozed through every word.

Miss Helen nodded. "Captain Clarke was better than most. He had a whole fleet of schooners that served as wreckers. He built the family fortune. And when that finally dried up, the family moved to marine sponging. They hired a bunch of Greek fisherman to dive down and harvest from the sponge beds—then they got in on all the land speculation up north. It's a shame really that the family left, but I understand from my mother-in-law that, after the storm in 1935, the island wasn't livable. That's why Frank grew up in Miami."

Her eyes grew misty with a faraway expression. "The Navy stationed Frank here during the war. It's how we met. I was a nurse at the Naval Air Station." She smiled. "Oh, we had so much fun, us girls in the barracks together. Then I met Frank. He was very proud of his family, and I was proud to be with him. He wanted to bring life back to his family's home… and we did." Miss Helen's eyes welled, a lone tear escaping. She dabbed at it self-consciously with a tissue.

Amelia patted the woman's hand as she collected herself. "Actually, Miss Helen, that's a little bit of the reason I wanted to bring Becca to the house today. I wanted to show her your beautiful art collection."

Helen pressed the tissue to her eyes and cleared her throat. "Just in time, too. Robert is finalizing all the paperwork for its donation to an art museum in Coral Gables."

Amelia eyes twinkled when they met Becca's gaze. "Miss Helen has an incredible collection of art. I think you'll like it."

The elderly woman picked up a small device that looked suspiciously like a garage door opener and pressed a button. A few moments later, Jason reappeared in the doorway. "Could you tell Robert I'd like him to open up our little collection for my friends?"

With a nod and smile, Jason disappeared again. Miss Helen continued with her story. "They bought most of it before I married into the family, but I'm proud to say we've never had to sell any of the pieces. The Clarkes have always been good with money. Sponging wasn't as profitable as the former family business, but they had the foresight to go north and get in on the Miami land boom." Helen winked at Becca. "And with the money the family amassed, it kept us nicely. There are a couple of pictures up there that Frank and I picked up along the way. He was a big fan of those New York artists."

Becca hadn't known what to expect when Robert led them begrudgingly up the wooden staircase. After seeing the other eclectic items in the home, Amelia's simmering excitement made it clear that whatever lay behind the door was exciting.

"Don't touch anything," Robert admonished before swinging the door open.

Nothing of what she had seen so far in the old home could have prepared Becca for the sight that met her. A long, high-ceilinged room stretched out from the doorway to the far wall of the house. Windows were covered with heavy blackout curtains, and a low whir drew her attention to several dehumidifier machines positioned throughout the room. Mouth agape, she took in the rows of paintings and professionally-matted photographs that lined the walls. Several pedestals stood in the center space, topped with both sculpture and decorative arts.

"They converted the attic space in the late 1960s. Miss Helen and her husband wanted to have somewhere they could enjoy their collection. Once Frank's parents passed, they brought the majority of the art from the family home in Miami," Amelia explained as she paced into the room.

"Not all of it. Just the ones they loved." Robert corrected her from his position by the door.

Becca wondered if the nasty look on his face was a permanent affliction.

"You don't need to stay if you have better things to do," Amelia informed him with a saccharine sweet voice.

Robert didn't even attempt to smile. "I'll stay. This collection is worth a lot of money. I can't leave it with every random person who swoops in on my aunt."

Amelia's lips tightened, but she held her tongue. Becca had lost interest in their squabble and instead stood dumbstruck in front of one of the paintings. "This is…" She looked with wide eyes at Amelia. "This is a Picasso, isn't it?"

Amelia grinned; Robert's presence forgotten. "It's crazy, right?"

"Oh my god!" Becca turned in a circle trying to take it all in. She pointed to each unique item in turn. "O'Keefe, Pollack, Cassatt…" The more she looked, the more she found. "It's every big name of the 19th and 20th centuries," she said in wonder before turning back to Amelia. "In an attic! In Key West!" She shook her head in disbelief. "How does no one know about this?"

"Miss Helen and Frank were very low key most of their lives. Doesn't pay to advertise what you have."

Becca nodded. The security in the home didn't appear sophisticated, and she was still having a hard time accepting that these valuable pieces were just sitting here.

"Are you done yet?" Robert asked, looking at his watch. "I have a meeting with an associate, and I don't want to be late."

"Go. We don't need you here." Amelia didn't bother to look at him, but Becca could see the man's face turning purple over Amelia's shoulder.

"We can go," Becca said, hoping to avoid an argument. With one last longing look at the room, Becca left the room, Amelia humphing behind her.

Later that night, when Becca was curled up on her couch with a cup of tea and her cat, she couldn't help thinking about the Clarke collection. It was a shame that it was going to Coral Gables before the residents of Key West could get a chance to view it. An idea popped into her head, and she typed out a text to Dana.

Becca: I have a great idea for a fundraiser for Art for Kids. No travel required, lol!

The response didn't take long.

Dana: Sounds gd. On date. Talk tmrw?

Becca held her finger to the text bubble until the thumbs up icon appeared, liking the message, and put her phone away, excited for the first time in a long while.

3

"So, why are we here again?"

Becca lifted her champagne glass to hide her smile. "I told you. Dana has the flu, so I had to fill in tonight. It's an important fundraiser for the charity. Dana has put so much work into helping with this party, and I'm hosting a workshop for the kids' next event. Though I still have no idea what I'm going to do. Besides," she tried not to giggle as Rey tugged at the collar of his tuxedo again, "you look nice, and it's an open bar."

Rey grunted. "True, not sure how you convinced me to put on this rig, though."

"It's a good cause, and I told you black tie was required. You didn't have to come," she reminded him.

"I had to be up here in Miami for work anyway, or we could have driven together. Plus, you promised you'd make me wings for the game next weekend."

Becca took another sip of her drink and rolled her eyes. Rey might complain, but there was no denying he looked impressive in the formal wear. "So, I did. C'mon, I need to make the rounds and represent the gallery. You can just smile and be my handsome date."

"Right, I'm going to hit the bar first for something stronger."

Becca smiled. "All right, I'm going to head down to the water and start with those groups. I'll find you in a bit."

Rey nodded. "I'll come as soon as I get a drink. Do you want anything?"

"I'm good. I'm having a hard enough time staying upright as it is." She gestured with the half-empty flute to her high heels. "I'm out of practice."

"I like them." Rey grinned appreciatively. "See you in a few minutes."

Becca walked across the coquina patio of the mansion to the steps leading down to a large expanse of Bermuda grass and an infinity pool that disappeared into Biscayne Bay. Carefully navigating the narrow steps, she walked gingerly to a group of guests by the water's edge. Becca didn't know most of the guests, but she recognized one of the women in the group as Barbara Ellison, "Bunny" to her friends on the charity circuit.

"Becca!" The older woman greeted her warmly. Bunny was dressed head to toe in gold Versace, her silver hair cut into a fashionable bob.

"I'm sorry to interrupt, Bunny, but I wanted to come say hi. Dana was so disappointed she wasn't able to make it tonight."

Bunny made a face. "I heard she was unwell. It's a shame because I really wanted to introduce her around. There are some heavy hitters here tonight." She winked conspiratorially at Becca. The three others in the group chuckled, clearly used to Bunny's forthrightness. "Let me introduce you to my friends. I'd love for you to tell them about the work you and Dana are doing for Art for Kids.

Becca put on her best social smile. She wanted to do a good job, not just for Dana, but because Becca loved helping the at-risk kids and sharing her love of art with them. Bunny introduced her to the two young women and the older man who stood with her. The younger women were gorgeous. Their dresses were in the bandeau style, leaving little to the imagination. Allison, the redhead, had pulled the side of her long hair up in a sparkly clip that matched the diamonds on her ears and wrist. Sara, the brunette, had hair hanging free in waves almost to her waist. Becca felt a spark of jealousy at their youth and the lovely glow that came with it. However, when the older gentleman in the requisite tuxedo slid his hand down to rest on the brunette twenty-something's rear, all nostalgia disappeared.

"Allison's date is around here somewhere, but Richard here is the one you want to talk to." Bunny bestowed an expectant smile on the man, who gave a good-natured chuckle.

"It's why we are here, after all," the man murmured, but it was clear he was far more interested in his date's curves.

Becca, irritated by the man's behavior and uncomfortable that both Richard and Bunny had dismissed the two young women as unimportant, bit her tongue. She had to play their social game tonight if she wanted donations.

He finally lifted his eyes from Sara's cleavage. "Tell me about this gallery of yours, and what you do for the charity?"

Becca took a calming breath and began explaining her role and why she felt that the Art for Kids charity benefitted their South Florida community. When her friend and boss, Dana, told Becca she would need to attend the event, Becca had put together a succinct pitch, and she fully expected to repeat it several times over the evening.

She was just finishing up her practiced remarks when Allison suddenly smiled, her face lighting up. "Oh, thank god! I'm parched."

Becca felt someone walk up behind her, close enough that he brushed her arm, a glass of wine extended past her. Becca's neck tingled, and her heart jumped into her throat when she caught a whiff of cologne. Even before he spoke, she knew it was him.

"Sorry, there was a line at the bar." Harry's deep voice hit her in the chest like an axe.

Sheer will kept Becca's smile in place, and she concentrated on not letting her legs buckle beneath her.

Stay calm. Don't embarrass yourself!

The last time she heard from Harry was the day he walked out of their hotel suite at the resort in the Bahamas. Dumping her.

Becca forced herself to pull her eyes off the ground and looked in his direction, her mask securely in place. Harry had moved so that he was standing next to the striking, young redhead, his arm around her tiny waist. The stab of pain in her chest took her by surprise, followed instantly by anger at herself for caring. Harry watched her silently, his green eyes unreadable and his face blank.

Is he really going to pretend he doesn't know me?

Was he worried about his girlfriend, she wondered. The thought only fueled her anger.

"Hello, Harry. It's been a long time. You seem well."

Understatement of the century.

He is just as sexy as ever. Even more so in a tux! Dang it!

If she hadn't been doing her own examination of him, she would have missed the way his eyes heated as they took in her tight black dress. When she'd first tried on the dress borrowed from Dana, she had worried it was too tight.

"You'll be perfect, trust me. It's Miami! There will be much more revealing dresses there." Dana had laughed.

Becca was glad she had listened to her younger friend's advice.

"Oh, you know each other?" Bunny was clearly surprised.

Harry's lips remained closed, his eyes still on Becca.

"Yes, we've met," Becca finally said.

"Here you are! I've been looking for you." Rey's voice was loud, breaking the odd tension that seemed to grip the group. "Babe, I just got a call from the office. I need to go in. I'm sorry to tear you away so early."

Harry glanced to where Rey had put a proprietary hand on the small of her back. "Agent Foster." Harry's voice was glacial.

"Brennan." Rey's voice was almost jovial compared to Harry's, and Becca guessed he did it on purpose to irritate the other man. "Who would have thought we would run in to *you* here. Sorry though, no time to play catch-up." He smiled at Becca, meeting her eyes. "I need to cut our evening short."

Becca caught his lifeline. "Bunny, I'm so sorry that I need to go but when you're with the FBI…"

"I understand. And don't worry, I'll get Richard here to get his checkbook out before he leaves." Bunny smiled.

With a brief smile and a round of 'nice to meet you's,' Becca turned and began to walk back toward the mansion. Rey's hand on her back kept her moving, one foot in front of the other. When she stumbled at the first step, she was grateful he caught her elbow and tucked her hand around his arm, holding her snug against him.

"You're shaking like a leaf." His voice was laced with concern, but he kept it pitched low so only she could hear.

"Was it obvious… back there? The shaking?"

"No, I don't think so, but you'd have to be blind not to see there was something going on between the two of you."

"Good… that it wasn't obvious I mean."

Rey steered her past the crowds and back through the house, keeping hold of her hand until the valet brought his truck around. Becca clicked her seatbelt in place and closed her eyes.

"What the hell is he doing here?" Rey asked.

"No idea."

Becca folded her hands tightly in her lap, ignoring Rey when he glanced at her before returning his eyes to the road. Becca hoped the darkness hid her because at the moment she felt like she had been flayed open, every nerve raw and sensitive.

It wasn't fair, she thought. She wasn't ready to see him without warning, and she definitely hadn't been ready to see him with his arm around someone else! Becca inhaled a shuddery breath. She hadn't expected it to hurt this much.

Rey's eyes cut to her again. "Do you want to stop somewhere? Get a drink?"

Becca shook her head. "Just take me to my hotel."

"That's the first time you've seen Brennan, right?"

"Mm hmm." Tears were building and Becca didn't want to risk opening her mouth. A few more miles passed in silence, and by the time Rey pulled into the entrance of her hotel, her breathing had calmed and she was in control of herself again.

Rey drove up to the front doors, shifted his truck into park, and turned off the ignition.

Becca sighed. "You don't have to go up with me."

Rey grunted, not bothering to answer. He flashed his badge at the valet who came forward to object to Rey's parked truck and said, "I'll be less than five minutes."

Becca stayed silent until they reached the elevators. "I'm good from here." She gestured at the elevator car when the doors opened. Rey simply rolled his eyes and followed her in. Becca didn't bother to argue and pushed the button for her floor.

"Are you okay?"

"Do I not look okay?" Becca countered.

"You do now. Beautiful." He shot her a grin. "But there was a second there I thought you were going to throw up in my truck.

"I was just surprised," she groaned. "I'll have to tell Dana we left early. How am I going to explain that?" This won't be embarrassing at all, she thought. What could she say? The sight of her ex-boyfriend had so freaked her out that she left before getting the donations they needed.

After returning from the Bahamas, she and Dana had grown close. Their relationship had deepened far past the normal work friendship, and the young woman knew some of what had transpired. She, along with Amelia, had made for great break-up sidekicks during the months after Harry left her.

"Just tell her what I told that fancy lady. I had a case, and we had to leave. Dana loves me."

Becca smiled. Rey was right. Every time he visited Becca, Dana practically cooed at him. "You love it," Becca said dryly as they reached her room.

"What can I say, ladies love the badge." He gave her another grin, and she felt herself smile back. "Well, most of them anyway." Rey winked, and she rolled her eyes. But his teasing had worked, and she felt much better.

"She would eat you alive."

Rey paused as he took the key from her hand and opened her door. "Good point." After giving the room a quick once over, he stepped back to let her enter. Becca pretended she hated his overprotective ways, but secretly she loved that someone was looking out for her. It wasn't something she was used to.

For most of Becca's life, it had been necessary for her to take care of herself. Over the last several months as she spent time with Rey, he had shown her that maybe she could count on other people if she let herself. Trusting still did not come naturally to her. Her main issue was that she needed to be a better judge of *who* she could take a chance on, because her track record sucked.

Harry was the perfect example. In the end, he tried to help her by making a deal with Sean for the USB that implicated her son in a money laundering scheme. But it had come at the price of their relationship. Her life had become too complicated, and he walked away.

Rey stepped into the hall and planted his open palm against the door to hold it open. "We left early but I still get my wings, right?"

Becca smiled. "Yes."

"Excellent. Are you sure you'll be all right? I'm headed to Marathon for a case. I have some interviews I have to do, but I can bunk with a buddy here in Miami until morning, and follow you part of the way back if you want."

Rey was now based out of the Key West bureau, but he'd bought a small waterfront home on Sugar Loaf Key because he said fishing from his own dock made the commute worth it. It was only thirty minutes from Key West, which meant it wasn't difficult to meet up. At first it had been odd spending time together without some sort of mystery between them, but they had quickly fallen into a rhythm over weekend hangouts watching football. Owen had even come down a few times and stayed with Rey. Guy time, they told her. It might have hurt her feelings a little that Owen hadn't chosen to stay with her, but she was glad that Owen had Rey as a man he could count on.

There had never been a repeat of the kiss they shared in the Bahamas. By unspoken agreement, they decided they worked better as friends. Becca also suspected she hadn't done such a great job at hiding her broken heart either. Even more proof she was better off single.

Rey leaned in and pressed a kiss on her cheek before letting go of the door. "Don't forget to put the top lock on."

"Okay, Dad."

Rey grunted as Becca shut the hotel door, loudly flicking the top lock closed. She knew Rey wouldn't walk away until he heard it.

Becca undressed, hanging Dana's dress in the closet, and attempted to block out her feelings.

At least if I had to run into him, I was wearing this.

Becca remembered the flash of heat in Harry's eyes. She hoped everything she had felt seeing him again wasn't advertised across her face. Rey said it hadn't been, but he may have just been being nice.

No, Rey isn't that nice. He wouldn't miss the opportunity to make fun of me.

What was Harry even doing there? Not once in the time they had been together had they *ever* gone to a fundraiser. On the contrary, Harry had always disparaged the pretension of the

South Florida fundraising circuit, wealthy people competing with each other to prove who was the most charitable. It wasn't that Harry wasn't generous. She knew he donated heavily to the environmental causes he was so passionate about. He simply hated the hypocrisy of spending as much money on a fancy party to collect donations as the actual funds they collected.

Becca rubbed a washcloth roughly over her face, scrubbing at her makeup.

Who was that girl? She's what, twenty-five?

Becca abruptly threw down the cloth.

Nope! I am NOT doing this! It's been months! He's dated his way through the Caribbean; I saw the proof myself. I will not make a fool of myself again!

Becca thought back to the night in August, after she had returned from the Bahamas, and the awful texts she had received. An anonymous number had sent her pictures of Harry with a variety of women. In that moment, her heart had broken.

When her marriage ended, she thought she had experienced the full depths of sadness, regret, grief... but seeing Harry with those women, mere days after they had parted, had hurt in a different way. She had opened herself up to Harry, been vulnerable with him... and he had betrayed her. It was a pain she didn't think she would ever get over.

During the months that followed, Becca worked on autopilot. Jake worked out his plea agreement with the government, and every day she and Owen waited for Nicole to be arrested. She didn't have time to think about her heartbreak for too long. Becca's focus was split between her work at the gallery and the constant worry over how Owen would handle it all. Jake had only agreed to be a witness to protect Owen, and Becca was concerned that her son would hold himself responsible for his father's incarceration.

Normally the detailed information would never have been shared with them, but Rey had been on the task force investigating her ex-husband and his wealth management firm. After the hearing, Rey called, and said that if he didn't tell her what was happening, Becca would "find a way to stick her nose in and probably mess everything up." She suspected he was only half joking. He explained that after Jake testified against the Olivera cartel, they would move him to a minimum-security prison to serve out his six-year sentence.

Before she had even hung up with Rey, Owen had walked to the ocean's edge and stared toward the horizon. After a moment, he turned back and informed her he was going ahead with his plans to spend a semester abroad after all. Owen said that everything in his life had felt like it hung in limbo that fall while they waited to find out what would happen to Jake. He was ready to go where no one knew him or his family's history.

It broke her heart to think of her twenty-year-old son an ocean away, but it was probably a good idea to put some space between him and the upcoming criminal trials of everyone involved in the scheme. Now that Jake's money was frozen by the government, Owen didn't have the cushion he was used to, but she had been determined to find the money to pay for it.

Becca put on pajamas and climbed into her soft bed.

There are much more important things in my life to deal with than worrying about an old boyfriend.

Her mind flashed to her favorite painting–the turbulent ocean and the sea turtle who struggled against the current, but kept swimming.

If Petunia can do it, so can I.

4

The stack of books in her bicycle basket made maneuvering more difficult than usual. Becca had checked out more books than she needed from the library because she wanted to be sure she had all the information possible. She had always loved the library. When she was young and broke, it was the perfect way to entertain her young son for free, while her now ex-husband Jake worked long hours to get ahead. Owen loved the computer games. The computer's electronic babysitting made it possible for Becca to settle into one of the bean bags nearby to read, still able to keep an eye on her child.

It took awhile for Becca to come up with the theme for her Art for Kids workshop, but once the idea took root, she threw herself in. It occurred to her that since the kids were being brought to Key West for the weekend, it would be good to expose them to a brief history of the area, too. She noticed that the previous events that year had focused on more common topics like the Old Masters or Impressionists. Becca hoped that learning how art reflected the cultural history of an area might interest them.

Becca was pleasantly surprised to find that the library had a large selection of books on Spanish Colonial Art. She supposed she shouldn't have been. Key West had been part of the Spanish empire off and on for three hundred years. As a result, she had forgotten her basket's limits and ended up with a wobbly stack of books.

There wasn't much time before she was supposed to meet Dana and Amelia for drinks, but she was itching to open the books she had found. Her two closest friends on the island were very different but had hit it off when Becca introduced them.

Becca tucked the bike against the side of her cottage, scooped up her load of books, and climbed the little steps to the door only to be greeted by a yowling cat.

"Sorry, buddy, I know I'm late. If you're so hungry, why don't you do something about all these lizards?"

The small chameleon perched on her doorframe turned its head as if it understood her. "Sorry," she mouthed. Unlocking the door, Becca almost tripped when Furball wound her way between Becca's feet.

"If I break a leg, you're not going to get fed." The cat sniffed and trotted ahead unimpressed. Becca poured Furball's food into her bowl, and grabbed a stack of colorful sticky notes, before settling with the books at the kitchen table.

She began flipping through the art books, tagging pictures she thought might interest the kids. Spanish Colonial art is colorful, and she thought it would catch their eyes. Her brain began to whirl, imagining the palettes she would put together and what craft might be best.

Her eyes were scanning through a history section when a small painting in the margin caught her attention. She stopped to read the accompanying description detailing the Cuzco School of Art from Peru. She flipped forward a few pages and found several examples of different paintings. She wasn't familiar with that particular school of art, but the vibrant colors of vines and vegetables depicted around the edges of the religious paintings were unique. Becca hesitated looking closer at the painting staring up at her. Something about the colorful vegetation seemed familiar but she couldn't put her finger on where she would have seen it. She studied art history in college, but she didn't remember ever hearing about this 18th century Peruvian School of painting.

Becca tapped her phone to check the time. *Argh!* She needed to get changed and head out or else she would be late. Nevertheless, she found herself flipping to the next page and then... stopped dead. A glossy painting featuring a religious figure on horseback surrounded by indigenous people took up three quarters of the page. In his hand, he held a large cross aloft, and the people in the foreground were on their knees in reverence.

A tingle ran down her spine. *It couldn't be.* Becca leaned so close to the book her hair fell onto the pages. The colorful cross in the painting was incredibly similar to the one she had seen at Miss Helen's just a couple of weeks before. *How cool!* Becca grinned, picked up her phone, and snapped a picture of the painting. Becca looked forward to telling the elderly woman what she had discovered. Miss Helen may not like the piece, but surely as an art lover, she would be interested in knowing the style the cross had been done in.

Becca stood, still smiling, when her eye caught the words "lost cross" in the caption under the painting. Her mouth formed an O, and she slowly sank back down into the chair. Feverishly, she read the paragraphs that described the importance of the famous Franciscan friar, Joaquin de Santiago, the man in the painting, and the cross he carried around Latin America converting the indigenous peoples. The book continued on to explain that the man had met an untimely death in the early 1800s, when he and his party were killed by a disease that swept through their camp. Only a handful of survivors escaped, and upon arriving in Havana, they recounted what had happened to the holy man.

"The cross which had become a symbol of Santiago's fame disappeared and is presumed to be buried with the friar."

Becca squinted at the painting again. *No way!*

She shook her head.

It's impossible... still...

Becca enlarged the photo on her phone. The colors were certainly brighter than the cross in Miss Helen's conservatory but... the vegetable vines winding their way around the cross certainly looked the same.

Becca shook her head again to clear her thoughts.

Okay, imagination. You're getting carried away. You only saw it for a moment. Still, how neat would it be if it were a replica?

Becca bit her lip. What had Miss Helen said? "It's not my style, but it's Frank's family's heirloom." She'd even mentioned that her husband's grandmother had taken it with her when the family fled the flood waters of a hurricane. It was frustrating that Miss Helen didn't have any more information about it. Surely if it were actually a religious antique of significance, the family would know about it? Clearly they were collectors... it must be a replica.

Becca blew out a stream of air, a little disappointed, and then laughed.

Not enough excitement in your life lately? No smugglers or murderers around?

A shiver ran through Becca at the errant thought. What was wrong with her? Those had been terrible events, and she was acting like she missed the excitement! Rey had called her a drama magnet. Was it true? Did she seek it out more than she thought?

Becca stood suddenly. She was being ridiculous! Overthinking as usual. She left the book open on the table and rushed to her bathroom to freshen her makeup. There was no time to change now. Becca retrieved her bicycle and headed back toward Duval.

THE LIGHT WIND BLEW HER CURLS BACK AS SHE PEDALED FASTER. She was definitely going to be late, but she couldn't wait to share what she had found with Amelia. Even if the cross was just a replica, it was exciting to find out more about its origin. Unless the style had been deliberately copied, it was safe to assume that it must be at least a couple of hundred years old.

Becca coasted to a stop and tucked her bike into the alley behind the Salty Oar.

"Hey, Becca!" Cole, one of Amelia's hot, young bartenders, waved at her from the bar. The crowds were smaller this time of year, but there were still plenty of people in the bar. Other than being cleaner than when it was owned by Charlie Silverman, the bar looked much the same as it had on Becca's first night in Key West. Her eyes drifted to one of the stools, and for a brief second, she pictured her friend Evie sitting there. The memory sobered her. Evie was gone now. Murdered a year and a half ago. For the second time in an hour, Becca shook herself to banish unpleasant thoughts.

"Hey, Cole. How have you been?"

"Good, good." He flashed an unnaturally white smile her way as he passed a beer to a man sitting at the bar.

Becca scanned the room, and not seeing either of her friends, she frowned. "I was supposed to meet Amelia and Dana…"

Cole angled his head toward the back of the bar where Amelia's office was located. "She's meeting with Silverman."

Becca rolled her lips in to hide her smile. "She's with Dan… interesting." She'd noticed over the last couple of months Amelia had been spending more time with her old boyfriend. Every time Becca asked, Amelia insisted they were just friends, but Becca suspected there was more going on. Was that why she was so interested in Becca's love life? She didn't want to examine her own complicated one?

Still smiling to herself, Becca slid onto the corner stool. Cole folded his arms on the bar and leaned toward her with what she was sure was supposed to be a flirty expression. However, he was closer to her son's age than hers, and while she could objectively appreciate his (ahem) physical attributes, she was more inclined to pat him on the head than anything else. Her tastes ran more to tortured, green eyes and thick dark... *Nope! Not going there.*

"So, can I get you anything while you wait?" Cole drawled.

"Just a beer when you get a chance." Becca pulled out her phone and texted Dana.

Becca: Where are you?

She continued to stare at her phone, pretending to be engrossed with what she was looking at, until Cole finally straightened to get her the beer. Becca smothered a sigh. It wasn't Cole's fault he reminded her of another young man who had stood behind this bar, and of Evie, who had given into Josh's charm with devastating results. Becca blinked hard banishing the memory.

The office door at the back of the bar opened, and Amelia emerged brushing at her skirts. When her eyes caught Becca's, she reached up and self-consciously tucked the stray, gray hairs that had come out of the braid behind her ear. Are you serious, was Becca's first thought, as Dan appeared behind Amelia, also adjusting his clothing. Becca felt bad when her next thought was... *Ewww!*

They rounded the bar, and Dan threw Becca a smile, before continuing out the door. Amelia joined her, offering a rapid air kiss to both Becca's cheeks. She picked up Becca's beer and drained almost half the glass. Becca bit the inside of her cheek to keep a straight face.

"Sorry if I rushed you."

Amelia let out one of her signature belly laughs, completely oblivious to anyone listening. "Don't worry, honey, you didn't." She looked at the delicate watch on her wrist. "Oh, dang. I didn't realize how late I was. Guess the time got away from me." She winked at Becca.

"You're as bad as Miss Helen with her poor, home health aide!"

Amelia's eyes twinkled. "I hope so."

A wave of exotic perfume arrived milliseconds before Dana's arms looped over both their shoulders, her bangles clattering together. "I'm so sorry I'm late!"

"I just got here myself." Amelia waved her hand in the air.

Becca had been late herself, so she simply smiled. "Do you want to stay here or go someplace to get dinner?"

"Somewhere else," Dana said immediately and then winced. "I mean someplace quieter would be better."

Amelia was unbothered. "Works for me. I'm not interested in bar food… or giving it to you ladies for free."

"What about that new fusion place near Casa Marina?"

Becca's nose wrinkled. "That's a little far." She didn't love the idea of riding her bike that far across the island alone in the dark. For the most part, Key West was a safe city but still…

"I'll pay for the rideshare." Dana clasped her hands in front of her and flashed a smile, her gold and bamboo earrings clinking with her exuberance.

Becca put her hands up in surrender. "You win! I'll get my bike tomorrow. Might make me a couple minutes late for work."

Dana smirked. "I'm sure it won't be a big deal. I'm tight with your boss."

"This isn't one of your fancy places is it?" Amelia asked.

"No." Dana rolled her eyes. "Though I have to admit I don't think hemp hearts in a lavender reduction is on the menu."

Amelia humphed and then said archly, "I suppose I'll have to make do. Lucky for you, I'm in an unusually good mood."

Becca tried not to gag when Amelia winked at her *but come on....*

Anywhere other than Key West, the friends would have looked odd standing next to each other—an aging hippie in a flowing kaftan and braid, a vivacious, young woman with a platinum pixie-cut and oversized sunglasses, dressed in resort chic, and Becca, the bridge between the other two women with her simple knee-length dress and hard-to-control reddish blonde curls. As different as the women were, they had found solidarity. Each of them had faced loss in their own way and gone on to forge a life they could be proud of.

Dana arranged for the car service, and when the women slipped in, and the driver confirmed the address, Becca buried her face in her hands in anticipation of Amelia's explosion.

"You said this wasn't one of your fancy places!" Amelia sputtered as Dana clicked her seatbelt. "It's the flipping Conch House!"

"Yeah, but it's their new casual restaurant." Dana shrugged, but Becca could tell by the curve of her lips she was pleased she had tricked Amelia into going. Under normal circumstances, it would have taken wild horses to drag Amelia into The Conch House, the luxurious hotel symbolizing everything she objected to.

It wasn't the prices. Becca had learned that appearances were deceiving, and her friend Amelia had more money than anyone would suspect. However, she had a deep aversion to anything that overtly spelled wealth. Becca knew Amelia had made a good bit of money as a smuggler, along with her deceased husband, in the 1960s and 1970s, but it didn't quite account for her seemingly limitless resources. Dana came from money as well, but was estranged from her conservative, New England family. Apparently they objected to what they called her "immoral lifestyle." Which meant that Becca was the only one who would have to worry about a budget that night. Oh well, she'd stick to one drink and an appetizer. That shouldn't be too expensive.

The car pulled up to the resort, and the women got out, Amelia making a point to loudly verbalize her unhappiness.

"C'mon. Let's have a drink and hang out. It'll be fine," Becca said.

Amelia grumbled something about overpriced drinks.

"Says the woman who owns a bar on Duval Street. What's the saying about the pot and the kettle?" Dana teased and squeezed her friend's waist to take the sting out of her words.

Amelia chuckled. "Touché."

Unfortunately, once they were inside, the hostess informed them that the restaurant where they intended to eat was reservation only. Undeterred, Dana led them to the bar.

"I bet they are thirty-dollar cocktails." Amelia groused and Becca winced. She made a good income working for Dana at the gallery and selling her own art, but funding Owen's semester abroad had led to definite cost cutting.

Dana rolled her eyes. "My treat, Debbie Downer."

Amelia humphed again but Becca didn't object. She usually preferred to pay her own way, but it was either that or make an issue about her lack of finances.

5

The bar was as elegant as one would expect for the premier waterfront property on the island. Becca looked down at her white sundress and felt a pang. If she had known they were going someplace this fancy, she would have worn something nicer.

They were seated at a table next to the large windows facing out over the water. The reflection of the low votives on the table flickered on the highly polished surface. Becca turned her gaze out to the Gulf where its black expanse was dotted with a variety of lights beyond the shore. Fairy lights happily bobbed on the sailboats at anchor as they rode the small waves. However, a few of the lights were stationary, and Becca knew they must be from the larger yachts moored offshore.

Becca swallowed hard and looked away. How long would it be before the sight of a ship at anchor ceased to remind her of the magical month she had spent with Harry on his yacht last summer? *Why am I even thinking about him*, she thought angrily?

It's only because I saw him at the fundraiser last weekend.

As far as excuses went, it worked. Becca wasn't about to

admit, even to herself, that she had never really *stopped* thinking about Harry.

Desperate to distract herself, she blurted out, "I found out something really cool today."

"Oh, yeah?" Dana set down the pyramid-shaped cocktail menu she had been perusing.

Harry momentarily banished from her thoughts, Becca smiled remembering what she had potentially discovered about Miss Helen's family heirloom. "I finally settled on Spanish Colonialism for the kids' workshop, so I went to the library today to get some resources."

Before she could continue, the server appeared at the table. "Have you ladies decided?"

"Absolutely." Amelia leveled a challenging gaze at Dana. "We will have three kombucha and tequilas, please."

Wait, what?

"Speak for yourself. I'm having the hibiscus martini," Dana said.

Amelia's smile was so sweet it was frightening. "I came to your fancy bar; you can drink my drink."

Oh god! If she thinks she is punishing Dana, how awful is this going to be?

Dana's lips twisted, but she nodded at the server, who did his best to hide his relief that there wasn't going to be a girls' night brawl over the drink order.

"Kombucha and tequila?" Becca asked weakly.

"It's good for you."

"I think I read about it on *People.com*," Dana said deadpan, though a smile almost broke through at Amelia's disgusted expression. "Very trendy." Dana leaned back as the server filled their water glasses and winked at Becca.

"Can you two stop bickering long enough for me to tell you what I found out?"

Amelia and Dana exchanged an innocent glance.

"Who's bickering?" Dana asked.

"So sensitive." Amelia sipped from her water. "So, what did you find out?"

The women's teasing didn't bother Becca. She took a deep breath. "I think Miss Helen's family cross might actually be a valuable antique."

Dana frowned. "Miss Helen?"

"She's an old friend. I've known her since... well forever." Amelia shrugged. "She's a member of one of the founding families."

"Amelia introduced me a couple of weeks ago." Becca quickly filled Dana in on the meeting, and when Becca began describing the amazing art in the home, a flush spread across Dana's cheekbones and her mouth hung open.

"She has a Cassatt? A Picasso and a Pollack? Here? How did they keep that a secret? That's... that's..." The server placed the drinks in front of them, and Dana took a large gulp.

"Incredible, right?" Becca grinned remembering her own sense of wonder at first seeing the paintings in such an incongruous place.

"It's... it's... I don't know what it is." Dana stared blankly at her glass before absently picking it up and draining it. "That's not bad," she muttered.

Becca was briefly distracted. "That was what I wanted to talk to you about, actually. For a fundraiser. But then you were sick, and other stuff came up."

"Fundraiser?" Amelia asked.

"I thought we might ask Miss Helen if she would let us display some of her pieces for a fundraiser to benefit Art for Kids. I think a lot of people here would jump at the chance to see such an eclectic collection. Then, when you add in that these rare paintings were here this whole time in one of the historic houses... a house that has been continuously owned since it was built by one of the founding families... I mean the ad practically writes itself. You said yourself Miss Helen loves this community. We could do a one-night-only kind of thing and make a ton of money for the charity."

Dana's eyes gleamed. "That is a fantastic idea?" She turned to Amelia. "Do you think she would be interested?"

Amelia pursed her lips. "Possibly. Can't hurt to ask, anyway." Amelia wasn't as interested in what Becca and Dana considered a newly discovered art treasure trove because she had known about the art collection for most of her life. She zeroed in on Becca's comments from before they had gone off on the fundraising tangent. "The cross? The family heirloom? What were you saying about it?"

Becca nodded. "I'm sure it's just a replica, but it looks so much like a cross in a painting I saw today—in a library book, I mean," she clarified. "It was a painting of a Franciscan friar from the late 18th century, Santiago or something. He apparently rode thousands of miles around Central and South America converting the native people."

"Sounds about right." Amelia's lips twisted.

"Whatever you think of what the colonists did... this painting... it showed him, Santiago, on horseback holding Miss Helen's cross. Well, not her cross but one very similar."

Amelia stared at her blankly. "You don't think this cross is *actually* the one this friar carried. I love your imagination but that's nuts."

"No, of course not," Becca averred. She didn't *really* think it was the same cross, but hearing Amelia say it, in that tone, took all the wind out of her. Maybe a part of her imagined that it really *was* the original. "But the style of painting on it does seem to date it to that time period," Becca insisted. "There was an artistic tradition in Peru, the Cuzco School," She paused. "It wasn't like, a physical school. It just means a bunch of artists were doing the same thing..."

Amelia raised a hand. "I understand what a 'School of Art'

is. Just because I grew up in the Caribbean doesn't mean I was raised in a cave."

Becca's brow wrinkled. "I know. I'm sorry. I tend to get carried away." Amelia arched a brow, and Becca rushed on. "That style, the Cuzco School, it took the western technique and melded it with the South American style." Becca's voice became more animated. "Their paintings were religious, as was most of the art at the time, but what was different about the Cuzco style, is that they incorporated native plants... elaborate flowers, vines, and vegetables along the edges of all their pictures. The unconventional use of native flora is their trademark style; they were the only ones to do it."

Becca missed the look Dana and Amelia exchanged as she pulled up the photo she had taken of the library book page and thrust it across the table. Amelia wasn't interested in art beyond what looked pretty, and despite owning a gallery, Dana wasn't as interested in art as Becca was. She had once told Becca that owning an art gallery in Key West was just another way to annoy her family. "See, the same vegetables and vines are on the cross in the painting..."

"Just like those ugly gourds on Miss Helen's." Amelia inhaled sharply, and took the phone out of Becca's hand to examine at it more closely. She expanded the photo, zooming in on the friar and the cross in his hand. "It does look very similar." Her mouth softened as she looked up at Becca. "Do you think it could be the same?"

A tingle of excitement spread through Becca even while her brain told her to slow down. "If nothing else, I think someone trained in that Cuzco School decorated Miss Helen's cross. Which probably makes it valuable."

"Let me see." Amelia passed Becca's phone to Dana, who peered closely at the picture before unsuccessfully trying to zoom in further. "I've never seen Miss Helen's, but that's a unique cross."

Becca met Amelia's eyes with a smile.

"Okay, I'll give them a call and find out when is a good time to go over this week."

Becca fairly shimmied in her seat. She couldn't wait to get a better look at the cross and to tell Miss Helen what she suspected. She had so many questions she wanted to ask her. How had her husband's family come to possess it? If it was connected to the friar or the famous Peruvian School of Art, how had the story been lost? Maybe the Clarkes had family records somewhere.

Her thoughts lingered on the cross as they were served their dinner, and the topic of conversation moved on to other things.

"So, I passed Dan Silverman looking awfully self-satisfied on my way into the Salty Oar tonight?" Dana said, widening her eyes at Amelia.

The older woman placed her napkin on the empty plate in front of her.

"I would imagine he *was* in a good mood," she said slyly, and Dana trilled out a laugh.

"Are you seeing him again?" The uncharacteristic blush tracing the older woman's cheekbones startled Becca. "You are!" Becca gleefully accused.

"It's still fresh." Amelia threw her hands up. "We aren't defining it as you young people say! It's fun and we are enjoying each other's company. That's all I care about right now."

A flush of happiness filled Becca as she looked at her two friends laughing across the table. The last several months had been hard, but here she was, on the other side, and things looked...

No freaking way.

The thought had barely formed in her mind when Amelia, sitting to her left, inhaled sharply, the blood rushing from her face.

"Son of a bitch!" She was half out of her seat when Dana and Becca each caught an arm and pulled her down.

"What are you..." Dana began.

"I see him, too," Becca said in a low voice.

Dana looked between the two of them before following their gaze to two men at the bar. "What's going on?"

A tight band of anxiety constricted Becca's chest. She wanted to tear her eyes away, but at the same time she had to keep looking... to be sure. Both men were attractive and polished... almost too polished even for a luxury bar in Key West. The younger man appeared to be near Dana's age, somewhere in his early thirties. He had a thick head of glossy, black hair and was dressed in a pinstripe suit and flashy watch. He had the well-groomed appearance only the über rich exude. However, the man who captured their attention, also handsome, and dressed superbly, was much older. His dark hair was liberally sprinkled with white, and even from across the bar, Becca could see the lines around his eyes and mouth, the result of years in the sun. As they watched, the older man extended his hand, and with a loud laugh, placed it on the man opposite's forearm. Becca couldn't take her eyes off the tableau, and a hot knot of anger began to build.

How dare he come back here? After everything he did to the people of this community... Eduardo's family, Dan... Harry...

Becca forced her jaw to relax as the memories Harry had shared of his troubled childhood tumbled through her mind. She would never forget the pain in his eyes when he told her his feelings of being unwanted... rejected. Even as her blood began to boil, Amelia stood and threw a wad of cash on the table making Becca blink.

"Damn, woman! I said I'd pay." Dana gave a half laugh.

But Amelia's eyes were locked on the man at the bar. Goose-bumps rose on Becca's arms. Amelia had her own history with James Brennan, and Becca wasn't sure exactly what her friend would do, faced with the man who had faked his death for so many years after defrauding people Amelia cared about.

"Let's just go," Becca said, catching Amelia's eye. Blue eyes blazed back at her with an intensity Becca had never seen there before. The older woman's face hardened, and she stood to her full height. In that moment, for the first time in their almost two-year friendship, Becca could picture exactly how Amelia had survived in the cut-throat world of Caribbean smuggling. James Brennan must have sensed his observers because he turned his head and looked directly at them. The three women were close together, but Becca saw that it was Amelia standing by the table, that had the focus of his attention.

He tipped an imaginary hat to the older woman, before his eyes flicked briefly to Becca, and then Dana, before he returned to his companion and continued the conversation as if the women were of no consequence.

Works for me.

Becca didn't want to be on his radar, and she certainly didn't want to see an older replica of Harry's handsome face. She didn't like the way her stomach knotted as she wondered if that was what Harry would look like in a few decades.

Stupid! Stupid! Stupid! Stop thinking about him!

"Ready to go?" Becca asked, keeping her eyes from the bar.

"What? Who is it? By the looks on your faces it must be the devil."

Dana jumped in her seat when a sound that could be loosely called a laugh exploded from Amelia. Becca refused to check if James was looking at her outburst.

"More like a rat," Amelia responded. "An insignificant rat." Her eyes slid to Becca, but Becca kept her eyes on her plate.

Dana observed both of them with eyebrows almost in her hairline. "Are you going to fill me in?"

Becca's smile appeared more like a grimace. "That's Harry's

mysterious father." She gestured to Amelia. "Her ex-friend, criminal, conman, and all around bad guy."

"Ahh!" Dana nodded giving James an appraising stare. "Looks the type. Too good-looking for his own good."

Another 'too good-looking' face flashed in front of Becca's eyes, and her chest tightened painfully. "You said you'd pay for the car? I'm ready to call it a night."

6

Robert Clarke was even less enthused to see them than he was the first time Becca had visited.

"My aunt didn't mention you were coming." His upper lip curled.

"We're early but Miss Helen likes surprises. I'm sure she'll be happy to see us." Amelia glared at the man.

"We have some interesting news about one of the family pieces," Becca inserted, her voice a few shades too bright. She worried that the obvious antagonism between the two would result in Robert slamming the door in their face.

The man's faded blue eyes shifted to Becca.

"I came across some information when I was doing research for an upcoming workshop I'm hosting, and I was hoping I could take another look at the painted cross in the solarium to be sure," she trailed off, as Robert sighed and put his hand on the door as if to shut it.

"My aunt is sleeping…"

"If I'm right, the cross could actually be a very important piece of art history."

"That ugly old cross?" he scoffed, and the door began to move.

"Becca says if it's what she thinks it is, the cross could be worth a lot of money," Amelia said, correctly guessing which of the man's buttons to push. His hand froze on the door, and while it was obvious he would have preferred to shut it on them, his curiosity won, and he hesitated.

Becca, seizing the chance, rushed on. "The paint on the cross —the flowers and vegetables—it's something I had never seen before, and recently I was reading about the Cuzco School…"

"I think Miss Helen should be the first one to hear this, don't you, Robert?" Amelia arched a brow. "Seeing as how she's the owner."

Robert grunted but stepped back allowing them to enter the home. Becca saw that the foyer was full of cardboard boxes and several pictures had been removed from the wall.

Amelia took in the scene with sad eyes. "I didn't realize the move was so imminent?"

Robert's lips turned down for a second, before firming again. "My aunt isn't well. It will be easier to take care of her near my home. Miami has much better facilities."

Amelia's mouth opened to say something, then thought better of it. "Is she in the solarium?"

Robert didn't deign to answer but extended his arm indicating that they should go ahead. As they walked to the room at the back of the house, Becca's eyes roved the walls. Many of the smaller memento photos were already down, and the knick-knacks that had crowded the little tables were gone, packed away.

She felt a wave of sadness. What was it like to pack up an entire life after almost seventy-five years in one home? It had been gut wrenching to pack up her house after her divorce, and she had been thrilled to leave. She had chosen what she would take with her into the future. How did Miss Helen feel knowing that many of her items would most likely end up in a charity shop because none of her family wanted them? Becca shook herself. By all accounts, Helen had enjoyed a long life and happy marriage. Did the material things really matter? Becca immediately squashed the unexpected pang of loneliness that struck her.

I'm not lonely... I'm just... alone. It's not the same thing.

But she wasn't feeling as confident about the truth of that statement as she had been in the past. It was just the reappearance of Harry that had thrown her off. She was only a little unsettled, she lied to herself.

"Aunt Helen?" Robert called softly, bringing Becca back to the moment. Helen's attendant, Jason, stirred in his chair. It appeared he had also nodded off in the peaceful, sun-filled room. He stood and walked to where the elderly woman sat in her large rattan chair. Alerted by Amelia's soft gasp, Becca scanned the scene. It was clear that in the weeks since they had been there Helen had lost weight her frail form could barely spare. Robert's haste to move her to Miami made more sense now. It wouldn't be much longer.

"She's sleeping. We'll come back," Amelia said in a voice Becca had never heard before.

Jason gave them a bright smile, and said softly, "She'd kill me if I let her sleep through a visit." He reached out and gently jostled Miss Helen's arm. "Ma'am?"

The elderly woman stirred, opening her eyes slowly. She blinked a few times before lifting an eyebrow. "Why are you all just standing there watching me sleep? It's decidedly creepy."

A smile teased around Amelia's lips. "Sorry to wake you, but Becca found out something exciting, and we couldn't wait to share it with you."

Helen moved slightly, batting at Jason's hands when he tried to help her sit up straighter. "Bah. I'm fine. Stop fussing." Despite her protestations, she accepted the glass of water Jason pressed into her hand. She took a sip, then glared up at them. "Are you going to tell me, or do I get to guess?"

Amelia and Becca sank into the chairs nearby, while Robert stood in the doorway his arms crossed tightly across his chest.

"I think I mentioned when I was here before that I help out at an art charity."

Helen nodded.

Becca explained, "I was doing some research for our upcoming event and came across a painting of Joaquin de Santiago. He was a Franciscan friar in the 18th century, renowned for converting the indigenous peoples of North America to Christianity. The painting wasn't all that remarkable, but what caught my eye was that he was riding a donkey and holding a large cross." Becca's gaze sought out the dark wood cross sitting on the table nearby. "A cross that looks an awful lot like that one. He was famous for it.

"He carried it to each community and used it as a physical symbol of what he was teaching. Because it was such a striking piece, stories about it spread through the Americas. It was distinctive from other religious items brought from Europe because it had been made in Peru in the Cuzco style." Becca rose from her seat and bent to examine the cross closely. "The painted flowers and vegetables were unusual... I'd never seen that style before. But when I saw the painting in the book, I realized your cross has the same unique details."

Everyone's eyes were on the cross now.

"And you think that cross is the same one?" Helen didn't hide her skepticism.

"No, I mean I don't know. But it did occur to me that it might be from the same school of art in Peru... which would give it significant artistic value if not monetary."

"I thought you said it was valuable?" Robert scowled again.

"Frankly, I'm not educated enough on the subject to say, but if you found someone who was knowledgeable, they would be able to tell you if it had any monetary value. Even if it's not worth a lot of money, it would be valuable as an historical piece. The Cuzco style was mostly utilized in paintings. That's why the Santiago cross was so special. I don't think it would matter if it wasn't the original item. Just the fact that it is of the same time period could make it valuable." Becca shrugged. "Like I said, I don't know enough about it, but I wanted you to have the information in case you wanted to get your own expert."

"Do you know anything about how the family came to have it? Other than just from wrecking I mean," Amelia asked.

Helen's eyes were fixed on the cross when she shook her head slowly. "No, nothing much was ever said. But when the family moved to Miami in the 1930s, they took it with them. And they didn't take everything, so it must have held some significance to them. But my mother-in-law was a religious woman. I always just assumed that was why."

Robert strode to where Becca bent examining the cross and snatched it off the table. He inspected it closely. "The wood's so dark it's hard to make out all the paint. Could that be cleaned?"

"Possibly," Becca said. "But you'd have to find an expert restorer. Before you do anything, I'd have it checked out." She hesitated. "I called the University of Miami, and they have someone there that is qualified."

Helen's bemused gaze met Amelia's. "What do you think, Melie? Could it be true?"

"It wouldn't be the first time treasure came out of these waters. I think it's worth looking into. Becca showed me a picture of the painting, and the cross looks just like the one in the monk's hands."

"Friar," Becca corrected quietly but was ignored.

"Let me see it," Helen demanded. Robert hesitated but dutifully handed the piece to her. The cross looked huge in her frail hands, and she clearly struggled with the weight of it, letting it rest in her lap. She traced her fingers over the faintly visible vines that twined down the wood. "Wouldn't that be something?" When she looked up, her eyes were wet. "Frank would have loved this."

The cross began to tip, and Robert removed it without saying anything. Helen stared at it in his hands for a moment before saying sharply, "Get the information for the expert. I want to know everything there is about this cross before I die."

Becca blanched at her comment, but Robert nodded. "I'll take care of it."

After Becca had given Robert the name of the historian at the University of Miami, she and Amelia left. The excitement had obviously exhausted Helen, and despite the fact she had been sleeping when they arrived, her eyes were starting to drift shut again.

"I hope they find out in time," Amelia said sadly, as they walked up Whitehead Street.

Becca frowned. "Me, too. To be honest, I don't have a lot of hope they will. Checking provenance and the tests they'll need to run to determine age can take months, if not years."

"Years is one thing Miss Helen doesn't have. You didn't ask about using the collection," Amelia pointed out.

"It didn't feel like the right time. Bunny just had the event in Miami, so I doubt they would schedule one for a couple of months, anyway. I'd like to wait until they get good news about the cross. Hopefully, that will make them more inclined to do me a favor."

Amelia cast her a speculative look. "That's the most mercenary thing I've ever heard you say." Becca flushed, and Amelia grinned. "Don't get me wrong, I like it."

7

The door to the cottage swung open with a whoosh of air.

"Oops, sorry! The wind caught it," Amelia said, shutting the door behind her. Thankfully, Becca had been reloading her paint brush and not actually applying color to the canvas because she was sure that her startled jump would have ruined what she was doing.

"You almost gave me a heart attack." Becca looked at Amelia's grin suspiciously. "What's going on? What have you done?"

If anything, Amelia's smile grew wider. "You were right, honey."

"I usually am," Becca joked. "But about what specifically?"

"Miss Helen called. They got the report back from the expert you found."

Becca set the brush down. "Already? It's only been a month!" Becca called after her friend who had already started toward the kitchen. "And? Amelia! What did she say?"

"Do you have any of that risotto left from the other night?"

Becca shook her head affectionately. Amelia was enjoying

the moment. "Refrigerator, top shelf, blue top. Now, tell me what the report said!"

Becca suspected it was good news, or Amelia wouldn't be dragging it out the way she was. Amelia dropped into a kitchen chair and peeled the top off the plastic container. "They did a bunch of tests…"

Becca waved her hand in a circular motion indicating Amelia could skip that part. "I already knew that. What did they find?"

Amelia finished chewing. "Definitely 18th century, definitely Cuzco. And based on some sort of mathematical mumbo jumbo, the dimensions match how it is depicted in all the paintings of that Santiago guy."

Becca's face grew hot and her ears buzzed. Could it actually be the original cross? "Is it…"

Amelia scrunched her mouth. "That's the not-so-great part. They can't say for sure because they don't have all the details of how the Clarke family got it. I mean they think they are clear on how it came into their possession, but they aren't sure how the previous owner got it. They have an idea, but it's not documented the way the experts," Amelia huffed, "would like."

Becca nodded. "That makes sense. Without the proper provenance, there is no way of saying with one hundred percent certainty that it is the same item. Still, this is an amazing find for the historical art community! One of the books I read said that there are very few original items left from that style of art, so this is very exciting!"

"I have to admit, the documents they found and the story they pieced together were pretty cool. Miss Helen had Robert hire a genealogist and a whole bunch of other people to try to learn more about the family with the hope of understanding the whole thing better. They turned up some neat stuff. Even some stuff I didn't know about Key West's history."

When Amelia began eating again, Becca grew exasperated. "Why are you torturing me? Tell me!"

"Hold your horses. I'm getting there, but I'm also starving."

Becca snatched the container off the small table and held it over her head. "Not another bite until you tell me."

"So bossy," Amelia grouched good naturedly. "Very well. It's actually a really interesting story. They were able to trace the cross back to a Cuban planter named Rodríguez. It was listed on the manifest this planter submitted for the steamship Fairhaven in 1863. And, in true Keys fashion, what do you think happened to the steam ship?"

Becca remembered what Miss Helen had said about her husband's family history of wrecking. "It sank."

"Bingo. On its way to New Orleans, it sank in the shoals. One of Captain Clarke's crews camping out on Indian Key brought it in after rescuing the passengers."

"The wreckers could keep what they found, right?"

"Sort of. When word went out that a ship had gone down or run aground, the different wreckers would rush out to salvage it. Whoever got there first was the wreck master, basically in charge of any other salvage groups that showed up. They even built a tower on Indian Key to scan the horizon for wrecks... just so they could be the first. Okay, okay, sorry, I just thought it was interesting," Amelia said when Becca glared at her. "Anyway, after 1823, that's when the Clarke family came from the Bahamas, the United States government made the wreckers bring whatever they had recovered to the Customs House for auction. The owners could try to buy back their cargos, but sometimes the reserve was assessed at ninety percent of the value. So, essentially, whatever they wanted back was going to cost them double the original price. Obviously not everyone could afford that so the unclaimed stuff would go to auction, and they had the chance to bid on their belongings."

"They had to buy their own stuff back? That's ridiculous. It was theirs!"

"Finders keepers?" Amelia gave a belly laugh. "It was a

different time. Wrecking wasn't too far off from piracy. The Clarke family was smart. By the time that steamship went down in 1863, the Clarkes weren't just wreckers, they also owned warehouses, and one of them operated as an auctioneer. Miss Helen showed me a drawing that showed Mallory Square was jammed with these places! Explains why Key West was the richest city in America for a while."

"You saw Miss Helen again?" Becca was disappointed she hadn't been included. She would have loved to talk about the research with the elderly woman, but she also understood that Amelia was closer to her.

"It was an impromptu thing, and you were working, but I have good news for you!"

"About what?"

"I asked Miss Helen about displaying the pictures for that charity fundraiser of yours, and she thought it was a great idea! Cranky pants Robert didn't like it, but she told him to work it out with the museum in Coral Gables. I guess they are due to take possession of the art soon, so you are going to have this party of yours earlier than you thought."

"Are you serious?" Becca clasped her hands in front of her. "Oh my god, that is amazing! Thank you so much!"

"Meh, it was nothing." But the flush of color along her friend's cheeks showed she was pleased by Becca's response. "They want you to come and talk about the arrangements. Better bring Dana if you can pry her away from that new girl she's dating."

"It was a vacation fling, and the woman's already gone back to Ohio," Becca said absently. The reality of what Amelia had said was beginning to sink in, and the first tendrils of panic curled through her. A fundraiser took a lot of work. She hoped she would have enough time.

"When does the museum take the collection?"

"Not sure," Amelia said, around her bite of food, "but soon.

I'm sure Robert will tell you when you get there. He seems to have taken up permanent residence at the house. Probably afraid some other relative will swoop in and take something he wants. Miss Helen wants you to come tomorrow evening."

Becca sat in the other chair at the table, mentally cataloging all that needed to be done. Maybe she should call Bunny for advice. Dana was going to murder her for the fast timeline, but the publicity for the gallery should be worth it.

"Do you want to hear the rest of the story?"

Amelia's words brought Becca out of her reverie. "What? Oh, yes! Sorry, I'm just so excited about having the collection at the fundraiser. This is going to raise so much money!" Becca couldn't contain her grin. "Where were we? 1820s?"

"1863. The Fairhaven goes down, and Captain Clarke is the first one to the wreck."

"So, he was in charge?"

"Exactly. From the wage rosters, it looks like he had a couple of ships, and they took the majority of what was recovered and brought it back to Key West to be stored in one of his own warehouses."

"That's convenient."

"Wasn't it though?" Amelia chuckled. "Rodriguez is brought back as well with the other passengers and wants to buy back his belongings. Only problem is most of his money was in gold, and it had also gone down with the steamship. He had money in Havana and New Orleans, so he sent word for a surety of funds."

"Couldn't they just telegraph it?"

"They didn't have the telegraph in Key West yet. They weren't wired until after the Civil War. But it didn't take long for a boat to cross to Cuba. Remember, it's just ninety miles."

"He bought his things back?"

"He didn't have enough for the reserve, so his property went to auction."

"Did he lose the bid on the cross?" Becca was getting confused.

"Not so fast. This is where it gets interesting. Apparently Captain Clarke had every intention of bringing the cross to the Customs House for auction. The researcher found the paperwork filed with the Customs House. However, it wasn't part of the final auction lot paperwork. And when she looked further, she found a newspaper article describing how the plantation owner, Rodriguez, pulled a gun on the Captain."

"What?"

Amelia nodded. "He must have been desperate to get it back. The article said Captain Clarke decided at the last minute not to sell because his wife had a *vision*." Amelia made air quotes around the phrase.

Becca's brow furrowed. "A vision? About what?"

"That the cross was touched by God, and they had to keep it." Amelia shrugged. "Sounds like an exaggeration but who knows. Helen did say the family always kept it with them."

"Was that even legal? I thought you said the government made them bring everything to auction that wasn't claimed?"

Amelia set her fork down having finished the risotto. "Not really, but remember Key West was a small town full of money at this point. Captain Clarke and his family had several businesses here and most likely the connections that went with them. I'm sure money changed hands at some point. What was Rodriguez going to do?"

"Apparently try to shoot him in the street," Becca drawled. "How could their family have forgotten that story? It's sensational!"

Amelia shrugged. "A lot of time has passed and other things happened."

"It's fascinating that, even though they didn't understand why it was important, the family kept it with them."

"Seems like there must be something special about it if the

planter was willing to pull a gun in a public street to get it back. The researcher thinks all of this is more evidence that it is the original... from the painting. Keep in mind, this was less than seventy years after that Santiago guy died." Amelia stopped, and when her eyes gleamed, it was obvious the older woman had held back something. "That and the fact that when the cholera survivors of Santiago's group relocated to Cuba after his death... it was to live in religious retreat on the Rodriguez plantation."

Becca's mouth fell open in shock. "Are you serious? Whoa! Then it could actually be the real one!" She squealed in excitement. "It's sad though for the Cuban guy and his family. It must have been precious to them... and then to lose it like that."

"Don't feel too bad for him. The whole reason he was relocating to New Orleans was because he didn't want to give up his slaves in the Cuban Revolution."

Becca made a face. "Scratch that. I'm glad he lost it. So, what happens now?"

"Without provenance, it's not worth as much as Robert was hoping."

"Even so, it would be a tremendous addition to a museum. There are so few examples of the Cuzco School left."

"Well, a museum might get it. The Clarke family has decided to auction it off."

"What? Why?"

Amelia's lip curled. "After hearing about its value, the heirs are already angling for who is going to get it. Miss Helen has agreed to sell the house, and I think she's hoping if the cross is dealt with before... well, there will be less family strife if it's just a matter of dispersing money. Plus, like you said, this way either a museum or gallery will get it, and it can be protected."

The next day at lunch, Dana surprised Becca at the gallery. "What are you doing here? I thought I was on my own today?"

"After you dropped that bombshell on me last night, I've been on the phone all morning with Bunny and the rest of the Art for Kids fundraising committee." By the grimace on Dana's face, the conversations hadn't been pleasant.

"They should be happy that this opportunity dropped in their lap!"

"Pfft. I'm not sure they like anything that didn't start as their idea. They have thrown up lots of barriers which basically boil down to they won't kick in any money to help set up."

Becca frowned. "That's so dumb! But it'll work out. I don't think their flashy style of fundraising is what we want, anyway. The whole point is to raise money not have an excuse to buy another outfit."

"Yeah, I don't think they see it that way. This is how they 'give back.' " Dana made air quotes but then sighed. "I'm a little biased. This is all a little too reminiscent of my mother and grandmother."

Becca squared her shoulders. "Then let's put on an event *we* would enjoy. Let's keep it low key, in true Key West fashion. No fancy dresses, no passed hors d'oeuvres or full dinner, no DJ."

"We have to have booze. People will expect it."

"Of course, but we could just do a signature drink or something. Keep it simple." She grinned. "We happen to know someone who owns a bar. I'm sure Amelia could hook us up with her distributor and possibly even a bartender or two."

Dana paced to the middle of the main room and perused the gallery thoughtfully. "We don't have a ton of space. If we take down some of the paintings in the back two rooms and move some of the floor pieces into my office, that would free up standing room."

"And protect the pieces." Becca patted the glossy head of a giant seahorse statue. "We can put up signs at the local bars and restaurants and post on the gallery's social media. Keep it easy. There are enough people who live in Key West, not counting the tourists, who will jump at the chance to see a collection like this in person."

Dana's enthusiasm was growing. "Hell, yeah! We are going to raise a bunch of money for the kids, and those stuffy rich women can shove it."

Becca laughed. "I'm supposed to go to the Clarke's house this evening. Come with me! They should meet you, and I want you to see the pieces in person. It will help us plan. Can you get someone to cover for me?"

"I'll call Sheree," Dana said, naming one of the part-time employees. "She'll be happy for an extra shift. I'll be in the office making lists if you need anything." She wrinkled her nose. "It may not be my mother's style of fundraiser, but I'm fully aware what needs to be done from watching her all those years."

AT SIX O'CLOCK, AFTER GETTING SHEREE SET UP, DANA AND Becca walked the brief distance to the Clarke home on Whitehead. Dana turned her head in shock when Becca reached for the white gate. "*This* is the Clarke house?"

Becca smiled, remembering her own reaction the first time she realized the grand house was actually a residence. "Yup. Wait until you see the inside."

Dana pushed her bright red sunglasses up onto her head, her head swiveling, taking in everything around her. "This is awesome!"

"It really is." Becca raised her hand to knock, but the door was pulled open by Jason, his face creased with worry.

"I'm glad you're here. Mr. Clarke is not happy."

"Is he ever?" Becca bit her lip. She hadn't meant to say it out loud, but Jason didn't seem to notice as he stepped back, ushering them into the hall. The space was tight as boxes were now stacked high throughout the foyer. It was a shame Dana wouldn't get to see the house as Becca had the first time, but at the sound of raised voices coming from the back of the house, that thought disappeared replaced by concern.

They strode to the back of the house where Robert stood with his hands on his hips facing his great-aunt. Miss Helen was a shrunken figure in her chair, but her eyes snapped with an angry fire.

"I will do as I choose so long as I am still breathing, and no one will tell me different," the elderly woman said. Her words were faint, but the conviction imbued in them resonated throughout everyone in the room.

Robert's hands fell from his hips as he turned to face Becca and Dana. "This is your fault."

Becca tried to keep her face blank, furious that the man had been berating his aunt. "Miss Helen, are you alright?"

Miss Helen closed her eyes briefly, and when they opened, they were laser focused on her great-nephew. "Of course I am. Just a family squabble, nothing important. Robert, you have something for Becca?"

Robert's frustration was palpable. He reached for a folder on the table and thrust it at Becca. "This is the information you need for your *fundraiser*." Becca moved to take the folder and saw that Robert's fingers were white along their edges where they clutched the folder tightly. "I hope you understand the value we are putting in your hands. That art is irreplaceable, and if your little gallery…"

"I'm the owner of the gallery. Is there a specific problem you are concerned about?"

Robert's eyes narrowed as he took in Dana's flashing brown eyes. Becca could tell he was making the same mistake many did meeting Dana for the first time. They saw her youth and beauty and immediately dismissed her.

"Yes, as a matter of fact I do. And so does the Coral Gables Art Museum. They are extremely concerned that you don't have the proper facility or security necessary to ensure the protection of our collection."

Dana lifted one eyebrow. "I have just had a state-of-the-art security system installed. I'm sure we can accommodate any other requests the museum might have."

Becca blinked but kept her mouth shut. She wasn't sure which had her more surprised—Dana's lie about the security system or her suddenly haughty tone.

"Robert, you are being rude," Miss Helen admonished. "These are guests in my home. I've said they can use some of the paintings, and that's all there is to it. The museum can gripe, but they are the ones benefitting from this donation."

Robert pressed his lips together but seemed to accept his defeat. He released his hold on the folder. "The curator that will be in charge of transport is named Hathaway. His contact information is in there, and you should call him as soon as possible. They already have plans to open their exhibition so you need to hold your event by June 1st."

Becca's mouth opened in dismay. "That's only a month away!"

"Take it or leave it." Robert's eyes were hard, and she knew he was happy to use this as an excuse to cancel Miss Helen's generous offer.

"I was only surprised. Of course, we will be ready." Her eyes fell on the cross sitting in its normal place and took a few steps forward. "Amelia told me what your researcher found. It's an extraordinary story."

"One we may have never known if not for you," Miss Helen said.

Her words apparently were meant for Robert, because after

taking a slight breath, he grit his teeth and said, "Yes, thank you for bringing it to our attention." He didn't sound grateful, but by his great-aunt's smile, he had clearly been told to say it.

"You are so welcome." She could be just as fake as him. *Jerk.* "You've decided to auction it?"

For the first time since they arrived, Robert's face eased into a smile. "Yes, Sotheby's is including it in their June fifteenth auction."

"So soon?"

Robert cleared his throat and looked toward where Jason still hovered in the doorway. "There's no reason to wait."

"What he means is the sale needs to be completed before I kick it," Miss Helen said dryly.

"I'd love to see the collection," Dana blurted out and then turned red. "Sorry," she muttered.

"It's all right, dear. It can be hard for the young to talk about mortality, but when you get to my age, it's just a fact. I'll be happy to see my Frank again. Robert, take them up."

The change in tone had sobered everyone. Robert moved to lead Dana out of the room but stopped after a few steps and looked back at Becca. He pointed at the folder. "We've chosen the pieces you can display."

"Oh, I'd hoped..." Becca stopped when Robert's eyes narrowed. "Great! Any one of the pieces will be great."

Becca hung back as Dana and Robert left the room. "Miss Helen," she paused. She couldn't believe she was actually going to ask, but ever since she had laid eyes on the cross again she couldn't get the idea out of her head. The older woman's eyes were beginning to droop now that her great-nephew had left, and Jason gave Becca a speaking look. The argument had taken more out of the elderly woman than she had let on, and now Becca felt guilty for even asking, but... "Now that we have the story of the cross and how it came to be in Key West, I'd love to be able to include it in the exhibition."

"Absolutely not!" Robert's voice exploded from the doorway. He must have left Dana in the attic space.

"It's unique history, the ties to a ship wreck... our gallery is only a stone's throw from the Shipwreck Museum. With the religious aspect, it would be a huge draw."

"No, it's too valuable to risk."

"There's no bigger risk to the cross than the other pieces," she argued.

"Jason, a glass of water please," Miss Helen's voice was weak, and it stopped Becca dead. Therefore, she was surprised when once the aide handed her the glass the woman continued. "Robert, we never would have known the significance about the cross without this young woman. There will already be security in place for the collection..."

"It would give it more exposure... probably even drum up interest before the auction," Becca pointed out.

Robert's expression grew speculative, and when Becca felt Miss Helen's shrewd eyes on her, Becca knew the woman realized what she was doing and approved.

"I'll think about it."

Becca decided to stop while she was ahead. She gave him a smile and pressed an impromptu kiss on Miss Helen's wrinkled cheek. She wished she had met the woman earlier. A wide-eyed Dana met her at the bottom of the stairs. Becca held the gate open while her friend laid out her plans for the fundraising event.

"You realize what the first thing you need to do is, right?" Becca asked.

The red sunglasses turned her way. "Get a security system actually installed?"

"Uh huh."

8

Dana reshuffled the brochures on the front desk. "What do you think? Does it look okay?"

Becca glanced around the front room of the gallery. Dana was almost never nervous, but Becca understood that this scenario was different from their normal challenges. Becca was a little nervous, too. They weren't the largest or fanciest gallery in Key West, and the two women had spent days removing the kitschier items intended for the casual, tourist shopper. The walls still held several of Becca's paintings as well as other more expensive pieces they sold. However, there was no denying that they *were* a local gallery and not a museum. She could understand why the museum in Coral Gables wasn't happy about them having first crack at displaying the paintings.

"I think it's looks good. Besides, Miss Helen promised us. So even if the museum staff doesn't love our set-up, there's not a whole lot they can do about it without risking her donation."

Dana glanced at her watch. "They should be here any minute. I better open the champagne."

Becca smiled reassuringly at her boss but wondered if champagne in the morning was the right look for them if they wanted to be taken seriously. Becca wandered to the center of the front room and inspected the specially constructed box that the cross would rest in. She felt a twinge of nerves. Were they in over their heads? Even though they were only displaying seven items, it was an extremely valuable collection. She was the one who had pushed to have the artwork as well as the cross. If anything went wrong, it would be her fault.

The loud pop of the champagne made her jump.

"Here," Dana held out a glass. "A little liquid courage can't hurt."

"It's going to be fine." Despite her words, Becca took the glass Dana offered. Mimosas in the morning were a thing... they were just skipping the orange juice part. When they had both finished their sparkly drinks, Becca set their glasses back on the tray Dana had brought out, slightly apart from the others so that she would remember which were theirs. Becca found herself arranging and then rearranging the glasses on the tray. Dana was shifting the brochures again when the two women caught each other's eye and laughed.

A flash of a blue fabric through the glass door was their only warning before the door opened. Becca froze. A man she presumed was Dr. Hathaway entered with an irritated expression, but what shocked Becca was the attractive woman who had entered with him carrying a leather portfolio. Becca forced a smile to her lips as recognition washed over the other woman's face. *Allison.* The young redhead's smile dimmed. They hadn't exchanged words at the gala, but the tension between Becca and Harry must have been obvious to his new girlfriend. *How had Harry explained it to her?*

"Dr. Hathaway?" Dana extended her hand enthusiastically. The older gentleman looked a little out of place in dress slacks, pale blue button-down shirt, and a linen sport coat. He inspected Dana's hand as if he was considering not taking it. When he finally stuck out his hand, he gave Dana a smile that closely resembled a grimace.

"Yes, you must be Ms. Mitchell. It's nice to finally meet you in person." His tone indicated it wasn't.

"Please, call me Dana." Her voice was determinedly cheerful in contrast to the man's condescending attitude. "And this is my gallery manager, Becca Copeland. She's spearheading the arrangements for the exhibition."

"Ah, you're the one who convinced the Clarke family to display it here in Key West before it joined our permanent exhibition?"

Becca hesitated. His attitude was seriously irritating, but she didn't want to rock the boat. This exhibition was important to her, and she needed the museum's cooperation to ensure the collection was transported safely.

"I am. I think it's wonderful that Miss Helen wanted to share this experience with the community."

"Becca's also the one who discovered the significance of the Santiago cross. She recognized the artistic style," Dana cut in.

The man's eyebrows rose. "Oh? Do you specialize in Cuzco art?" He cast a dubious look around the gallery. Standing behind him, Allison sent Becca a sympathetic smile.

Don't be nice to me.

She was being petty and childish. It wasn't Allison's fault that Harry had moved on with her... but it also didn't mean Becca had to like her.

"Not at all. I came across the information by accident. I was doing research for a workshop I'm hosting for the same charity this fundraiser is benefitting. That's actually how I met Allison." Becca wasn't sure what prompted her to make the comment. Was she trying to prove that the encounter hadn't made her jealous?

The younger woman's eyes widened slightly.

Hathaway frowned. "What charity?"

"Art for Kids," Dana answered absently, looking curiously

between Becca and Allison. Dana had picked up on the uncomfortable energy between the two women. "I'm sorry, I don't think we've met before. Are you involved with the charity as well?"

"Oh, no, though from what I've learned it's a wonderful organization. Ms. Copeland and I met at a fundraising gala a couple of months ago. But I was there," her eyes flicked to Becca, "with a date."

Ouch. It shouldn't have hurt; Becca knew it was coming, and she was pretty confident she hadn't shown how much the words affected her... but still...

"The fundraising gala." Dana made a sympathetic face. "That's right. My stupid flu ruined it for you because I got you sick. But thank goodness you healed quicker than I did. I couldn't believe you were able to drive all the way back the next day. I was down for the count for days!"

Dang it! I forgot I lied about that. Maybe Allison won't...

"Were you ill? You did rush off so fast, but I thought it's because the guy you were with had a work thing or something," Allison asked, her forehead furrowed.

Dana's questioning eyes were on her, and Becca was more than grateful when she was rescued from an unexpected source.

"Ladies, perhaps you could chit chat later. We have a lot to go over, and I was hoping to get back to Miami before dark."

"Of course, let me show you around." Dana gave Dr. Hathaway and Allison a tour of the gallery, pointing out which remaining pieces would be removed for space consideration. Becca chimed in with where the refreshments would be and how they had several volunteers to stand by the works of art during the evening to protect them.

"I want them crated and on their way to the museum the same night as your event. It's bad enough they will be here overnight the night before. Regardless of what the Clarkes say, I'm not comfortable with your security system."

Dana's lips tightened. "Since you are paying for transport,

I'm sure it can be arranged. Let's go into my office to discuss the logistics."

"I'll stay out here in case we have a customer."

Dana nodded. Her friend was going to want the whole story after the museum staff left, but for now Becca had been granted a reprieve. She heaved a sigh of relief when they disappeared into Dana's office and shut the door. Becca had had enough of the man's pompous tone, and the appearance of Harry's new girlfriend made her want to scream.

Her excuse about customers was thin at best. Becca found most sales came in the afternoon after boozy lunches lowered tourists' shopping inhibitions. Suddenly people were willing to spend more than normal on a piece of art to take home as a remembrance of their vacation.

Becca cleared the tray of untouched champagne into the kitchen. With the awkwardness of their meeting, Dana had never offered the museum representatives a glass. Alone for a minute, Becca slipped out of her low heels. She wasn't used to standing in formal shoes for so long. Typically, she wore flat sandals and a sundress, but Dana had wanted them to present a more sophisticated impression, and so Becca had put on one of the last Ann Taylor structured dresses in her wardrobe.

Before she returned to the main room, she stabbed at the air conditioner. It was too hot for the heavy polyester dress, and the zipper was scratching at her. She wiggled uncomfortably wishing she could run home to change into her normal comfortable clothes.

Two steps out of the kitchen she stumbled to a stop. A familiar figure stood in front of a large painting of a sea turtle. Could she retreat before he noticed her?

"I see Petunia is doing well."

Too late.

"Thank you." At least her voice sounded normal.

He turned his head slightly back toward her before facing the wall where her paintings were displayed.

"You've done a lot. You must be proud." His velvety voice made her insides clench, and her heart thudded painfully.

How many times would she see him before that stopped happening?

Becca kept her voice bland. "Yes, it came out exactly as I wanted." She squinted at his back.

Why is he here?

He turned; his brows knit together over his striking green eyes. "It's... different from how I remember."

Becca's breath caught. He was right. She had begun the painting in his villa at Turtle Bay, and he had only seen the painting that one afternoon. The memory was clear because that same night Harry told her he loved her for the first time. The next day, they had sailed to his friend Sean's resort and... her whole life changed.

Emotion flickered in his gaze before he looked away. Was he remembering that afternoon, too? Longing warred with anger. What right did he have to come here now, acting as if they were friends? He had shipped the painting of Petunia, along with the rest of her belongings, back to Key West without ever returning a single one of her texts.

She had completely reworked the painting after that. The turtle had been symbolic of where her life was at the time. Just as Petunia, the giant sea turtle, swam among the turbulent seas on canvas, Becca was determined to keep going—to follow her dreams regardless of the heartbreak threatening to drown her.

"She *is* different," Becca confirmed.

I am different.

Harry took a few steps toward where she still stood outside the door of the kitchen. Unwilling to be a sitting duck, Becca evaded him by pacing to the far end of the wall.

"Are you interested in buying some art today?" Her voice

was sharp. Memories rushed through her, and combined with her physical response to him, her temper had risen.

"Maybe."

It irked her that he seemed so calm.

He lifted a finger to indicate the large canvas with the turtle. "Is this for sale?"

"No," she snapped. Not to you, she added silently.

He looked pointedly at the price tag beneath the frame, and then cocked his head observing her. It took all of her will power not to look away. Seconds ticked by and the air seemed to thicken around them. Almost as if they had a will of their own, Becca found her feet moving her closer to him, even as Harry, compelled by the same invisible pull, closed the distance meeting her halfway. They stopped a foot apart staring at each other silently. What was it she wanted to say? His chest rose and fell rapidly. Was he as affected as she was? He was so close she could smell a faint hint of his cologne, and a low thrum pulsed through her. Why did he always have to smell so good? Harry's eyes fell to her lips, his eyes darkening, and Becca unconsciously leaned forward.

BREEP BREEP BREEP

Becca jumped back with a gasp, flushing bright red as the office door flew open.

Dana glared at the flashing emergency lights by the ceiling. "Again?"

A phone rang in the office behind Becca, and Dana dashed to answer it as Dr. Hathaway and Allison walked back into the gallery space. Becca could hear Dana telling the security monitoring company that it was another false alarm. Becca seized the distraction to get her body back under control, acutely aware of Dr. Hathaway's pinched expression of disapproval and Allison's suspicious glances between Harry and Becca. The fire alarm shut off abruptly, and Becca's heart resumed a relatively normal rhythm. Harry turned his back on the group and walked several paces away.

The alarm had saved her. She had almost done something colossally stupid, and she vowed she wouldn't let it happen again.

"Sorry about that. The older wiring in this building isn't as compatible with this new security system we've installed as we'd hoped," Dana explained. "That's the third one this week!"

"Hardly reassuring," Dr. Hathaway said darkly.

Dana sighed, "Look, the Clarkes, as well as the museum's insurance people, think it is acceptable. This exhibition has been so widely advertised by Robert Clarke no one is going to try anything. It would be impossible for them to sell the pieces."

After Miss Helen agreed to let them display the cross, it felt like Robert had made it his mission to let everyone in the Western Hemisphere know about the possible discovery of the Santiago cross in the hopes of building buzz for the auction.

Allison finally took her eyes from Harry's back. He had returned to his position by the wall and was ostensibly studying Becca's paintings, effectively removing himself from the conversation. "Dr. Hathaway, the board has gone over the setup, and while it may not be state of the art..." Her voice had an edge to it that it hadn't before. The sight of Harry with Becca had apparently cooled her previous friendliness. "They don't believe it's much of a risk because these pieces would be difficult to sell."

"The paintings are perfectly safe," Dana bit out, offended at Allison's implied insult. "Key West is covered in cameras. If someone were to break in, the police would be here momentarily, as you saw." She gestured back to her office. "And they could track the thief's every movement on the traffic cams."

Normally, Becca would have felt compelled to help defuse the situation but her brain felt like slush, and it was all the fault of the handsome man nearby. She stared blindly at the polished concrete floor.

You are pathetic, Becca! He dumps you, and the second he's back, you are ready to throw yourself at him just because he remembered a painting?

But he had remembered...

"Becca?" Dana's voice broke through her whirling thoughts, and Becca's head snapped up.

Dang it! Were they talking to her? Her cheeks heated again realizing the group was staring at her. "Um, I'm sorry..."

"I was telling them that there are no security concerns, and that you're actually dating an FBI agent, so we could always rope him in if necessary."

Dana's eyes begged Becca to play along. Her friend knew very well that she and Rey weren't together. Becca's gaze flew to Harry. The tightness in his shoulders indicated he had heard the comment about Rey. *Why does he care?*

"Hmm." Becca made noise she hoped sounded like agreement.

"That's right. We met him at the gala. Harry?" Allison chirped.

"Yes." His voice was clipped. He turned, no longer pretending he wasn't listening. "I've met Agent Foster."

Becca did *not* want to have this conversation in front of Harry, but she couldn't ignore the little thrill that coursed through her.

He's jealous. Good!

Allison's inclusion of Harry seemed to distract her boss, and he frowned darkly.

"Is this a guest of yours, Allison?"

Allison squirmed. "This is Harry Brennan... my boyfriend."

Becca didn't outwardly react, biting the inside of her cheek to keep herself from saying anything. She felt the heat of Dana's eyes but refused to look at her friend.

To Becca's dismay, Harry didn't seem to mind the label. "I happened to be in town, and since it was a Friday, I thought I could take my girl to lunch." His flirty tone was so unlike him it made Becca cringe.

That's new!

"Hmm, I suppose it's all right," Hathaway grouched. "By the time we get back to Miami, the day will just about be over anyway, and we are done here." He glared balefully around the gallery. "I'll see you on Monday, Allison."

Without a proper goodbye to either Becca or Dana, he left, leaving Becca to shift her gaze between her friend and the couple.

Now what? Am I supposed to make small talk with them? I'd rather stab myself in the eye!

Harry slipped his arm around Allison's waist and gave Dana and Becca a cool smile.

Dana openly scowled at him. "If you aren't here to purchase anything, it's probably best if you go, Harry."

Allison's mouth opened slightly in surprise, but Harry didn't flinch.

"It's nice to see you again, too, Dana." With his arm still around his girlfriend's waist he guided her to the door.

Dana turned, her mouth open to speak.

"I can't…" Becca said, her voice catching. Dana closed her mouth and pulled Becca in for a hug.

"It's okay, babe. It'll be okay."

Would it?

9

This might not be the worst day of my life, but it is definitely climbing the ranks, Becca thought. Glancing at her watch, she sighed. Still another hour until closing time. She scanned around the gallery relieved that only two couples remained browsing the rooms. Normally, Becca loved talking about the art the gallery displayed for sale, particularly her own, but today she was totally spent. She hated to admit it, but her emotions had taken a beating seeing Harry again today.

Can't pay your bills if you don't sell something.

Acknowledging the voice in her head was right, Becca evaluated the two couples. She recognized one of the couples was just window shopping, but the younger couple had been lingering in front of one of her smaller pieces for quite a while. Becca squared her shoulders, put on her friendliest smile, and approached them, determined to find the painting its new home.

Half an hour later, the happy couple was leaving, and Becca was filing their paper work away detailing where to ship the painting. The tropical sunset had found a new home in Colorado.

"They bought it?" Dana asked, coming out of her office.

"Yup," Becca said happily. The couple's enthusiasm over her

work and their excitement to add it to their home had buoyed Becca's spirits. That's what she needed to remember—her love life might be dismal, but at least her professional life had never looked better.

"I think this calls for a little celebration. There's still half a bottle of champagne left." She winked at Becca. "It's almost closing time, and I don't see any reason we shouldn't enjoy it. Good bubbles should never go to waste."

Becca grinned. "Sounds good to me." She retrieved the bottle from the little kitchen, and the two women finished the bottle while discussing the upcoming exhibition.

"Dr. Hathaway was pretty peeved that we didn't have motion sensors and indoor cameras," Becca said. She didn't blame him; the Clarke collection was valuable, and he was ultimately responsible for it.

Dana waved a hand. "It's all good. We have the security system for when we aren't here, and the street is covered by cameras, both by the city and all the other businesses around us. He's just cranky because we are getting the first publicity out of it," she said, smugly. *"I'm sure you'll do the best you can... being such a little gallery."* Dana imitated the man's pompous tone. "I wish he hadn't insisted on accompanying the pieces though. I just bet he's going to lurk over everyone's shoulders. Can't let the peasants get too close." She crossed her eyes and made a face.

Dana set down her glass and glanced at her watch. "Do you mind if I head out? You can go ahead and close up if you want. It's only ten minutes early."

"No problem. I'm just going to rearrange the wall where the sunset hung before I leave so there aren't any empty spots." Becca wished that she had another piece she could bring the next day, but with as busy as she had been, nothing was ready yet.

"Don't stay too late!" Dana called as she gathered her purse and waved from the door. Becca collected the glasses and the empty bottle, carrying them back to the kitchen where she gave the glasses a quick rinse.

"Hello?" A deep voice called from the gallery.

Damn. I should have locked the door. I can't exactly kick them out before closing.

A tall man stood with his back to her, inspecting the wall with her paintings, much as Harry had done earlier in the day. Becca stiffened. Her heart raced as recognition hit her. She had only seen the man a couple of times, but even with his back to her—his build and hair so similar to Harry's—she knew exactly who he was. Though they'd exchanged only a handful of words, it had been the most dramatic introduction of her life. She'd never met a dead man before.

For a second, she thought about pretending she didn't remember him, but it was futile. He'd seen her with Amelia a couple of months ago, and he would see through her facade.

"Mr. Brennan." Becca sucked in a breath as he turned to face her, a mischievous smile on his face. He closely resembled his son, but they weren't an exact match. There were differences, not just in structure, but in the eyes. Both Harry and his father James had gorgeous deep green eyes, but despite the smile on James's face, his eyes were cold and somehow reptilian. Even angry, Harry's eyes could never look like that.

"How can I help you?"

James Brennan's smile spread wider, showing all of his teeth. "You remember me. I'm so pleased."

His smile was meant to be disarming, and his tone oozed charm, and in that moment, she could easily see why he had been such a successful conman. But, Becca knew better. She was familiar with who this man truly was and all the horrible things he had done. She had zero desire to play whatever game brought him there.

"Of course. Are you here to buy some art?" She kept her

arms at her side, her tone unwelcoming. "I was just getting ready to close."

James's smile dimmed a bit before he upped the wattage, and Becca thought she glimpsed his back molars.

"You have several lovely items. These especially." He half-turned to indicate her paintings. Becca's lips pressed into a thin line, and she bit back what she wanted to say. Her name was clearly displayed on a metal plaque in the middle of the wall. Did he really think she was going to fall for such blatant false flattery? Instead, she opted to stay silent.

"It's nice to finally meet you. I had to leave so suddenly the last time we met." He smirked.

Becca stayed expressionless. She couldn't believe he had the nerve to bring it up!

"I'm sorry we didn't have a chance to meet again after that." He shrugged. "These things happen though, I suppose."

"Is there something I can help you with, Mr. Brennan?" She not so subtly looked at her watch.

"I just came in to admire the beauty." His stare didn't waver, and Becca began to feel uncomfortable, suddenly aware that they were alone. She wasn't about to show how much he affected her because she knew full well that was his intention.

"Well, the gallery opens again tomorrow at nine. You're welcome to come back then."

James pursed his lips. "You're having a big exhibition here in a few days?"

"That's right." Becca didn't elaborate. She wanted this conversation to be over.

"Harry mentioned it this afternoon… he was here earlier today, wasn't he?" James's voice was casual, but the intensity of his expression gave Becca the impression he was waiting for her to verify his statement.

"He came to pick up his girlfriend. She works for the museum responsible for the pieces being displayed." Becca was surprised she didn't choke on the words. Her instincts told her he was trying to see if she was upset, and she would grind her back teeth to the nub before she let on just how much it did hurt.

"Ah, the beautiful Allison."

James had met her? Becca didn't love this new evidence about how serious Harry's relationship was, and that he had so intimately let his father back into his life.

"You and my son were together quite a while weren't you?"

He took a step closer and Becca watched his face carefully.

What is his game? Is he trying to embarrass me?

"What do you want?"

His eyes widened with mock innocence. "I just wanted to see. I heard you were a talented artist, and I also wanted to see what type of woman got my son to settle down… at least for a while, anyway. Sean implied that the two of you were serious, though Celine had a different opinion," he chuckled. "But then again, I think she was jealous."

A sudden image of the photos Becca received last September of Harry on dates with a variety of women flashed in front of her.

Could Celine have sent them? James? For some unknown reason, he seems to get joy from needling me.

"Harry and I are no longer associated," she bit out. "Today was the first time I've seen him in a long time."

"I can certainly see why he came to see you. You're a beautiful woman." James reached out with one finger to tug a curl where it hung over her shoulder.

Shocked, she slapped his hand away. "Don't touch me! What the hell do you think you're doing?"

He held his hands up in surrender with a laugh. "Beautiful, fiery hair, with a temper to match. My son does seem to have a penchant for redheads."

Becca's stomach rolled.

"It's time for you to leave." She was proud her voice didn't shake giving away how much he had unnerved her. She stormed to the door and held it open. James's lips twitched, but he followed her to the door, pausing in front of her. A sharp ache stabbed in her chest. He looked so much like Harry; it was disconcerting trying to reconcile her memories of one man with the disgust she felt for the older doppelganger standing in front of her.

"I didn't mean to upset you. I'm just curious. You seemed so close when I met you in the Bahamas. And then it was just over." He snapped his fingers close to her nose, and she flinched.

"Goodbye."

James leaned toward her slightly. If he was trying to intimidate her, it was working. "I hope we meet again."

"Can't wait."

After he was gone, Becca flipped the lock with trembling fingers. Feeling exposed by the glass door, she retreated to Dana's office and sank into her chair. She covered her face with her hands and concentrated on breathing evenly. It took her several minutes before she calmed enough to leave the office. Long enough, hopefully, that James Brennan wouldn't still be lingering in the street.

Unlocking her bike from in front of the gallery, Becca ducked into the alley that ran along the side of the building. It would add a few minutes to her commute, but it was worth taking a circuitous route to avoid another run in with the man. Sure enough, when she made her way across the first intersection, she looked up the street toward Duval. A block north of her, she saw James Brennan standing on the corner.

Suddenly, Harry appeared, and James threw an arm around his shoulders. Becca exhaled the air she didn't realize she was holding. He wasn't waiting for her after all, but as she slowly pedaled home, she couldn't shake the sadness that swamped her at the sight of the two men together.

It didn't matter that she *wanted* to believe Harry was

someone different–that he was the man she had fallen in love with. The interaction with James proved Harry had gone back to whatever life it was he had led before they met. She still couldn't understand why he let his father back into his life after everything he had told her. But she was starting to doubt if anything he had told her was true.

Had it all been a lie?

10

"Is there a sign up in the local library or something?"

"What?" Becca looked up from her drink.

Amelia gestured behind where Becca sat at the bar. Becca pivoted on her stool and was impressed that she didn't fall off at the sight that greeted her. Two of her former friends, Michelle and Candice, were standing just inside the bar doorway. They seemed oblivious to the bottleneck they created by blocking the entrance. Candice's lip curled as she took in the tourists, but Michelle waved enthusiastically when she saw Becca.

"What the hell?" Becca resisted the urge to rub her eyes, certain she was hallucinating.

What in the actual…

"Incoming," Amelia muttered, as the two women made their way to the bar. Becca was immediately on alert. Michelle's squeal of excitement, before she bent to hug the still stunned Becca, didn't help. To anyone else, it would have looked like the reunion of great friends. What they wouldn't be able to see was the ten years of toxic friendship that had been capped with a scandal and betrayal that made them, at least Becca and Candice, virtual enemies. They had worked together in a hotel room last

August, when they saved themselves from Michelle's husband Brad, but Becca hadn't kept in touch with either woman. Would she ever fully escape her old life?

"Is there a mass exodus from that town or something? Something in the water?" Amelia raised her eyebrows at the women.

Michelle appeared unaware of the sudden tension their arrival had caused. "Oh my god! Becca it's *so* good to see you! I was going to call you to tell you I was here but... Surprise!"

"It's definitely a surprise." Becca mustered a weak smile.

"I saw the gallery's Instagram post about the exhibition and couldn't believe that my work is going to be displayed with Picasso! I mean can you even?" Michelle clasped her hands to her chest and pretended to swoon.

Oh, no!

It hadn't occurred to Becca that Michelle would follow the gallery on social media. Now, she thought her photographs would be displayed alongside the Clarke collection.

Michelle had a talent for photography, and several months before, Becca had talked Dana into displaying a few of her photographs for sale. She empathized with Michelle, trying to rebuild her life after her husband was arrested for murder. Becca had experienced first-hand how difficult the transition from stay-at-home mom to a career woman could be.

Becca had been lucky the day she met Amelia. The older woman effectively changed her life, and Dana had taken a chance on her. She wanted to offer the same opportunity to Michelle. Except now, Michelle thought her photographs were part of the exhibition! How was she going to tell Michelle that her photos, in addition to several other pieces, had been taken down for the night so that the Clarke collection could be displayed properly? Maybe Michelle would never know?

"I bought a ticket for the fundraiser."

There goes that hope.

"Of course," she continued, trying to hook Candice's elbow

with her arm, "Candice came for moral support because she's the best roomie ever!"

The tall blonde yanked her arm away with an irritated huff. "Why are you always touching me?"

Michelle didn't seem bothered by the rejection and giggled. "She puts on a good show, but she loves it."

The look on Candice's face made it clear that she, in fact, did *not* love it.

Wait? Did I hear that correctly?

"Roomies?" Becca slanted her eyes to Amelia, who leaned forward on the bar, not bothering to hide the fact that she was entertained. Amelia thought the suburban life Becca had lived before running away to Key West was fascinating, in a soap opera kind of way.

Michelle's eyes widened. "Oh! You didn't know?"

Uh, where exactly did she think I'd come by that info?

A major motivator behind Becca's move to Key West had been the allure of escaping the incessant gossip loop in Sun Coast.

"After everything that happened," Michelle waved her hand, "it made sense. We were both suddenly single…"

"Really, Michelle?" Candice's voice was sharp.

"It's not like Becca wasn't there." Michelle rolled her eyes. "Anyway, Candice still had some money, and I didn't…" Candice elbowed Michelle hard, a glance passing between them. "She was super sweet and invited me and the boys to move in with her."

Super sweet or guilty conscience, Becca wondered? Rey said that there was no evidence linking Candice to the investment scam that had set Brad's breakdown in motion, but Becca wasn't convinced. Where did Candice get enough money to support two households? The last time she ran in to Candice, the blonde had insinuated that at least part of the reason she was with John Raybourn was because she was broke after her divorce.

"Michelle told me about the exhibition. Sounded like a great time to get away."

Candice's words brought Becca back to the immediate problem. She needed to tell Michelle that her pictures wouldn't be displayed.

Before she got a chance, Michelle said, "I'm going to go to the bathroom. Will you order me something, Candice?" She took a few steps then turned back with a big smile. "Where is it?" Amelia pointed to the back of the Salty Oar. "Okey dokey! Back in a sec."

Amelia watched her go. "Fascinating."

Becca turned her attention to Candice who shrugged. "She's a little high strung lately."

"You drove all the way down here with her just to see an art exhibition?" Becca's voice dripped with doubt. She'd never known Candice to do anything that wouldn't benefit her.

Candice grimaced and leaned closer. "Honestly, I had to get her out of town. She's been on edge ever since Brad's trial. It was a foregone conclusion. I mean the jerk held us at gunpoint after all, but I think hearing him plead guilty, and then realizing their assets were still frozen because of the federal case, she kind of..." Candice twirled her finger next to her temple. "Lost it. It was starting to affect her kids."

Understandable, Becca thought. Michelle's entire life had been turned upside down. However, she was surprised by Candice's actions. Had everything the three women survived led Candice to actually make some changes in her life? Had she decided to not be such a selfish bitch all the time?

"So, I thought we'll go see her little photos, have a couple of days with boat drinks, and meet some hot guys."

Maybe not.

"Then there's the fact that she kind of got herself and her sons kicked out of Three Palms," Candice blithely concluded.

Becca's brow furrowed. Three Palms was the exclusive

private academy all of their children had attended, and it wasn't cheap. Was Candice paying the school fees, too?

"What happened? I'm surprised the boys were still enrolled. The Three Palms I remember was allergic to scandal."

Candice's mouth twisted. "Yeah, you'd think they'd have ostracized her the way they did me."

Becca grit her teeth and bit back the words she wanted to say. Typical Candice to make herself the victim. Candice had brought her problems onto herself. Michelle had been clueless as to what her husband had done.

"It turned out Three Palms had invested their teachers' pension with John's business," Candice explained. "They were pretty upset that their finances were frozen, because of the money laundering investigation, but they ultimately got it back. They let Michelle's boys stay. I think there was some sympathy because people could kind of understand what drove Brad to that point."

"So, why did they kick her kids out now?"

Amelia pushed two drinks across the bar.

Candice looked toward the back of the bar, making sure Michelle wasn't returning from the restroom, then tilted her head conspiratorially.

"Last week, Michelle totally freaked out in car line during morning drop off. Some mom in an Escalade in line in front of her got out of the car with her kids and then opened the tailgate to get something. I think Michelle said it was a backpack. Big no-no." Candice pursed her lips and shook her head to convey just how serious an infraction this was.

Amelia looked totally bewildered. She had never been forced to sit through hundreds of morning car lines or deal with school politics.

"Michelle jumped out of her car and started yelling at them. Waving her arms around… the whole bit. She was still in her bathrobe, so you can imagine how crazy she looked." Candice smirked. "Now, Michelle's version is she 'explained' to the other mom that she wasn't allowed to get out of her car. You know, the whole, 'have your kids ready when the door opens,' speech the principal always gives. Michelle must have been really out of control though and totally freaked out this other lady because several parents complained to the board. I think, at that point, the school board decided that Michelle was more trouble than the benefit their image was getting for their good deed in letting her stay at the school." Candice's sneer made it clear what she thought of the school's philanthropic attitude.

"Wow!" Amelia breathed, then looked from Becca to Candice suspiciously. "You're making that up."

Becca assumed Candice was exaggerating for drama's sake, but there was likely a core of truth in her story. Becca sighed. She would have to put the photographs back up. She couldn't kick Michelle while she was down.

Candice reached for her drink. "Anyway, while her kids are between schools, and she figures her mess out, her mom and dad have taken over homeschooling the boys. Michelle isn't, what's a nice way to put this, particularly *stable* at the moment." She took a large swallow and licked her lips. "That's why she's staying with me. What else could I do?"

Kindness had never been Candice's strong suit, and Becca couldn't figure out what the woman's angle in helping Michelle was. Was she trying to rehabilitate her reputation?

"Here she comes. Don't tell her I told you." Candice winked.

"Hey, Becca." Michelle's voice was overly bright when she reached them. "Where's that sexy boyfriend of yours? Does he have any friends you could set Candice up with?"

Becca flinched immediately drawing Candice's eye.

"Problems in paradise?" Candice couldn't hide the gleam in her eyes.

"Not at all," Becca said, keeping her voice as smooth as possible. "We haven't been together in a while."

She took another sip of her drink. She didn't want to talk about it, but she knew there was no way either of her former friends would let it go.

Michelle made an exaggerated sad face, sticking her bottom lip out. "Oh no, I'm so sorry! You guys were so cute together."

"It's okay." Becca forced a smile. "It all worked out for the best."

Liar.

Michelle's face brightened. "Yay! That means you can be a single lady like us! We can totally be cougars." The woman held her hands up like claws.

"Do you have to be so embarrassing all the time?" Candice groaned.

Deciding that was her cue, Becca drained her glass, and with an excuse about work the next day, made her escape.

11

The crowd in the gallery continued to grow, and as Becca glanced around, she recognized several faces. For as much as Key West is a top tourist destination, at its essence, it is still very much a small town. Becca was pleased by how many locals had turned out for the event.

She gave a little wave to a few of her regulars, people who would come into the gallery just to browse and chat for a few minutes. The doors opened again, and Becca caught a glimpse of Michelle and Candice. Both women were dressed in short dresses more appropriate to a club, and Becca thought they might be the only ones in the room wearing stiletto heels.

Michelle's eyes immediately began searching the room for her photographs. Her brows creased in a frown when she didn't spot them. Candice also surveyed the room, her face scrunched with revulsion. The eclectic Key West crowd was clearly not up to her standards.

Becca wasn't in the mood for whatever snark Candice planned to throw her way. Her nerves were stretched tight already. She and Dana had worked hard to prepare for the night, work made more stressful by the short timeline and value of the collection. Becca wanted the event to be a success and raise a lot of money for the charity, but the worry foremost in her mind was that she would run into Harry again.

Dr. Hathaway and Allison had been in the gallery earlier in the day overseeing the installation of the art, before they returned to their hotels to change for the fundraiser. Becca tried not to think about the fact that the beautiful redhead was probably sharing a room with Harry. Robert Clarke had also arrived early, but unlike Allison, he stayed, standing watch next to the Santiago cross. She was pleased at how the Lucite box looked, staged in the middle of the main room on top of a four-foot podium, surrounded by four stanchions connected with ropes. He held court, happy to regale whomever stopped with the importance of his family and their history in connection with the object.

With a sigh, Becca put on a smile and snagged two glasses of champagne from a passing waiter.

"Hi, ladies! I'm so glad you made it." Becca extended the glasses. Candice took hers with a lifted eyebrow, her attention on a man nearby wearing a floral shirt, shorts, and flip flops.

Michelle's fingers gripped the stem of the flute tightly. "Where's my art? I thought it was by the front door."

When Becca had first displayed the photographs Michelle had mailed her, she had texted Michelle a picture of them in situ.

"They *were* by the door, but because this is a special exhibition, we had to move them."

Michelle's face fell. "You took my art down?"

Becca placed a hand on her friend's arm. "It's still displayed, just in a different spot. Over here." Becca led them through the first room, into the larger, back gallery space, stopping by the back wall near the office door. She gestured to the grouping of Michelle's photographs.

"Oh."

"Just for the show," Becca assured her. "Then they will be

back up front. You are still exhibiting in a show with Picasso. That's pretty important!"

"You're in an art show. That's more than you had before." Candice sounded bored, but Becca was still taken aback by Candice's words. They were almost... nice.

Michelle grinned. "That's true."

First crisis averted.

Becca left the women and walked back to the front room where the majority of the crowd had gathered. She stopped to talk to Amelia and Dan for a moment, before checking in with Dana.

"Everything going smoothly on your end?" Dana asked.

"So far, so good."

"Any sign of you know who?"

Becca gave a slight shake of her head. She had been edgy all day, and Dana correctly guessed the reason.

"Maybe he has the decency to stay away... out of respect I mean."

Becca looked to where Allison was deep in conversation with Robert next to the podium. The young woman wore a high-necked, minimalist dress that somehow only accentuated her curves. "Maybe." She watched as they were joined by an older man in a loose linen suit.

"Stop glaring at her," Dana muttered.

"I'm not." Becca tore her eyes from Allison.

"You were."

"Whatever. I'm heading back out to mingle. See you on the other side."

Becca made a couple more loops around both rooms, answering questions about the charity and the workshop she had planned for the next day, before finding herself back at the podium. The older gentleman in the linen suit was still staring at the cross, completely absorbed. She watched the man in profile for a few moments before saying anything. He seemed mesmerized by it.

"It's extraordinary. Isn't it?"

"More precious than gold." The man's words were quiet but firm, as if he were stating a proven fact. Still, with the surrounding chatter, she wasn't sure she had heard him correctly.

Did he think it was made of gold?

"I wasn't familiar with the Cuzco School of Art until I unexpectedly came upon the cross." She gave an encouraging smile. "Are you a fan?"

He turned, his neatly trimmed moustache twitching above his lips. He was older than she had first thought. Early seventies, she guessed, with deep lines running down his darkly tan cheeks.

"A fan? I don't think that is the correct word. A devotee would be more accurate. Is it true you discovered this beauty?"

"I did, though it was completely accidental." Becca laughed. "I was doing research on something else and came across a picture of Joaquin de Santiago. The unusual, painted vegetation on his cross reminded me of the Clarke cross. I'd seen it just a few days before."

"What a lucky coincidence." He smiled charmingly, and she found herself returning the smile. "Are you often lucky?"

"Not even remotely! More like unlucky. I'm Becca, by the way."

He paused, and his smile faltered. He reached for her hand and pressed a kiss to the back of it. "Encantado. I'm Juan." He bowed his head, and she was charmed by the gallantry.

"When did you first become interested in the Cuzco style?" she asked.

Juan's brows lowered then cleared with understanding. "Ah, no. I'm a Catholic. I collect relics and various religious artifacts. Though this one has a special attraction for me. Santiago should have been made a saint for all the conversions he performed."

"Hmm." Becca wasn't touching that with a ten-foot pole.

"They ground real gold into the paint," Juan said reverently. "It's why it glitters in spots." His face flushed, and his breathing became rapid and shallow.

Becca tried to keep her frown from her face. Was he unwell? Seeing things? She peered at the cross trying to find something glittery. It was still the same dark wood with dulled paint. The Clarkes had decided not to risk cleaning it before the auction in case of damage, so there was still only minimal gold paint visible. She cleared her throat and glanced around to see if any of the people standing near them appeared to be with the older man.

She cleared her throat. "Well, the Spanish certainly liked gold…" It was inane she knew, but she wasn't sure what to say.

"Everyone likes gold." Juan's voice was surprisingly harsh. "Without it you are powerless."

Umm. This is getting awkward.

Just as Becca was trying to figure out a smooth exit, a younger man approached them, and Becca blew out a sigh of relief until she recognized him as the man from The Conch House bar. The man who had been with James Brennan.

"Gold is a treasure, and he who possesses it does all he wants in this world, and succeeds in helping souls to paradise," the man next to her said reverently.

"Oh, that's nice."

Weird is more like it.

"Christopher Columbus." Juan met her eyes. "He was right, you know. With gold, one rules the world… and controls people's souls."

Something about the way he said the words was disturbing, and it made her uncomfortable. She was grateful when the other man finally reached them.

"Papa, are you flirting with this young woman?" Even though the man was several years younger than Becca, he exuded confidence.

"I'm old, not blind, Andréas."

"Your father was just telling me that he collects religious items? This cross is going to auction soon. You could acquire it there."

"I'm afraid I am a bit short on gold at the moment," Juan laughed. "Andréas, I'm ready to go."

"Of course. I'll get Brennan, and…"

Becca's heart stopped. Which Brennan did he mean? As much as she didn't want another unpleasant encounter with James, she also didn't want to see Harry with Allison again. In keeping with her statement to Juan about being unlucky, she saw Andréas wave to someone in the crowd. Like a bad movie, a group standing nearby parted, and Allison and Harry approached holding hands.

Harry's eyes met hers, and she thought he paled a little. He leaned down and whispered something in Allison's ear.

I can't do this right now. Not in front of all of these people.

"If you'll excuse me… it was nice to meet you," Becca muttered, her throat tightening. She spun on her heel and scurried away. As an exit, it wasn't graceful.

It's over. My worry came true. They are here together at my event, and I survived. At least there shouldn't be any more surprises.

BREEP BREEP BREEP

Not now, Becca moaned silently.

Around the room people stilled, not sure what to do. Dana lifted her hands and called out to the crowd over the alarm's piercing tone. "Nothing to worry about. Sorry, everybody, we've been having trouble with the alarm."

The unmistakable sound of a phone ringing reached them from the office. Dana met Becca's eyes across the room. Two spots of color rose on Dana's cheekbones, and when she jerked her head in the direction of the office, Becca nodded. "It will be off momentarily," Dana promised.

Becca rushed into the office and snatched up the phone

receiver, providing the security phrase when prompted. The alarm went silent, and clapping echoed throughout the gallery. Becca hung up the phone, and placing both hands on the desk, she took a deep breath, before blowing it out in a steady stream of air. Her heart slowed a little.

It was always going to be a hectic night, but seriously?

"A land line? Really? How adorable."

Becca's eyes widened but not because of Candice's sarcastic words. A group of people had gathered in the doorway watching her. In her rush to answer the security company's call, she had forgotten to close the office door. She straightened, taking in Michelle and Candice's delighted expressions. She expected them to enjoy the drama. What gave her pause, however, was the sight of Harry and his father James standing with them.

Great. I'm so ready for this night to end.

"Always so much excitement around you," James chuckled, and Candice gave him an appraising look. Unlike many in the crowd, both Brennan men were dressed in dress shirts and slacks. She caught Candice checking out James's shoes and watch.

I could warn her, but they deserve each other.

Becca brushed past the group pulling the door closed behind her. She ignored the onlookers and tried not to react to Harry's cologne. At the sound of Candice introducing herself to James, Becca quickened her pace. For a fleeting second, Becca thought she felt Harry's fingertips brush her arm, but when she looked over her shoulder, he was watching his father flirt with Candice, a bored expression on his face.

Her brain still focused on the group behind her, Becca ran straight into Juan, knocking him back a step.

"Oh! I'm sorry!" she exclaimed. Her cheeks flushed hot under the scrutiny of his son and Allison with whom he'd been talking.

He flashed her the same charming smile he had before, his

eye's sparkling. "It's quite all right. I hadn't expected so much excitement tonight. Besides, beautiful women should never apologize."

Becca smiled wanly. She could do with a little less excitement. In fact, she was starting to be anxious for the evening to be over. She settled for, "Me, either. Hopefully, that will be the last of it." A waiter walked by, and she looked longingly at the tray of glasses.

"Did you want one?" Juan asked, and started to raise a hand to signal the waiter.

"No, thank you. But I should probably make sure the caterers have enough." It was a total lie. In reality, Becca just wanted a moment alone to get her emotions back under control.

"We should leave," Andréas said in a low voice to his father. "You've been out in the open long enough."

That sounds like he really is ill. Poor man.

Candice let out a loud peal of laughter, and Becca turned to see her with a hand on James's arm leaning into him. *Gross.* Michelle had disappeared, but movement in Becca's periphery caught her eye, and she realized Harry was watching her.

Yeah. I definitely need a break.

Becca disappeared into the kitchen, joining the handful of caterers in the tiny space. It took several deep inhales before she felt she was in control of her emotions again. By the time she had calmed her heart rate from the events of the last few minutes and returned to the main room, Harry was gone.

She quickly scanned the room. Candice and Michelle were looking at the cross with glasses of champagne, but Candice definitely looked less than enthused. Was that because, along with Harry, James seemed to have left as well? Becca took a few steps forward in order to see into the other room, and to her dismay, she realized it was disappointment she felt when there was no sign of Harry.

What is wrong with me? One minute you dread seeing him and the next you are sad he's not here!

Over the next thirty minutes, the crowds dwindled until there were just a few strangers and... Allison. Becca was a little surprised that Harry hadn't waited with his girlfriend. Maybe they aren't that serious, the traitorous voice in her head whispered, igniting hope in her before she ruthlessly extinguished it.

When the last guest had left and the door had shut behind the caterers, Becca and Dana exchanged a look across the room.

"Hang on." Her friend disappeared into the kitchen and came back with a plate of hors d'oeuvres and two glasses of champagne, precariously balanced in her hands. "I set these aside earlier. I figured we should at least get to sample the goodies."

She collapsed into one of the chairs they had set out and released a giant whoosh of a sigh, loud enough for the museum's movers to pause while wrapping one of the frames. Becca popped one of the tiny quiches into her mouth to cover her smile.

"Girl, that was a lot." Dana waved her champagne at Becca. "I am dying to get out of these heels, but Hathaway will be here soon to meet the movers. Allison left to pick him up. Why don't you head home? They aren't going to let us touch anything anyway, and as the boss, I can get a catnap in my office."

Exhaustion suddenly swamped Becca, still she hesitated. "Are you sure?"

"Go! You've done so much to get ready for this show. We had to have made a ton from ticket sales. This place was packed." Dana winked. "Besides you have the kids' event tomorrow. Plus, you have to get everything set back up for when we open again."

12

The ringtone blared out, startling Becca. She cursed as her coffee splashed over the counter top. *Dang it!* She snatched a rag to wipe up the spill before it spread over the hardwood floors. She recognized "Walking on Sunshine," the ringtone she had assigned to Dana.

The song's chorus played again illuminating the screen, the time displayed in large numbers in the center. Damn! She was fifteen minutes late already. Becca was never late, but she had stayed up the night before working out her frustrations on canvas. Dana was opening so Becca hadn't been as concerned. She was confident she had set the gallery back in order after the workshop, but if Dana was already calling, it wasn't a good sign.

"Hello? Becca?" Dana's voice was tense.

"Hey, I know I'm late! I'm leaving right now."

"So, you *are* coming in." Dana's voice changed. "I told them that! I told them you wouldn't have anything to…"

A gruff voice replaced Dana's on the phone. "Ms. Copeland, this is Detective Ryan of the Key West Police Department. I'm sure you remember me… from…"

Becca's heart sank. Of course, she remembered the detective.

He had questioned her twice after Evie had been murdered. Something must be very wrong.

Becca licked her suddenly dry lips. "Yes, Detective Ryan, I remember."

"Dana tells me you're late for work." His tone was brusque, and Becca was a little discombobulated by him calling her friend by her first name when he was normally so formal. "Will you be here soon?"

"Yes, I was just telling Dana that I was leaving now."

"Great." His tone was flat. "I'll expect to see you in a few minutes then. Don't stop anywhere."

It took Becca a second to realize he had hung up. She stared at the device confused.

What in the world happened that the police are at the gallery?

Ignoring her coffee, Becca grabbed her purse off the entryway table and biked as fast as she was able through the streets of Key West. About a block from the gallery, she could see the road was partially blocked by two police cars. Yellow crime scene tape strung across the shop front made her chest squeeze painfully. In the past few years, she had had more interactions with the police than anyone would ever want.

Is Rey right? Am I the unluckiest person alive?

She grimaced, leaning her bike against a lamp post, not bothering to secure it. With a deep inhale, she squared her shoulders and walked to the entrance. A young officer, not much older than her son, stood holding a clipboard, checking people in. Becca's heart sank at the shattered glass door.

After explaining to the officer who she was, he gestured for her to enter the gallery. Becca scanned the front room full of law enforcement personnel, looking for evidence of what had been taken, but everything seemed just as it had been when she had left the night before... minus the glass shards she stepped over.

"Ms. Copeland, nice to see you again," Detective Ryan

drawled, walking toward her in his customary khaki pants and loose Cuban shirt. The wry smile on his face indicated he found her appearance there comical.

"It's nice to see you, too," she automatically answered, and then blanched at the inappropriate response. Becca looked past him and saw his partner, Detective Alvarez, talking to a group of people clustered around the box where the Santiago cross had been.

Had been? Becca's heart thumped hard in her chest. *Please, not Miss Helen's cross!*

She closed her eyes, and when she opened them, a space had opened up between the crime scene technicians. She could clearly see that the Lucite had been broken and the cross was gone.

"We're dusting for prints, but it doesn't look like they're going to find much usable. They are telling me it's a smorgasbord of fingerprints on that base. I guess you ladies didn't clean so well after your event."

Becca glared at him. Miss Helen's family heirloom was gone, and Becca was not in the mood to joke. She wanted to throw up.

"What happened?" She couldn't tear her eyes away from the jagged edges of what remained of the display box.

"That's a good question. You were the last one here last night?"

Becca nodded. The technicians were bent over the pedestal again, blocking her view.

"I closed up around eight o'clock. I left a little early... I'd done a workshop earlier in the day and got the gallery in decent condition to open." She hadn't made the gallery perfect. She had been exhausted and left early.

"You were here alone?"

Becca finally looked the Detective full in the face. "I know you have to ask me these questions. But you can't think I had anything to do with this. I'm sure the bars on the street have cameras. They'll show that I left when I said I did."

Detective Ryan made a humming noise. "Hope so. We've requested their video. Did you set the alarm before you left?"

"Of course." She had, hadn't she? Her mind returned to the moments before she locked the door. She had been thinking about Harry... Becca frowned.

"What is it?" Detective Ryan eyed her closely.

"Nothing. I'm positive I set the alarm and locked up." Becca nodded emphatically. She was. She clearly remembered keying in the code and pulling the door shut snugly behind her. "But the locked door wouldn't have mattered if they shattered the glass, right?"

Detective Ryan ignored her question. "Who else knows the key code for the alarm? For the security company?"

"Just myself and Dana."

"No one else?"

Becca thought for a moment. "I can't think of anyone else, right now," she said slowly.

The detective jotted something down in his notebook "Your boss tells me you've been having some problems with the alarm."

A pause stretched between them. Becca bit her tongue. What was he implying?

Detective Ryan watched her expectantly, but she couldn't figure out what it was he wanted her to say.

"Yes. That's right. It's been going off... something about the wiring... not being up to the specifications of the new system. Dana put it in for the exhibition." Her brow furrowed. "Did it not go off?"

The detective's questions didn't make sense. Becca was certain she had set the alarm, but she couldn't figure out how someone could have broken in and escaped with the cross before the police responded to the alarm. Even though it was a Sunday night, the street should have been crowded.

"It went off," Detective Ryan said.

"Then I don't understand. Why didn't the police respond? The security company always calls, and if I don't answer with the right code word, they are supposed to send the police immediately!"

"They did call." The detective rubbed a finger over his top lip. "But it seems you guys have had a lot of false alarms lately, so they were a little slow to respond. Both your fire alarm and the security system have had issues, right? By the time they realized this wasn't just another accidental trigger and notified the police, the perp was gone."

"Slow to respond," she echoed. "Why didn't they come immediately? No one is supposed to be here in the middle of the night! Did someone answer the phone?"

Detective Ryan cocked his head at her and rolled his lips in. "I didn't say when the alarm was triggered."

Becca sighed and tried to hold on to her frustration. The man's short responses were grating on her nerves, and her thin smile failed to hide her irritation. "I just assumed. There are always a lot of people on the street, so I figured a thief would want privacy."

Detective Ryan had an equally fake smile. Becca had spent enough time with the man to be suspicious of the glint in his eyes.

"See, it's curious you say that. The alarm sounded just before 8:15 PM. The security firm said you are supposed to still be open at that hour. They assumed you were going to get to the phone. Normally you are open until 8:30. Is that correct?"

Becca's stomach clenched. If she hadn't left early, she could have come face to face with the burglar. She swallowed hard. "Yes, I left a little early. How did they know I wasn't going to be here?"

"Exactly. Your boss tells me you aren't in the habit of closing early, so this is out of character for you."

Becca could tell by his tone where he was going with his questions, so she wasn't caught off guard when he asked, "Why exactly did you close early?"

"I was tired. The gallery wasn't open to the public yesterday. We closed so that we could host an Art for Kids event. After two days of back-to-back events, I was exhausted."

"Has there been anyone around that you would be suspicious of? Loitering, etc.?"

Becca's mind flashed on James Brennan. He was a known criminal, but he hadn't given any indication he was interested in the cross.

"Where were you at 8:15 last night, Mrs. Copeland?" The detective repeated.

"I picked up some food at the restaurant on the corner and then went straight home. I'm a regular; they should remember me."

"Okay, next stop was home... alone?"

Becca nodded. He grunted before scribbling in his notebook again.

"Your boyfriend wasn't there with you?"

Harry's face appeared in front of her, but before she could answer he continued, "The FBI guy?"

"Rey isn't my boyfriend."

Why does everyone think that?

Key West wasn't large, and she *had* spent a lot of time with Rey over the last few months. Becca supposed it made sense for people to link them except for the fact that Rey was a serial dater much like Dana.

Detective Ryan shrugged. "How are your finances, Mrs. Copeland?"

Becca blinked rapidly.

"They are fine. I had no reason to steal the cross! Besides, if it happened at 8:15, I would have been almost home. I'm sure with all the cameras around that will be easy enough to prove."

"It's unlikely this was a one-man job. Someone had to have let the perp know the place would be empty and about the faulty security system. Seems to me, you easily fit that description. Not to mention, you were the one who convinced the Clarke family to put this cross thing on display."

Becca's mouth hit the floor. *Is he serious?*

"This was your idea, right? At least that's what," he gestured to where Dana was still talking to his partner, "she said."

"But... but it wasn't like that!" What had Dana said? Becca felt a sharp stab of hurt. "I did ask... I mean I arranged it. But the family are the ones who agreed to show the cross. I did the advertising for the exhibition, but it was Robert's idea to include the cross in the ads. He paid to advertise the cross's involvement, in order to drum up interest in the auction."

"Now see, I heard that was all you. That you wanted to keep it an extra day so that you could use it in your little charity workshop." Ryan's eyes were shrewd, and Becca had the first sensation of misgiving.

Phrased like that, it didn't sound great.

"That's true, but..."

"How well are you acquainted with the family? The Clarkes? Seems a little odd that this super rare cross, going up for sale and displayed for the very first time in public, is suddenly stolen. I don't live under a rock; I've heard the reports about what this thing might be worth at auction. Surprising that they'd put it in a tiny gallery with no guards."

"I can understand why you'd think that," Becca agreed with him. "But *most* galleries don't have guards, and we installed a brand-new security system!"

She didn't mean to sound so desperate, but the detective's penetrating stare made her nervous. Becca's phone buzzed in her pocket.

"Mrs. Copeland, I just have a few more questions."

He's right, she thought. Of all the items, why would the cross be stolen? It wasn't as if somebody could sell it easily. It was too well known now. Robert and the auction house had flooded the region and the internet with its image for the upcoming sale.

"It doesn't make any sense," Becca muttered, pulling her phone from her pocket as it began buzzing angrily again.

Rey's number was displayed across the screen. "Hold on a second." She held up a finger to Detective Ryan.

"Mrs. Copeland!"

Becca ignored the Detective's reddening face. "Hey, Rey. Where are you right now?"

"On my way to you." His tone was brusque. Becca wasn't sure how Rey had heard already, but she was grateful that he had.

"Guess who was the last one here last night?" She tried to keep her voice light, but a trace of worry slipped through.

"Have you talked to the police yet?"

"Yes, I'm with Detective Ryan now." She smiled at the Detective whose scowl darkened in response.

"Keep your mouth shut."

Becca's lips parted in surprise. Was 'Mr. Duty Before All Else' FBI agent telling her not to cooperate with law enforcement?

"Tell them you have nothing else to say until you have an attorney present."

Becca ears buzzed. This couldn't be happening again. She put her hand to her forehead and rubbed furiously at a sudden, sharp tightening between her eyes.

"Rey…"

"Hang up the phone and call an attorney," he barked. "I spent the night up in Key Largo on a case, but I'm heading back now. Tell the police if they want to question you, you want an attorney present. Do you understand?" he repeated.

"Yes."

For a second there was a pause of silence. "You managed to stay out of trouble for a few months at least. Don't worry too much. I'll be there soon, Nancy Drew." He hung up before she had a chance to reply.

Becca turned back to the glowering Detective Ryan. "That was my friend, Rey. The 'FBI guy.'"

Ryan's eyes narrowed at her joking tone.

She gave an apologetic smile. "He says I shouldn't talk to you without an attorney present."

Ryan threw up his hands before slapping them back down on the tops of his thighs in exasperation. "You want an attorney? I'm just trying to ask you some preliminary questions, and you want an attorney. You know that makes you look guilty, right?"

Becca squared her jaw. Unfortunately, over the last year and a half she'd become familiar with law enforcement tactics, having spent time both in police interrogations and in Rey's company. The detective was trying to guilt her into talking.

"Regardless, I'm not talking any further until I have an attorney."

Ryan glared at her. "Suit yourself, we can do this the hard way. Get an attorney and tell them to meet you at the station." He looked at his watch. "One o'clock. I'd say don't make me come find you, but if history tells me anything, it's that you won't be able to stay away."

Becca had half expected him to say that she needed to go to the station with him right away.

He shooed her with his hand dismissing her.

"Can I talk to Dana before I go?"

"No. Unlike you, she doesn't need an attorney, apparently."

Becca tried to catch Dana's eyes across the room, but the woman was busy wringing her hands and speaking with an officer.

Becca remembered seeing the name of a local woman she had sold a pair of paintings to in the news as a criminal defense attorney. Becca located the attorney's number in her phone contacts and arranged to meet her in front of the police station. Rey offered to come with her, but they both realized his presence might only antagonize the local police.

"Thank you so much for coming, Greta."

The attorney's hair was cut in a dark, shoulder-length bob. Dressed in a bright blue skirt suit, she looked like the portrait of a successful lawyer which instantly calmed Becca's nerves.

"I appreciate it on such short notice."

"Happens more than you would think." Greta smiled. "Do you have a dollar?"

"What?"

"A dollar. We'll call it a retainer."

"Oh, yeah, I should." While Becca rooted in her purse, Greta pulled a manila folder out of her briefcase.

"If you will just sign this, we should be all set to get started. If anything comes of this, then we will have to reassess a fee schedule." She placed her hand reassuringly on Becca's arm. "But from what you said on the phone, I'm confident that won't be necessary." Rey had said the same thing, and Becca hoped they were right.

The two women were escorted to the same interrogation room Becca remembered from when she was questioned the last time. It probably hadn't been intentional, but goosebumps rose on her arms as Becca fought against her anxiety.

Detective Ryan entered the room alone. "Now that you have an attorney with you, I hope you are ready to answer my questions."

"Of course."

The detective started with an overview of the day before. Where had she been? Who had she seen?

Becca explained about the Spanish Colonialism workshop she had hosted for the charity, and that afterwards, she had cleaned up and put back many of the pieces that had been shifted around for the exhibition.

"What's that mean, 'Art for Kids'? What exactly does the charity do?"

"It's an outreach program essentially. The charity introduces at-risk children to the fine arts. Many of the schools these kids go to no longer have an arts budget due to budget cuts, so the charity tries to make up the difference."

"How old are these kids? Elementary, middle school…"

"Yes, both."

"Any older kids?"

Becca frowned. "You aren't suggesting one of the kids had something to do with it?"

"Just covering all the bases."

"It couldn't have been one of the kids at my workshop. After it was over, the chaperones put them back on a bus to Miami. They wouldn't have had the opportunity to come back."

Detective Ryan grunted. "Did you notice anyone lingering? Watching the shop?"

"I don't think so." Becca thought back. "At least no one that stood out. But I was pretty busy inside. I'm not sure I would have noticed. It's a busy street."

"You said you left early?"

"Yes."

"Any particular reason?"

"No, I was just tired. It had been a long couple of days on my feet. I knew Dana wouldn't mind."

"Is that something you did often?"

"I wouldn't say often, but we did occasionally."

Detective Alvarez paused his writing. "That's interesting. Your boss, Dana, said that was out of character for you."

Greta interrupted before Becca could answer. "I would think out of character to be in keeping with what Ms. Copeland said... not often."

The detective grunted again. "Walk me through your closing up routine."

Becca quickly explained how she turned off the lights, set the alarm, and locked the doors. "That's it. We are pretty low tech."

Suddenly the detective leaned back in his chair and pinned her with his eyes. "You're sure you set the alarm?"

"Yes." Becca pictured herself keying in the code. "I remember because you only have thirty seconds to be out the front door so you don't trigger the stupid thing. But earlier you said they were slow to respond—it had to have gone off. That's proof I set it!"

"Stupid thing?" The detective ignored her question.

Greta's hand landed on her leg, and Becca swallowed her frustration.

"Not stupid. I only meant it constantly goes off."

"Explain."

Becca blinked. "I'm sure Dana told you about the wiring problem."

"I'd like to hear it from you."

Greta tensed beside her but didn't indicate that Becca shouldn't answer. "Dana had a new security system installed, so that we would have proper protection for the event. It's just for the exterior door and smoke detectors. Dana didn't think we needed anything more elaborate because we are in such a busy part of the city. Plus, we don't sell anything that's easily pawned and don't keep cash onsite."

"So, you're saying it was Ms. Mitchell's decision not to have more security."

"No, I mean, yes. But it wasn't because Dana didn't *want* more security. She didn't think we needed it. I agreed with her!"

Greta's hand was back squeezing her leg.

"You said you were frustrated with the alarm system?"

Becca glanced at Greta who nodded. "The building we are in is pretty old. Ever since it was installed, we have had a ton of false alarms."

"How many would you say?"

"I don't know for sure, but I had issues yesterday, too."

"Issues?"

"I just meant I'd had an alarm issue earlier that day."

Detective Ryan watched her closely. "What happened then?"

"It was just another false alarm. They called, I gave them the code, and that was it."

"How quickly after the alarm went off did the security company call you?"

"Right away. They always… wait a second. If the alarm was triggered and no one answered the phone, why didn't they send the police?"

Detective Ryan cocked his head. "Who else has access to the security code?"

"Just Dana and me. No, wait. Sheree and Isaac. They work part-time helping out."

"And you've never given the password to anyone else?"

"Of course not." Becca shook her head.

"There was never anyone in the room with you when you gave the code over the phone?"

"No, they call on the office phone, and customers aren't allowed in there. We've been lucky for the most part. The alarm hasn't gone off while people were in the gallery. Except for…"

"Except for when?"

Becca's thoughts returned to the night of the exhibition and the crowd in the doorway when she had gotten off the phone with the security company. She didn't know for a fact they had overheard her giving the code. Becca swallowed. "The night of the exhibition, the alarm went off, and in my rush, I didn't shut the office door. Several people could have heard me." The detective picked up his pen again. "But, I'm sure…"

"I need the names."

Well, this is going to make me popular.

13

"Miss Helen, I can't tell you how sorry I am."

After leaving the police station, Becca had called Amelia and asked her friend to join her at the Clarke's house. The police had already informed them about the theft, but Becca's guilt forced her to go in person to speak with them. The cross never would have been there if she hadn't asked for it to be part of her event.

Amelia had pulled a chair next to the elderly woman and took Miss Helen's thin hands in her own. The blue veins were more prominent than they had been when Amelia and Becca had visited weeks before, the skin almost translucent.

Tears welled in Miss Helen's eyes. Becca blinked furiously against her own. This lovely woman had been nothing but kind to her, and Becca felt terrible that this had happened in what appeared to be her final days.

"You're sorry?" Robert bellowed at them. "You're sorry you browbeat my aunt into letting you display our family's most priceless possession in your ramshackle, low-rent, local gallery!"

"Robert." Helen's voice was faint, and he ignored her.

"And this is what happens! It's a *coincidence* that the first art theft in Key West in thirty years..." he scoffed. "The police, when they were here talking to us, said they suspect an inside job." Robert's eyes narrowed at Becca. "Considering the company, you keep..." His glare flicked to Amelia.

"Robert." Helen's voice was stronger and had a pleading quality to it.

The man finally looked down at his aunt and noticed her distress. His lips pressed into a tight thin line, but he acquiesced to her silent plea.

"It does look suspicious," Becca said, "but I swear to you, neither Dana nor I had anything to do with it. I don't understand how this could have happened. I'm really am so sorry," she finished miserably.

What could she say? She had jumped at the chance to display the cross, and now it was gone. Ultimately, in her mind, it was her fault. She had been responsible for it.

"So, you say," Robert muttered.

"Give it a rest. You've never cared about the family history before, besides..." Amelia looked shrewdly at him. "You had it insured, right? Who knows? I wonder if your payout is more than you would have gotten at auction?"

Becca bit her lip. This wasn't going in a good direction. Was Amelia implying that Robert had stolen it?

Helen pulled her hands from Amelia's and raised her eyes to Robert. "As he should have." The tiny woman took a deep breath and let it out in a shuddery sigh. "No good can come from pointing fingers at friends." She sighed again. "Could just be karma."

"What do you mean?" Becca asked.

Helen's smile was a little sad when she shrugged one bony shoulder. "It fits the story, doesn't it? It didn't really belong to our family. Even by the time it came to this country, it already had a tawdry legacy, didn't it? The Cuban planter lost it at sea, fleeing his country with his wealth because he wanted to keep slaves. Our family recovered it after a disaster at sea... *recover*."

She let out a quiet chuckle. "Let's be honest. Wrecking was just a form of legal thievery. As long as they made an attempt to save the crew, whatever they fished out of the water was theirs. Even though the owner was right there wanting it back. No," she said as she shook her head, "that's all the wrecking was... legalized thievery."

"We did everything we thought was necessary to protect the art..."

"Ha! Obviously you didn't do enough!" Robert glowered.

"Wait a second," Amelia said. "If someone were going to steal something why wouldn't they have come when the pieces intended for the art museum were there?"

"They were just as valuable as the cross, if not more so," Becca mused. "But they were only in the gallery that one day."

There was another faint shuddery sigh, and Becca saw two tears tracking down the older woman's creased cheeks. Her stomach dropped.

"I don't blame you," Helen assured Becca, catching her eye. "But I am a little sad. I'm afraid this has worn me out a bit. Getting old is so tiresome!"

Amelia shifted, and Becca, understanding the unspoken message, rose to her feet alongside her friend. Amelia patted Helen's hand on her lap and brushed a quick kiss against her cheek.

"I'll come see you again soon," she promised.

Robert stalked to the front of the house and opened the door wide enough for them to pass through. "There's something fishy going on," he hissed. "You're right. It's too big a coincidence that *you* were the one who realized the importance of the Santiago cross, and *you* were the last one at that gallery before it was stolen." He stabbed his finger at Becca with each accusation before shifting his focus to Amelia. "And *you* are a notorious smuggler! Am I just supposed to believe that our family's heirloom isn't on one of *your* family's boats? It's probably already on its way to whoever bought it from you!"

Becca gaped at him in shock, but Amelia's expression hardened. "I'm not a smuggler anymore, and I can't speak to what my family does... but this girl right here had nothing to do with it!"

Amelia's defense was comforting, but Becca couldn't help but wonder where the cross was. Robert was correct. They were on an island surrounded by boats. Over the water *would* be the fastest way to get away, with the Overseas Highway as the only other escape route. With an angry *harumph,* Robert slammed the door behind them.

Becca swallowed over the lump in her throat. "I'm so sorry, Amelia. We thought the arrangements we had made were enough... I don't understand why the alarm company didn't send the police! Did someone give the right code? How did no one notice a shattered door? The detective wouldn't tell me what the police think happened."

"It was dark and most everybody on Duval at that hour is drunk."

After parting from Amelia at the Salty Oar, Becca wandered aimlessly. She found herself sitting by the marina where she lived when she first came to Key West. She couldn't get Miss Helen's sad face out of her head.

The heirloom was in the Clarke family for over 150 years. If I hadn't pushed to get it displayed, it never would have been stolen.

Her rational brain told her she wasn't completely responsible, but her heart was overwhelmed with regret.

I just don't understand how it could have happened!

14

Becca's phone rang and, for a moment when she saw Dana's number on the screen, she didn't answer. At the last second, she found herself swiping to accept the call. "Hey."

"Oh my god! You're not gonna believe it!"

Becca couldn't imagine what could make Dana so excited on such a terrible day. Becca didn't have to wonder long because the words spilled out. "The cops got the footage from the bar across the street." Becca perked up. "They caught the whole thing on tape!"

Becca grinned. "That's fantastic news! That means they can identify whomever it was and get the cross back."

"Not exactly. I don't have all the details. But from what I was told, they saw what looks like a guy wearing a hoodie and pants. He threw a rock through the glass doors and climbed in."

Becca frowned. It hadn't taken the police long to get surveillance footage, and she was sure there would be more. Key West had cameras everywhere, both for security and for live streams aimed at tourism. A smashed window and a crime caught on tape… that didn't sound like any art robbery she'd ever heard of. She knew about groups of people doing things like that in malls and jewelry stores, but an art gallery? How did the thief think he could get away?

"So, the police think it was a smash and grab?"

"I don't know. That's all he could tell me."

"He?"

Dana laughed. "I have my sources."

Becca didn't even want to guess.

"Wow, Dana! One of these days you are going to get yourself in trouble."

"Spoilsport."

Becca was still thinking about the odd nature of the robbery. "Some guy decides to throw a rock through an art gallery door and chooses a Christian cross protected by a Lucite box that he would also have to break into?" It didn't make sense.

"Hmmm, good point. He could have snatched one of the smaller paintings off the wall or one of the smaller statues. Heck, if he was looking for fun he could just smash stuff up."

"Right! So, why the cross? What about the office? Was anything taken from in there?"

"No, they had me give it a once-over to see if anything was missing, but it didn't appear like anyone had even gone in there."

"Whoever it was, they went straight for the cross and then left? They had to have walked pretty far into the building to even see it. That Lucite box couldn't have been easy to break."

"True. We did advertise pretty heavily. Maybe it's some religious freak. The only bright spot out of this is at least I'm off the hook for the insurance. The alarm went off, and it's not my fault they didn't respond like they were supposed to."

Becca understood her friend had to think of the gallery, but for Becca, the most important thing was the loss of the cross.

"Hang on. What do you mean the security company didn't respond?"

"I don't know the specifics of why, but they didn't alert the police right away like they are supposed to."

Becca was furious. "Why not?"

"I just told you. I don't know! The police said they would find out. I guess they'll tell me then."

"Yeah, right. Knowing Detective Ryan, it could be months before he fills you in." Becca thought for a minute, Rey's voice in her head, telling her not to get involved but… "Do you mind if I call them?"

"Who? The security company? What good will that do? Oh god, this isn't you trying to solve another crime is it?"

Sometimes, Becca wished she hadn't confided in her friend about helping solve her friend Evie's murder, as well as the nightmare in the Bahamas last summer.

"I'm curious. It can't hurt, can it?"

"Knock yourself out, honey. Hey you wanna get dinner with me? After this morning, I think an early happy hour is justified. I saw your sexy FBI buddy was in town. You should invite him along." Becca laughed.

Ever since Dana learned that Becca and Rey were just friends, she had been angling for a set-up. "Not tonight, besides I'm sure Rey's still at work."

"Huh! I could have sworn I saw him and that behemoth of a truck today."

"You probably did. He told me he was heading back when I spoke with him."

"I still don't get why you needed an attorney."

"It's easier to listen to Rey than be lectured for the rest of my life."

"Whatever. Hey, the cops said we can open tomorrow. Are you up for it?"

"No problem, I'll be there to open."

Becca was almost back to her cottage when she pulled out her phone again. She was disturbed by what the security company had told her on the phone and the timeline she had pieced together.

What would have happened if I'd still been there? The police haven't caught the man yet. I could have been a target! Why would the man break in when the gallery was supposed to be open?

She was getting ahead of herself, but she couldn't stop the thoughts that shot rapid fire around her brain. Logically, it made sense that whoever did it saw that the lights were off. They wouldn't have looked for the hours of operation before picking up a rock!

You have got to get it together, Becca told herself.

But what if... Panic began to claw at her throat.

Is it all just coincidence? Is it rational to think so many bad things keep happening around me?

With trembling fingers, she dialed the FBI agent's number. The phone rang several times before Rey's voicemail picked up.

"Hey, Rey, it's me." She let out an uncomfortable laugh. "Could you call me when you get a chance, please? I need to ask you something... it's kind of important."

She was just entering her front garden when she heard her phone ringing.

"What's up, babe?"

"Rey, I just spoke to the security company..." Becca glanced around her but she was alone in her tiny garden. She was being paranoid. She'd tell him her fears, and Rey would tease her about her overactive imagination. She would feel silly and everything would be okay.

"Why were you talking to the security company?" he interrupted her.

Becca frowned. "Because I'm trying to find out what happened? The whole thing feels wrong..."

"*Becca.*"

She hated when he drew her name out like that. "What? I could have been there! The security guy said the break-in happened during our normal business hours. Don't you think that's weird? Why not wait until late at night when all the surrounding stores are closed?"

Rey took a beat too long to answer, and suddenly the panic was back. This was not the 'put Becca at ease conversation' she had hoped to have.

"Hey, I'm finishing up some paperwork right now, but I think we should meet. How about that cantina you like on Big Pine Key?"

"Sure, I'll meet you there." Becca exhaled.

Why isn't this making me feel better?

Rey must have heard frustration in her voice. "Give me forty minutes or so. I'll make some phone calls, see what I can find out. Does that work for you, Nancy Drew?" he teased.

"Yeah, see you soon."

Furball yowled a hello when Becca unlocked the front door. She pocketed her phone and leaned down to scoop up the cat. The orange tabby tucked her head under Becca's chin with an aggressive purr. She snuggled the cat for a few more minutes before carrying her into the bedroom. Setting the cat down, she quickly slipped into jeans and a T-shirt, gave Furball one more quick rub, and poured some food in a dish. "I'll be back in a little bit. Promise."

True to nature, the cat had already dismissed Becca, and was crunching happily at her dinner.

15

Traffic leaving Key West was light for once, and Becca made it to the restaurant a little early. A rideshare driver introduced Becca and Dana to it one night when everything else had been closed, and they weren't ready to call it a night. It wasn't fancy, but the nachos were fantastic! The sun was starting to set, and in keeping with the atmosphere, instead of a lot of overhead lighting, the small, partially-grassed parking area was lit by strings of colored lights. On the opposite side of the building was a small dock where boats could tie up, and she could hear the water lapping despite the cars passing by. Had a boat just pulled in? Becca rubbed the goosebumps that rose on her arms, as she hurried to the door. There was no logical reason for her to be this jumpy. You are being overly dramatic, she told herself in a stern voice.

Becca chose a seat in one of the corner booths and ordered a margarita from the server when he set down the chips and salsa. As the seconds ticked by, she fidgeted, turning the bowl of chips around and around while she waited. The server delivered her drink, and she took a sip of the frosty beverage, her eyes glued to the door. It opened a few times, but only strangers came through. She checked her phone.

Rey is late.

Rey is never late.

Stop it!

Becca closed her eyes, and let her breath out slowly. She was spiraling, as Dana liked to say whenever Becca's imagination took control. When she opened them, she saw Rey just coming in. Becca gave a little wave and a smile, but when he met her eyes, her heart dropped. She could tell Rey wasn't going to spend the dinner making jokes about her wild suspicions.

"Hey." He stopped as the server approached the table and pointed at Becca's drink. "One of those please, and a plate of nachos, extra jalapeño on half."

When the man walked away, Rey propped his elbows on the table and leaned forward. "Tell me again... why did you call the security company, Nancy Drew?" Unlike in their previous conversation, his nickname for her didn't sound affectionate.

Becca kept her face blank. The implication was clear. Once again (in his misguided opinion), Becca was sticking her nose in where it didn't belong. But her nose did belong! That was where she worked! She should have been there when the break-in happened. If the lights had been on, there wouldn't have been the same opportunity for the thief, not to mention that the cross would never have been at risk if she hadn't asked Miss Helen.

Unless it had nothing to do with the cross, and instead of finding an opportunity, the bad guy had actually missed one because she wasn't there. Was the robbery a cover?

"Becca!" Rey's sharp tone reached through her thoughts. "Why did you call them?"

"Dana told me that the alarm had gone off, but the security company didn't respond. We were just curious about why they didn't respond the way they should have, the way they always have."

"We?"

"I think she's concerned about her insurance claim. She is worried that if there were a problem the insurance might not pay." Becca shrugged. It was just a teensy lie. Dana hadn't actually said that, but it *could* be true. She had been just as baffled as Becca, at the security company's lack of response.

Rey's eyebrow arched high. "Dana, I'm trying this gallery on for size, is already thinking about issues with her insurance?" He snorted in disbelief, and Becca bristled on her friend's behalf. "Just because she's only been doing this for a couple of years doesn't mean she doesn't know how to run a business. She loves that gallery!"

Rey put his hands up in surrender. "Got it. Sorry."

"You just don't like her."

"I don't dislike her." He seemed surprised. "She's cute in her way. She's just always so… what's that word… extra?"

Becca almost choked over his use of pop culture slang. "That's fair, but only in the best ways."

She smiled. If nothing else, this nonsense conversation had relieved her anxiety for a few minutes, but she wanted to know what Rey made of the whole situation. "Were you able to get any information out of the police?"

He leaned back to let the server place the platter of nachos on the table between them. Rey turned the plate so that the jalapeño side faced him. Plucking a loaded chip from the pile, he stuck the whole thing in his mouth and proceeded to chew uncharacteristically slowly.

Becca glared at him. "You eventually have to swallow." She held up a finger as he choked back a laugh. "Not in the mood, Rey."

His eyes were laughing as he finished his bite. "Such a dirty mind for a mom."

He reached for another chip, but Becca grabbed his hand to stop him.

"Rey, seriously, I need to know what the police think. Was this a random theft?"

"It's actually a co-investigation now between KWPD and the art crime division of the FBI."

Becca's eyes widened. "The FBI is involved? That's great! That means you can help me find the cross!"

"You aren't going to find the cross, Nancy Drew. You are going to leave it to law enforcement to do their job, and you are going to stay out of their way."

Becca refused to let him squash her hopes. "But you'll be able to help them, right? I'm much less likely to get in the way if I know what's happening."

"How do you think the FBI works? I'm not even in the art crimes division. And even if I were, I wouldn't be able to talk to you about the details of an ongoing investigation. Just making the calls I did ruffled feathers."

Becca's face fell. "I'm sorry. I didn't mean to get you in trouble."

"You didn't." He gestured from her to him and then back again. "But they were already cognizant of the connection between us and about the previous two cases you were involved in."

"Do they think it could be connected to any of that?" Becca held her breath. She hoped that the theft had nothing to do with the Olivera cartel, but if it was just an isolated crime, they might never recover the heirloom.

"They don't have any evidence that this is connected in any way." Despite the words, something in his tone had her nerves jangling.

"What's wrong?"

He grimaced. "It's not 'wrong' exactly. It looks like this is more serious than a smash and grab. Which is concerning for the island."

"What the heck does that mean?"

"The security company told the detectives the same thing they told you. On a side note, you might want to look into another monitoring company because, even without their complete failure to act, they are awfully chatty for people in the security business."

"No kidding. Stop stalling!"

"The first alarm was triggered about 8:15, but they didn't call the police until ten minutes later, after the third unanswered phone call to the gallery."

The meaning of Rey's words hit her. "They waited ten minutes? What if I was being murdered?"

Rey's face darkened. "It almost goes beyond incompetence, but they explained that because they knew it to be regular business hours, and that you had had several false alarms, including one that day, they thought that maybe... one of you couldn't get the phone."

"That's ridiculous! If we couldn't get to the phone while the alarm was going off, shouldn't that have been a concern for them?" Becca was outraged.

I could have been dead on the floor!

"They had notes in your file describing a couple of previous occasions where that was precisely what happened."

Becca groaned internally. *Great! We look like idiots!*

"It was the wiring. The stupid thing was triggered all the time." She hated how defensive she sounded.

A smile played around his lips. "Chill out. I know it wasn't you. They had Dana's name in the notes. Anyway, by the time the police were on scene, the perp was long gone."

A chill raced over her. "If I hadn't closed early, and something happened where I couldn't get to the phone, help might not have come in time."

"He just wanted one thing. He must have known that the sound of smashing glass would bring attention. He would have been in and out even if you had been there." His mouth tightened. "Provided you didn't do something dumb like try to stop him."

Becca's gaze slid to the nachos. She'd been known to make some dangerously rash decisions in the past. She decided to ignore his implied question. "Why would anyone break in someplace like that... in the middle of a commercial district? It seems pretty risky just to grab some art. There are nice pieces, but the really expensive ones would have been too big to run away with. He had to have gone straight for the cross. He bypassed all kinds of smaller stuff, things that would have been easier to sell."

Rey made a noise, and Becca glared at him. "I'm not being dramatic. I'm serious. Whoever broke in *had* to be there specifically for the cross. Why else would it have been targeted? And don't say, 'we don't know.' Not only did they go straight for the box and smash it, they walked by a couple thousand dollars of smaller pieces to get there. I doubt pawn shops take old wooden crosses."

"The cross is why the FBI was brought in. That and everything about this is all wrong." He grimaced. "They found a body by the water."

Becca paled.

"It matches the description of the thief on the street cams."

"The cross?"

Rey shook his head. "Drag marks in the sand make it look like a small boat could have been present. He must have had an accomplice, and that individual shot him."

Becca gasped. "It doesn't make any sense. The cross's value hasn't even been established yet. It's never been sold, and there's nothing to compare it to. It's value mostly comes from its connection to the Clarke family. It has limited provenance, and without it being sold from the family's collection, it has none at all. Why would someone kill over it?"

"Criminals kill each other all the time. We can't be sure if this murder is directly related to the robbery, or if it was settling another problem between them."

"Have they identified the thief yet?"

"Probably. They aren't going to tell me, though. I asked, and the agent in charge told me to stay out of it."

Becca frowned. If the cross had been handed off to someone in a boat, it could be anywhere by now.

"If they identify him, then they can talk to his friends. Hopefully, someone will know who he was working with, and the police will be able to get the cross back."

"I wouldn't count on it." He waved his hands at the nachos. "That's all I got. C'mon eat. I've already almost finished my half. You barely made a dent in yours."

"That's because I don't take the anaconda approach to eating," she teased. "I like to chew my food."

They ate for a few minutes. Becca asked about his current case knowing he wouldn't tell her much. She finally voiced the niggling worry in her brain as she pushed her plate away.

"You're *sure* it's not the cartel?"

Rey set down his glass. "I'm never sure about anything, but trust me, if I thought you were in danger, I wouldn't hide it. I'd have you in a safe house somewhere." Becca believed him. Rey was nothing if not overly protective. "Relax. Owen's statement was anonymous, and Jake is serving his time. The cartel accounts have been seized, and the majority of their key players have been arrested. From what we can tell, over the last couple of months, everyone else has scattered. It's real hard to make payroll when you don't have any money. Without money, the Oliveras have lost their power. Criminals don't work pro bono. The only real targets we are still after are Olivera and his youngest son. They've gone underground, but if they are stupid enough to show up in a major city, there are international warrants waiting for them.

"It would be better to catch them in an actual criminal act to be honest. I'd only admit this to you, but some of the evidence those other warrants are based on is shaky at best. Olivera has always been shielded with layers of other people to do his dirty work for him. But they aren't stupid. The cartel won't do anything to draw attention to themselves." He laughed. "I'm not saying you weren't a giant pain in their ass... I can sympathize with them on that front..."

"But in the movies..."

"They have bigger problems than getting revenge on an artist in Key West."

"You're right." Becca shook herself mentally. She imagined dragons where there were none. "The last year or so has been so crazy, I guess..." She paused her hand reaching for a chip. The sensation of being watched tickled the nerves on the back of her neck.

Her eyes rose to the door. She jerked her hand back from the chip bowl, almost knocking over the remains of her drink. Rey, alerted by her action, turned his head, his face immediately rearranging into a scowl. Harry, framed in the doorway, gave them a brief nod of acknowledgement before moving aside, allowing his companions to enter.

"Because that's all this day needed," Rey muttered.

James Brennan didn't look their way, but Allison spotted them and whispered something in Harry's ear. When Harry turned his face to answer her, Rey reached across the table and squeezed her hand.

"Breathe," he said quietly.

Becca sucked in a mouthful of air. She hated that Harry could still affect her so much.

"Crap! They are coming over."

Becca saw with dread that he was correct. Allison approached, a bright smile pasted across her face, followed by an expressionless Harry. Becca's chest tightened and her hand twitched under Rey's. In one smooth motion, he squeezed her hand again before turning it over and interlacing their fingers. Becca had a split second to register what he had done before the couple was at the table.

"Wow! What a small world," Allison gushed.

"Apparently," Rey said with a smile of his own. He sent Becca a look, and she pulled her old social mask out of the reserve it had lived in for so many months.

"Yes, how funny that we keep running into you." Becca must have been out of practice because her tone was sharper than she meant, and Allison's eyes flickered uncertainly. Becca snuck a peek at Harry and then wished she hadn't. The glint in his eyes told her he recognized her fake social voice and was amused.

Jerk!

"It is." Allison's eyes fell to where Becca and Rey were holding hands, and her body relaxed. "Do the two of you come here a lot?"

Ha! Harry's not so amused now.

Harry was glaring at her, his eyes a stormy green. Becca fought to keep her eyes on Allison and not let them stray back to Harry.

The loud scraping of a chair being pulled back drew everyone's attention. James seated himself, looking as if he was holding in a laugh. Becca's lip curled. Harry's father seemed to relish the uncomfortable tableau and made no effort to hide it which immediately brought back Becca's anger.

Why the hell was Harry so cozy with his father? How could he be close to the man who brought so much pain to Harry's family and friends? It didn't make any sense, unless the time Harry had spent with her was as fake as she was beginning to believe it was. She felt a little like Alice after she'd fallen through the looking glass, and nothing was as it seemed.

"It's a shame about the gallery."

What was Allison saying? Becca forced herself back to the conversation.

"Dr. Hathaway was thrilled that we had removed the valuable art before the break in. Can you imagine if the paintings had still been there?" Allison shivered with exaggerated fear. "This is the exact scenario he was worried about! Thank goodness nothing valuable was taken."

Becca's jaw dropped. *Is this twit serious?*

"I don't think the Clarke family feels the same."

"Oh, I'm sorry! I didn't mean that the way it sounded." Allison giggled.

Does she think that's cute? She's a grown woman!

Becca was getting ready to snap the young woman's head off when she noticed Harry looking at Allison askance.

"Right, no problem," Becca murmured.

She wasn't proud of the spark of happiness she felt at Harry's obvious annoyance with his girlfriend, but she wasn't sorry either.

Allison's gaze turned speculative, before she said, "This is your boyfriend, right? The FBI agent?" She winked at Rey, who didn't respond.

Becca opened her mouth with the intention of correcting Allison, instead what came out was, "Yep, Rey's my boyfriend."

A muscle ticked in Harry's jaw.

Rey's eyes twinkled, and a slow grin, clearly intended for Harry's benefit, spread across his face. He brought Becca's hand to his mouth for a quick kiss, and Becca fought the urge to smack him. Rey was enjoying this a little too much. The skin across Harry's cheekbones tightened, and for a brief unguarded moment, Becca saw murder in his eyes.

That shouldn't be a turn on, Becca!

He doesn't get to care now, she reminded herself. *He* left *me.* Not to mention the fact he's standing there with his new girlfriend.

"Oh! How sweet! How long have you been together?"

Is she really this oblivious to the tension at the table?

"We should be seated. My father is waiting." Harry's smile was tight when Allison patted his arm with a laugh.

"You are always so cranky when you are hungry." She wiggled her fingers at Becca and Rey as Harry none too gently steered her away.

Rey's lips were still twitching when Becca finally summoned the courage to look at him. "Well, honey, that was fun."

"Shut up, Rey. This isn't funny."

Rey cupped his jaw with his free hand on the side that faced Harry's dinner party so that no one watching could guess what he was saying.

"Boyfriend, huh?"

Becca closed her eyes embarrassed. "I'm so sorry…"

"Nope, keep smiling. So, do I get boyfriend benefits? No? Too soon?" He gave her a reassuring smile and finally let go of her hand. "It's okay. I get it. Loverboy's got a new girl. Though she is clearly a downgrade."

Becca snorted, "Right, young and gorgeous, men hate that."

Rey waggled his eyebrows. "Well now, since we are trying to save your pride… how far are we gonna go to sell it? Should I call you sweet cheeks? Honey pie?"

"This isn't funny! I don't know why I said that. I'm happy being single."

"Got it. Strong independent woman. So… honey pie then?"

He was openly laughing at her now, and the ridiculousness of the situation combined with her stress made her burst out laughing. She finished the last swallow of her drink, and as she set the glass down, she caught Harry watching them.

Rey reached forward and with a single finger stroked her cheek. Becca jerked back, her smile less pleased, more a baring of teeth. "What are you doing?"

"You were staring. Can't give away our charade that fast," he said quietly, before continuing in a louder voice. "Ah, sweet cheeks, you had a little bit of cheese on your face. I figured you didn't want me to lick it off. Save that for later."

Allison tittered, and Becca realized he had said it for the other table's benefit. Becca narrowed her eyes at him. "Knock it off."

"Okay, okay. I was just trying to be a good boyfriend," he smirked.

Becca picked at the remaining chips. She wanted to leave but didn't want Harry to think it was because of him. She couldn't stop herself from looking over again. James and Allison looked happy, and a laughing Allison reached up to touch Harry's hair. Becca wanted to rip the hand off.

She frowned.

You are being stupid. It's been months. Get over it. I can't believe that I made up a boyfriend like I was in junior high. She put her hand on her forehead. *I think I'm losing it.*

"Are you all right?" Rey asked.

Becca returned her hand to the table. "Yeah, just feeling guilty about Miss Helen. I need to fix this." It wasn't a complete lie. She was partially responsible for the cross's theft.

Rey cocked his head, his face serious. "You can't."

"Can't what? Don't you understand? Miss Helen never would have given the cross to the gallery if I hadn't pushed for it." Her face lit with a brief hope. "Do you think there's a chance they'll recover it soon?"

"Doubtful." He shook his head. "If the dead guy did hand it off to somebody in a boat, that person is long gone. They could have been in the Bahamas in a couple of hours, Cuba..."

Becca's shoulders slumped. "I hoped..."

Rey covered her hand again, but this time his face was full of sincerity. "It isn't your fault, Becca."

"But, don't you think there is a bunch of stuff about this that doesn't add up? Why break into an art gallery when there is a jewelry store one block down? And why do it when he could have been easily seen? Why wasn't he worried about an alarm? Why go to all that trouble and take the hardest item to sell? It has no value without its history, and if they try to sell it on the antiquities market, they'll be revealed! There has to be a reason that explains all of that!"

"Becca!" Rey took his hand away. "Crime happens all the time.... to good people... to bad people..." He pinched his nose. "It doesn't always have a deeper meaning. Sometimes, it's just bad luck. You are seeing a grand plot when it most likely was a simple robbery."

"But someone killed the thief. That sounds like it was more serious than just a robbery."

Rey stilled. She could see she had him with that one. Then his body relaxed. "Contrary to popular belief, honor among thieves isn't really a thing. More often than not, criminals are murdered by other criminals. It could have been for any of a hundred reasons." He held up a finger when she opened her mouth to speak. "But I'm sure both the KWPD and the FBI are looking into it. All right?"

Becca's mouth flattened, and she crossed her arms over her chest. He was wrong, she knew it!

Becca had known Rey long enough to recognize when he was done with a discussion. He didn't understand how badly she felt. Miss Helen didn't have much more time, and Becca hated that she was responsible for the woman's last days being full of sadness. She had to at least *try* to find the cross!

"Stop it." Rey's voice was serious. He gave a quick glance over his shoulder at Harry's group. "I know you're not yourself lately. It's been a hard couple of months for you. You're at loose ends... your kid's gone off to another country... you want some excitement back in your life... I get it. But you can't invent a drama, then get yourself in trouble because you stepped on a landmine you didn't know was there."

Her eyes narrowed. She didn't appreciate his reference to her inadvertent discovery of a drug smuggling ring in the Keys.

"I'm not." Becca bristled. "My life is very exciting and I am very happy…" *Argh!* She hadn't meant to say that part out loud.

"Don't be defensive. I'm just saying this isn't a 'Becca needs to save the world' situation."

"I'm not trying to save the world! I'm not doing anything. I'm just asking a few questions." Becca had moved past irritation and was getting angry. She ignored the voice in her head that said Rey wasn't the man in the restaurant that had sparked those feelings.

"Tsk, tsk. Are we having a lovers spat?" Rey drawled.

Becca exhaled hard. "I'm sorry. I don't mean to take this out on you. I'm… frustrated. Maybe a little unnerved that I could have been in the gallery when that rock came through the window."

"I understand." He sounded like he meant it.

"It just seems *too* coincidental." She couldn't help herself.

"Again… most crime is."

Becca wrinkled her nose, but her anger had dissipated, replaced by confusion.

Rey was by nature suspicious, so why was he disagreeing with her? Did he really believe what he said, or was he trying to dissuade her from asking about it?

Becca truly didn't believe she was being dramatic. There were *way* too many coincidences. She studied his face trying to figure out what he was thinking.

He cocked an eyebrow back, fully aware of what she was doing.

"Whatever," she muttered.

"Want me to go back with you tonight? Ya know, cause you're nervous and all."

Becca rolled her eyes at his flirting but allowed him to take her hand when they stood and lead her out of the restaurant. It was petty and childish, but she couldn't help but feel gratified when Harry's eyes tracked them.

However, the moment was short lived. Becca took a step outside and then made the mistake of looking back. Her stomach plunged, and her heart climbed into her throat when she met Harry's gaze. If Rey hadn't been holding her hand so tightly, she would have yanked it free.

In that one unguarded moment, Becca saw pain in Harry's eyes. She didn't want to hurt him. Did her being with Rey bother him that much? She wouldn't deny she wanted him to be jealous, but the pain in his eyes brought back a memory of the times he had made himself vulnerable to her.

The stories of his difficult childhood and his feelings of abandonment—not just from his family, but also the friends who had been swindled by James Brennan and blamed Harry as well—her heart hurt for *that* Harry. Unfortunately, she wasn't sure if she knew who the real man in the restaurant was.

Once they were outside, Becca pulled her hand back under the guise of searching in her purse for keys. The parking lot was small with just a few cars, Rey's truck dwarfing her small VW. Had Harry come by boat?

"Do I get a kiss goodnight?"

Rey was joking or at least half joking, but as she looked up at his handsome face illuminated in the moonlight, she just felt sad. Why couldn't she date him? Why couldn't she let go of Harry… or rather who she thought Harry was?"

Something of what she was thinking must have shown on her face because his face slackened. "Just kidding. You know, ha-ha."

Becca forced a little laugh. "Yeah, sorry."

"Do you want me to follow you home? If you're still feeling uneasy, I mean."

Becca shook her head. She gave him a quick hug and then a wave as she turned the car south. The lump in her throat grew, and her chest clenched tighter and tighter. By the time she had parked her car on the street and let herself into her cottage, the ache was almost unbearable. She tried to convince herself it was guilt and worry over the cross's theft, but the voice in her head would not be silenced, and she finally agreed with it.

After everything that happened, how much he had hurt her… despite how strangely out of character he was behaving…

"I'm still in love with him."

16

The next day, when she reached the gallery, she was grateful Dana had already cleaned up the mess of broken glass. The ragged pieces of the Lucite box and the podium it had sat on were gone. She presumed the police had taken it with them. Other than the temporary wood covering the broken glass of the door and a new padlock, once inside it looked like nothing had happened.

Becca watched customers come in and out. Visitors were sparse, most likely deterred by the makeshift wooden door. One man lingered in front of her paintings longer than most. She should go over and make a pitch to sell a piece of art, but she wasn't sure she had it in her to be light and friendly. She was still nauseous from stress and lack of sleep. Minutes ticked by, and when the man finally left, he flashed her a flirtatious smile. The charming expression triggered a sudden memory. What about the man at the exhibition? The one who had been so fascinated with the cross and made the weird comments about gold and faith?

Becca stood straighter. He certainly appeared unusually interested, and he had been extremely chatty. Could he have something to do with it? Her brow wrinkled. She didn't even know who he was—only his first name. *Wait!* He was there with his son, and she had seen the son at The Conch House. Maybe they were staying there. If he was still in town... but how could that help? Becca didn't know, but she didn't have any other ideas.

Becca: Do you want to go for drinks at The Conch House?
Dana: Duh. What time?

Becca smiled when the next bubbles appeared.

Dana: Why don't you invite sexy FBI guy? He's in town, right?

Becca rolled her eyes but sent Rey a text asking if he was available to meet her at The Conch House later. She intentionally left out the part about Dana also being there. The return bubbles started and then disappeared. Becca shrugged. She had fulfilled her promise to Dana and wasn't going to push for him to come. If Rey were there, he'd figure out what she was doing, and she wasn't in the mood for another lecture.

The day dragged, and when the light through the windows changed from afternoon to evening, Becca began to feel nervous. She was jittery and kept glancing at the door. The plywood on the door prevented her from having a full view of the street, and that made her feel vulnerable.

She'd never felt unsafe in the gallery before, or while biking home in Key West after dark. In general, Key West was a very safe city. However, tonight as the sun started its descent, she began to worry.

You're being dramatic. Everything is fine.

Still, she found herself locking up early again. She wanted to be home well before sunset. Becca unlocked her bicycle from the lamppost and headed for her cottage. The faster she pedaled, the easier she breathed. She was being silly. It probably had just been a onetime thing. A fluke.

Then why are you bothering to try to find this man, she asked herself.

Even if he is there, what am I going to say? "Hi, remember *me? You were super interested in the cross at the gallery. Did you steal it? Will you please give it back?"*

She growled softly. Even her internal voice thought she was insane.

Becca changed into a wrap dress with a deep V neck and slipped into low heels. Not particularly dressy, but more appropriate for the upscale bar. She took extra time applying her makeup and pulled her hair up at the sides with a gold clip, leaving her curls to cascade away from her face onto her shoulders. It can't hurt to look nice while you're trying to get info out of people, she thought. Becca poured out a bowl of food for Furball, before calling a car. After the rideshare dropped her in front of the hotel, Becca began to have second thoughts.

This is nuts. Completely totally nuts!

Feeling deflated, Becca reminded herself that, worst-case scenario, she and Dana would have some overpriced cocktails and forget about what happened two nights ago.

"Hey, sexy lady!" Dana called with a wave from her seat at the bar. She gave Becca a kiss on her cheek as she seated herself. "You dressed up! Not that you don't always look nice… but damn. Are you trying to hook-up with somebody?"

Becca smiled and surveyed the bar. No sign of the older man. She slumped on the bar stool. What had she expected? She ordered a glass of wine and tried to relax.

"How was business today? Sell anything?"

"Uneventful." Becca scrunched her nose. "I think the wooden door is a deterrent. A reminder of something unpleasant isn't really what happy tourists want when shopping."

"I called and ordered a new one today, but they said it's going to take a week to deliver one." Dana laughed. "But then I said the magic words, and suddenly our door is scheduled to be installed in three days."

"Magic words?"

"Amelia told me to call."

Becca snorted, "That woman knows everyone!"

"It's a little scary."

Becca hummed her agreement before taking a sip.

"Uh oh! Don't look now, but Robert Clarke just walked in."

Never one to follow directions, Becca looked over her shoulder directly into Robert's fierce glare.

Dana looked annoyed. "He can't honestly blame us! We didn't steal it."

"When I spoke to him yesterday, he was very angry. He definitely holds us responsible."

"Huh! From what you told me, I thought he'd care more about the money. An insurance payout is more of a sure thing than an auction."

Becca chewed her lip. "There's no way of knowing how much it would have brought at auction. To be fair, I think he is upset on his aunt's behalf, too."

"Don't be so worried. There's nothing he can do. My insurance company has assured me that since the security company didn't respond, he doesn't have grounds for a lawsuit."

"I'm not worried about a lawsuit." Becca frowned at her friend. "I just feel terrible about the whole situation. You didn't see Miss Helen's face yesterday."

Dana, pragmatic as ever, shrugged. "I feel bad for her, too. It's been in the family a long time, and that kind of thing means a lot to some people. Trust me, I got an earful about that stuff from my grandmother daily, but you said she didn't even like the thing. Robert doesn't exactly strike me as the type to form a sentimental attachment to something just because his family had it for a long time. I think it was a business transaction for him. Speaking of insurance, I wonder how much he's going to get?"

"I have no idea. It didn't have complete provenance... I think he just named his amount."

"The insurance company wouldn't have given him a huge amount. There aren't any comparable sales. They would have hit him with massive premiums. It wouldn't have been worth it to insure it for too much."

Becca's thoughts whirled. "It was going to auction this month. He wouldn't have had to pay more than one or two of the premium payments. It might have been worth it for a big guaranteed payday."

Dana's eyebrows rose and she looked around the bar again. "What are you saying? You think he did it for the insurance money?" She lowered her voice. "He looks like a jerk but not the type of jerk to murder someone."

"Murderers don't have a look." Becca knew that better than anyone.

"I don't know. That feels like a stretch."

"Think about it." Becca leaned forward. "I mean somebody stole it. Even the police think it might be an inside job. It can't just be a coincidence that the only time we are robbed is one of the few nights the cross is there. It's not like we're a jewelry store where someone can smash a window, run in, and grab a bunch of watches. We're an art gallery. Think of all the shops near us. Much easier things to steal and pawn."

"You're not wrong. But isn't it more likely to be someone connected to the security company?" Dana scowled. "They didn't respond because of all the false alarms. That's what gave the guy time to get away. But how would the thief know that? He should have expected the police to be called immediately."

"Except a false alarm went off during the exhibition. Robert was there for that, along with a hundred other people."

Dana groaned, "Can we stop talking about this? You're making my head hurt."

Becca was frustrated, but she let the topic drop, and Dana ordered them another round.

"Didn't you say Rey was coming?"

Becca shook her head with a smile. Dana was incorrigible. "I invited him, but I don't know if he's coming or not."

Dana pushed her lips out in a pout.

"Oh god. You aren't going to make a play for Rey are you? You two would make each other crazy."

"I like his energy."

"Talking about things like 'his energy' is exactly why the two of you would be a disaster."

"I didn't say I was looking for a relationship." Dana winked.

Becca couldn't help but laugh, trying to imagine the straight-laced agent and her free-spirited friend. She could understand the attraction though. Rey was handsome. Maybe if Becca had met him at a different time, things might have been different. Seeing Harry again, she realized that her resolution to get over him had failed miserably, and she was starting to wonder if she ever would.

"Ladies! How nice to see you again."

Becca jumped. She had been so lost in thought, she hadn't even noticed that the very man she'd come to find had approached them. Some detective she was, she thought wryly.

Dana looked confused and clearly tried to place him.

"Yes, nice to see you, too."

He stood about a foot away, and while there was nothing overtly threatening about him, the oddly awkward sensation she experienced the last time they spoke returned.

"Juan," he reminded them. "We met at the gallery exhibition the other night. Wonderful event. So many lovely things. I enjoyed having a night out for once."

In that moment, hearing his innocuous comments about the event, Becca realized that her plan had been utterly ridiculous. He was just a nice, possibly lonely, old man who had appreciated the relic and wanted conversation.

"Yes, the fundraiser was very successful. We really appreciate everyone that came out. Having such a wonderful collection to center it around made it easy."

"There were many lovely things there..." He angled his head

trying to meet her eyes, and for a horrified moment, Becca realized he was referring to her.

Oh god, she was such an idiot! He wasn't obsessed with the cross after all, he had only been harmlessly flirting. She really needed to get her people radar checked, because she couldn't read anyone correctly.

"Yes, like I said, we were very fortunate that the Clarke family shared their collection with us before it's permanent installment in Coral Gables," she said, hoping to head off his interest.

His mouth turned down. "I read about what happened to the Santiago cross. It's a tragedy."

Dana grimaced. "Do you want to get a table?"

Becca understood why Dana didn't want to discuss the robbery with a stranger, but her abrupt response was rude.

"It has been awful." Becca agreed, ignoring Dana's irritated sigh.

"I'm going to the restroom. Get a table while I'm gone." With a last glare at Becca, Dana disappeared into the lobby.

Juan shook his head, sadness plain on his face. "It's sad that the cross was locked away for so long by those who didn't fully appreciate it. Beauty should be out and admired."

Is this flirting again?

"The Clarkes didn't intentionally keep it locked away. They had no idea of the piece's significance."

He lifted his hand. "It's true. Many people don't realize what they have until it's gone."

"Mmm," Becca agreed, reaching for her glass.

Dana better hurry up, she thought, not sure how to extricate herself without hurting his feelings. "I guess I should get that table. It was nice seeing you again. I hope you enjoy the rest of your stay here."

Becca shifted to stand but paused half way up when Candice wearing a form-fitting dress with a low, heart-shaped neckline entered the bar. She paused when she saw Becca and then turned back slightly. The man Becca recognized as Juan's son entered just behind her and placed his hand on the small of her back. To her dismay, they made their way to where she was speaking with Juan.

It had never occurred to her that the luxury hotel would be as popular as it was proving to be tonight. Then again, Key West wasn't exactly known for its formal locations. It typically lived up to its unofficial motto of "Come as you are."

If Candice was looking for another rich boyfriend, this would be the best place in town. Had she come here trolling for her next victim?

"Becca." Candice's voice was friendly, which immediately put Becca on guard. Clearly the woman was trying to pretend they were friends.

"Candice, I didn't realize you were still in town."

"I had originally planned on going back today, but then I met this lovely man at your little get together, and he convinced me to stay."

"I couldn't let you disappear when we were just getting to know each other. Your friend is quite a unique woman. I don't think I've ever met anyone like her," he said to Becca.

"Hmm, yes. That is a great word to describe dear Candice. She is certainly a..." Becca paused dramatically, and Candice's eyes narrowed, "a special type of person. She has definitely changed the lives of her friends. None of us are the same from knowing her." Becca smiled sweetly at the couple.

"What a lovely sentiment," Juan said.

"Yes, what an unexpected compliment. Thank you." Candice ducked her head with false modesty.

"If you ladies will excuse us for a moment, I need to discuss something with my father. It will just be a moment, darling."

The second the men stepped away, Candice shot Becca a

death glare. "You better not screw this up for me. I can't believe you are still so jealous."

"Jealous?" Becca's mouth fell open. "Happy to see all of your delusions are still intact. Where is Michelle? Did you abandon her for your new target?"

"She's at the condo I rented, and Andy isn't a target. I really like him."

"Didn't you meet him two days ago?"

"So what?" Candice challenged. "He's handsome and rich. What's not to like?"

Becca rolled her eyes. "Right, I forgot those were the only qualities that matter."

"You like living a little life, painting little paintings on a little island. I want bigger things. I want travel and excitement. Andy's taking me on his yacht tonight. If it all works out, I plan on sailing away with him." Candice didn't appear to be the least bit ashamed of her mercenary plans, but her words sent a chill through Becca.

"Trust me, excitement isn't all it's cracked up to be, and neither are men with yachts."

"Just because you couldn't figure out how to close the deal doesn't mean I can't."

Becca pushed down the angry words that sprang to mind. It wasn't worth arguing with Candice. The woman would never listen to her. She had to be better off with "Andy" than she would have been with James Brennan.

"Suit yourself. Just keep your eyes open. I'm going to get a table." Becca stepped away to leave just as the two men rejoined them.

"You aren't running off already are you?" Juan asked.

"I'm having dinner with a friend. In fact, I should probably find her. She seems to have gotten lost on her way back. Have a great evening."

Becca walked to the end of the bar to settle their bill with the bartender, only half-listening as the group behind her made plans to continue their evening.

Where the hell was Dana? She had been gone way too long for an average bathroom break. If she had ditched Becca for a cute somebody, Becca was going to murder her! Becca signed the receipt and headed toward the lobby to search for her friend.

"Becca!" Dana hissed at her from an alcove just off the bar.

"What are you doing? You ditched me, and I was forced to watch the world's worst episode of Love Connection."

Dana didn't answer. She grabbed Becca's elbow and began moving her down the hall toward the side exit.

"I called your phone like fifty times," Dana groused.

Becca pulled her arm free. "Why? What's wrong?" Becca's phone was in her purse, and she must have set it to silent.

"I ran into Rey on my way back from the bathroom. He took one look at the bar and told me to get you out of there. He's pissed about something." Dana pursed her lips. "I mean, he always kind of looks like he's pissed off, but this time seems worse. What did you do?"

"I have no idea." He couldn't know about her plan to question Juan tonight—which was a good thing since it turned out to be nothing. "What exactly did he say?"

"Just that I needed to get you out of there and meet him in the parking lot. I teased him about being so serious all the time, and he practically growled at me." Dana pouted though her eyes had a light that Becca recognized. She didn't have time for Dana to crush on Rey.

BECCA DIDN'T SPOT REY'S TRUCK RIGHT AWAY. HE HAD PARKED at the far end of the parking lot. As she got closer, she saw that he was sunk low in the seat, a baseball cap pulled low over his face.

"If you are trying to be inconspicuous, it's not working," she said, opening the passenger door. "What's going on?"

"Get in... both of you."

"Not until you tell me..." Becca started, but Dana took one look at Rey's face and pushed past Becca, sliding into the truck and up against Rey. Becca had no choice but to climb in and shut the door.

"Where do you live?" he asked Dana.

"Why, wanna come over?" Dana flashed her best smile, and Rey glared back. Dana's face fell and she gave him the address.

"Are you going to tell us what's going on? Why you made us leave?" Becca asked, as they pulled out of the parking lot and headed in the direction Dana had indicated. Rey didn't answer, every line of his body tense. Dana slid her a worried glance, but Becca wasn't impressed by Rey's mysterious routine. In fact, she was starting to get mad.

"Hello? Are you going to explain why you rushed us out of there?"

Rey turned his gaze from the road toward her, and Becca stilled.

Something is wrong.

The energy in the truck suddenly changed, and Dana shifted uncomfortably.

"Are ya'll in a fight?"

"Not that I'm aware of." Becca tried to smile reassuringly. By the expression on Dana's face, she hadn't been successful. Fortunately, the ride to Dana's house was short; however, by the time they arrived, Becca's stomach was a knot of anxiety.

What could have happened?

The truck came to a stop in front of Dana's condo building. Becca slid out, allowing Dana to do the same.

"Sorry about the drama. I'll call you tomorrow." Becca gave her a quick hug before rejoining Rey.

They rode in angry silence for a few minutes as Rey made his way back across the island. "Are you out of your mind? Don't answer that because I already know the answer!" Rey's voice was fierce, and for the first time, Becca realized just how upset he was.

"Are you going to tell me why you are so mad, or do you want to play twenty questions?"

Rey's jaw clenched tight. When the tense silence continued, Becca crossed her arms and leaned against the door. *Fine*! He wanted to play silent and brooding then she would do the same.

Instead of dropping her in front of the cottage like he normally did, he pulled his truck into a spot on the side of the road. He slammed his truck door and stalked up to her porch.

Okaaay!

Becca slowly counted to ten before she joined him, purposely staying silent. She fished her keys out of her purse and made a point of unlocking the door as slowly as possible, fully aware she was being childish.

"Wine?" She started for the kitchen.

"Becca." At his tone, she stopped and turned back. Hands on hips, his expression was stormy. "You going to tell me what the hell was going on back there? You've done some seriously dangerous and stupid things, but are you actually suicidal?"

Becca's cheeks flamed. Whirling around, she yanked open the refrigerator and pulled out a half-full bottle of wine. "Do you want some or not?"

"Not." In a few angry strides, he reached her, snatching the bottle out of her hand. "I'm serious. Why were you talking to him?" Rey was angry but also… worried?

"Who?"

"Olivera," he bit out. "I almost had a heart attack. There you are sitting at the bar sharing a drink with him!" He ran his hands back through his hair. "You will be the death of me."

Becca blinked. Her brain seemed to work in slow motion, as she tried to process what he was saying. "Olivera was there?"

"You were talking to him!"

Horror crashed over her. "Are you talking about Juan?"

"Juan Olivera. But I'm glad that you two are so close you call him by his first name."

Becca took the bottle back pouring two glasses of wine while processing what Rey's revelation meant.

"Juan? The guy I was talking to in the bar? The one with the son that Candice is flirting with... is part of the drug cartel?" Her forehead wrinkled. "That can't be right. He was sitting in the middle of a public hotel. You said he was in hiding... you said I didn't need to worry because they wouldn't come here and risk being arrested." Her voice raised an octave with each word.

Rey took a large swig of his wine. His shoulders dropped, and he no longer looked like he was going to murder her. "It's just a coincidence that you were there?"

"Of course it was!"

She wasn't about to tell him the real reason she had gone to the hotel that night. Her finger tips tingled. "Is he here for me? For revenge?"

She didn't wait for his answer. Shaky legs carried her as far as the small sofa before they buckled under her.

It was happening.

Her worst nightmare.

Well, maybe not her *worst*. Thankfully, there was an ocean between her son and this man.

Hope sprang inside her.

"Is he important? His last name is Olivera, but Juan is a pretty common name. He could be a cousin, a low-level guy that has no idea who I am?"

Rey winced at the shrill tone, then joined her on the sofa.

"No, Olivera. As in the boss. The man with him is Andréas, the last son standing."

All the blood in Becca's body plunged to her feet, then rebounded back to her head. Ears buzzing, she put out a hand to anchor herself on the arm of the sofa. She held onto the sensation of cool cotton stretched over the strong frame of the sofa like it was an anchor. Her stomach pitched; her vision narrowed...

Rey gripped her shoulder. "Hey! Stay with me."

Becca blinked rapidly and forced herself to breathe. In. Out. In. Out.

"That's better. Your color is coming back."

Her measured respiration seemed to calm Rey as much as it had her.

"Did you approach him, or did he come to you?"

"He spoke to me." Becca licked her lips. "I met him at the fundraiser. He came up to me again at the bar."

"At the gallery? What did you talk about? Did he know who you were?"

"I don't know. I don't think so. At least he didn't seem to." Becca struggled to recall the moment. "I can't remember if I introduced myself. I think I did? We were talking about the cross. He had some quote about gold..." Becca stopped suddenly turning wide eyes to Rey.

Rey zeroed in on her expression. "What?"

"I'm sure I introduced myself to him. But... but... he didn't even blink." She buried her face in her hands. "He had to have known. He kept flirting, being normal..." Becca's hands rose to her mouth, and for a second, she thought she would be sick.

Rey rubbed her back in soothing circles. "Tell me everything you remember about the conversation."

Becca told him about Olivera's fascination with the cross, how she had thought he was senile, and how Andréas had joined them.

"At one point," she confessed, "I thought because of his fixation he had something to do with the robbery. It sounds dumb now, but I felt so guilty... I wanted..." She clutched a throw pillow to her chest. "Before you say, I should let the police handle it, or... or, I need to trust that it's under control... I couldn't."

The enormity of the situation hit her, and she suddenly felt exhausted. "I did that, remember? I finally said I would trust someone, after my ex-husband taught me that nobody could ever be trusted. I trusted Harry, and he betrayed me."

"So, you being at the hotel wasn't a coincidence after all, then?"

Becca gaped at him. She made herself vulnerable sharing her insecurities, and *that* was his response? "I didn't know who he was."

Rey stared at her in silence for a full minute, a range of emotions playing across his eyes. When he finally spoke, his voice was gentler. "I get that you want to find this cross for your friend, that you feel responsible. But the truth is, it's gone and there's nothing you can do about it. I know you, and I know that's not what you want to hear. But you aren't going to be able to fix this one." He pulled one of her hands away from its death grip on the pillow and squeezed.

"It's okay. You don't have to fix everything. Despite what you believe, the cross getting stolen isn't your fault. However, it *will* be your fault if you keep putting yourself in danger. You have to stay away from these people!"

"I've got it."

Rey stood and walked to the kitchen placing his glass in the sink. She twisted in her seat to watch him.

"I'm serious, Becca. Deadly serious. These are not people you play with. Even on the extreme off chance Olivera is involved, you can't trick them into saying something revealing. Besides, there's no evidence that they had anything to do with stealing the cross, and I can't even imagine why Olivera would take a risk like that…"

"I just," her voice caught, and she swallowed hard. "I don't know what to do anymore. It feels like my life is crumbling around me." Tears suddenly filled her eyes. The shock of finding out she had been so close to Olivera, combined with the stress of the robbery, and Harry walking back into her life… she was near her breaking point. "I've tried so hard to keep it all together, and create this new life. Be everything I'm supposed to be, create a new career, be a good mom, find someone new to love… every time I turn around something catastrophic happens! Each thing that has happened over the last couple of years, it has fallen to me to fix it."

"That's not fair or even true. Think about it, Becca." He paused, and then choosing his words carefully, he said, "You can't do everything alone. You always had people around that wanted to help you. You refused to believe it."

Becca ground her teeth. He didn't understand. She'd essentially been alone, her whole life, with very little support. Her parents, her old friends, Jake, even Harry. They had all left her on her own when she needed them most. Life had shown her that she couldn't rely on people, and if she wanted things to work out… if things were going to turn out for the best, then she was the one who was going to have to put it together. So far, Amelia, Dana, and Rey had been different, but she didn't know if she could rely on her judgment. She had thought Harry was different, too.

She rose to her feet and joined Rey in the kitchen. "Everybody says it's not my fault, but if I could find the cross for Miss Helen, if I could figure out who…"

"Stop!" His hands slashed through the air. "Just stop."

Becca froze.

"This is exactly what I'm talking about! You. Are. Not. Wonder Woman. You cannot solve all the world's problems. You certainly cannot take on some art thief all by yourself. Particularly when the cartel is sniffing around. Jesus! You have got to let go of this savior complex."

"I don't have a savior complex," Becca scowled.

Rey's jaw dropped. "Do you hear *any* of the things that come out of your mouth? *I'm the only one that can fix it. I'm the only one I can rely on,*" he mimicked her. "Do you have any idea how insulting that is for you to say to me? After everything that I thought we had built between us as friends. I care about you. I care about your son." He sighed suddenly deflated. "You have this need to control all the stuff around you so that you don't get hurt. I get it."

"Somebody's been talking to the FBI psychologist." Becca immediately regretted her tart words.

Rey's expression shuttered.

"Yeah, I have actually. You know why? Because that's what adults do when they are struggling. Coming in from the field after so many years undercover and having to learn what it's like to be part of a community again." A harsh laugh burst from him. "You think it's tough learning to trust again after going through a bad marriage? Try pretending to be somebody else. You slip up, you die. You aren't the only one in the world who has trust issues, but you seem to be the only one in this room who can't even acknowledge they have them."

Becca was taken aback by his vehemence and felt horrible that she hadn't realized what he was going through.

"Think of it this way," he continued. "When we carry out an operation, you know the people with you have been trained to take down the bad guys. The FBI doesn't send an agent out there alone and say, 'good luck, hope you do well.' " He made a sound of disgust and walked toward the front door. "We have whole teams of people helping each other. We *rely* on each other, and I thought, if nothing else over the last year, you knew that you could rely on me. You have friends who care about you. You just won't allow yourself to believe it."

He was out the door, slamming it behind him, before Becca even realized what had happened.

How dare he judge her!

However, the ache low in her stomach and the tears rising in her throat forced her to acknowledge that there was more truth in what Rey said than she wanted to believe. Becca walked to where she had left the wine bottle on the counter. If ever there was a night she wanted to forget, it was this one.

17

Becca jerked to a sitting position. *Is someone outside?* Furball let out an aggrieved meow and jumped to the ground. Slightly bleary from being awakened suddenly, Becca tried to take in her surroundings. The TV was still on, playing quietly, the only light in the otherwise dark cottage. It was a safe neighborhood, but after finding out that Olivera was on the island, she wasn't taking any chances. She picked up a large candlestick and crept to the back door.

Wait! Should I call the police? For a noise? Doubtful they'd even come out.

Becca peeked around the edge of the curtain that partially covered the narrow window next to the door. The yard was dark. Still pressed to the glass, she reached to flip the light switch that powered the porch light.

"Ah!" The small shriek was involuntary. Harry's face appeared only inches away on the other side of the glass. Frowning, she set down the candlestick and opened the door. "What are you…"

"Turn off the light."

Becca was stunned. "What…"

He tore his eyes from hers long enough to gaze past her into the house. "Are you alone?"

"It's the middle of the night, of course I am." The response was automatic, and it wasn't until she saw the flash of relief, followed quickly by satisfaction, that she understood what he was really asking. He wanted to know if Rey had stayed overnight.

A rush of emotions swept over her, and her nervous system already frayed almost went into full meltdown mode. There was Anger—*what right did he have to care?* Which led rapidly to Confusion—*why does he care?* And the most insidious of them all—

Hope.

Harry took a step closer, crowding her back into the house. "Turn off the light," he repeated softly, but Becca's brain was scrambled by his proximity. She tamped down on the errant thought that if she took a deep breath, they would be touching. Then again... if her sudden lightheadedness was any indication, she wasn't positive air was still flowing through her body at all. Her hand blindly found the light switch, and they were plunged into darkness. Neither of them moved. As her eyes adjusted, they traced along the familiar lines of his face, and her heart lurched.

"Invite me in," he murmured, his lips grazing her ear. She recognized that tone, and her body tingled in response. He was already standing inside, did he mean...

Stop it! Her brain commanded. *Don't fall for this... he broke your heart...*

Her body ignored her brain and stepped backward. She'd left enough space for him to slide past her, but his chest brushed against hers, and her breathing hitched. Gritting her teeth against the sensation, she stepped away to turn on one of the lamps.

The room had shrunk with him in it. Memories of him in this very room flooded back threatening her resolve. But, Harry's attention wasn't on her. Instead, his eyes were drawn to the front of the cottage. He paced closer, stopping in front of three in-process paintings she had set on easels. He bent closer, she assumed to see them better, but then he twitched the blinds closed behind them.

"Worried someone might see you here?" The second the words left her mouth, she realized. "Oh, Allison!"

Her eyebrows drew down into a tight frown. She had drunk the rest of the bottle of wine and fallen asleep on the sofa, but she knew it had to be past midnight.

Why is he here so late? Why is he here at all?

Harry looked bewildered for a second, then his face cleared. "Allison is in Miami working."

"Still, I can't imagine she would be thrilled you are sneaking around visiting your ex in the middle of the night."

Harry ignored the comment. He crouched so that he was eye level with her paintings. "You are so talented. I'm glad you didn't give it up."

I'm sorry? What?

Indignation coursed through her. "Why would I give up painting? Because we broke up? Was that supposed to have broken me?" Her tone was scathing, revealing more than she wanted to expose to him. Fury and disappointment washed over her. She wasn't sure if the emotions were directed at him or at herself for believing he was different. Rey's voice sounded in her head, something about overreacting, but she ruthlessly silenced it.

Harry's lips quirked. "I can't imagine anything that could break you. I only meant that after everything you've been through in the last couple of years… it would have been enough to crush anyone's dreams. I shouldn't be surprised I suppose. I've never known you to back down from a challenge."

Becca's eyes narrowed. She needed to concentrate on her suspicions and not how his words made her melt. She didn't want him to pay her a compliment or say nice things. She wanted to hate him.

"It hasn't been easy," she bit out. "There was a lot going on this fall, but my friends were there to support me. I'm incredibly grateful that *they* stuck by me."

Her words found their mark, and Harry flinched. His eyes went again to the paintings.

"Why did you change Petunia?"

The question out of nowhere threw her off balance. "What?"

"The sea turtle. I remember that day." Harry faced her again. "You were so excited about it. You were in your groove." He gave her a wistful smile. "You are so beautiful when you are painting. You looked as if you were lit up from inside…"

Becca unconsciously leaned toward him, and he took a step forward hand raised. His hand dropped and he cleared his throat. "But the turtle was brightly colored. I remember there was a lot of blue sky in it." His words were so matter of fact compared to the ones that came before, and Becca straightened. He was giving her emotional whiplash.

"I paint what I feel." She refused to break eye contact. Let him see how he had hurt her.

Harry nodded and passed a hand over his mouth. "And what you felt was… dark?"

"I wouldn't say 'dark.' It's not as bright as it once was, but Petunia is keeping her head above water. She's still swimming."

The message wasn't lost on him, and she was having a hard time keeping up with the emotions that played across his face.

The moment was broken when the glare of headlights from a car driving past slipped through the blinds. Harry stepped quickly to the window, using one finger to move the covering enough to peek out. Whatever he saw satisfied him because his shoulders dropped with unmistakable relief.

"Harry, what the hell is going on? What are you so worried about?"

He stared at her in silence, unnerving her. He could have been a statue but for his chest rising and falling under the linen shirt.

"Harry, please talk to me."

"Are you and Foster together?"

Becca stiffened. "That's none of your business."

"None of my business?" His eyes widened with outrage.

"Not anymore," she retorted.

"Are you in love with him?" His ragged voice tugged at her in a way it shouldn't.

Becca considered lying, to hurt him the way he had hurt her, and her hesitation seemed to serve as an answer for him. In two quick strides, he was standing within inches, looming over her. She hated that she backed up, but when he stood so close, her brain didn't function the way it should. Anger and frustration rolled off of him, but she knew it wasn't directed at her, which only made her more unbalanced.

What is going on?

Harry's eyes fell to her lips. Becca's pulse raced when Harry slowly lifted his hand, and so lightly that she barely felt it, smoothed back the curls behind her ear.

"Why are you here?" she choked out.

"I don't know." He looked as bewildered as she was. "I needed to see you...to... I *shouldn't* be here." He shoved a hand roughly back through his hair, the lines of his body taut. He started to step away, but Becca clutched his forearm forcing him to stay. His body stilled. The glow from the lamp cast shadows across them intensifying the illusion of intimacy. They weren't standing under the happy string lights of the gala in Miami anymore, or the bright lights of the gallery surrounded by strangers. The shadows made her bold.

"Then why did you?"

Harry ducked his head. When his eyes rose, to meet hers, the heat in them almost took her breath away.

"I can't stay away. I *have* to stay away, but I can't." His voice broke. "Why do you think I came to meet Allison that day at the gallery? There was no reason for me to do it. I knew I shouldn't be there... near you. I had every reason in the world to stay away from you, and I couldn't. You were so close. I had to see you. It's easier to bear when you're far away but knowing you were a mile away…"

Becca felt his rough voice in her chest and swallowed hard. He sounded sincere, as if the connection they shared hadn't disappeared and instead drew her toward him. But the reminder of his girlfriend stopped her. She dropped his arm.

"If you wanted to see me, you've had almost a year. You never called. Not once. Even after you left me at the Royal, I tried. I wanted to fight for us. We were worth fighting for. Or at least I thought we were."

Harry's eyes slammed shut, and he winced. "I wanted to, Becca. God, you will never know how much I wanted to, but I couldn't."

Becca's chin jutted forward. "Why? Because I didn't turn out to be the perfect woman on a pedestal you wanted me to be? I admit it. I should've told you the truth long before. It was a mistake, but you didn't want to hear it. You cut me out of your life and acted as if I never existed. Do you have any idea how much that hurt, Harry? I loved you and you broke my heart." Her voice cracked, and she bit her lip to stop the quiver that betrayed her. She hadn't meant to tell him.

Harry's eyes widened. He understood the significance of what she just said. She had never put into words how she felt about him. Had never told him that she loved him.

"Becca." His hand reached out to cup her face, but just as his fingertips grazed her jaw, his hand dropped away. "I didn't want to hurt you. I didn't know any other way. I've never felt the way I do when I'm with you. It was uncharted territory, and yes, I handled it badly. But I had my reasons."

Her mouth twisted. "I'm aware. Celine was more than happy to tell me about how my messed-up life gave them the chance to blackmail you. I'm sorry for that, but it wasn't completely my fault. Why didn't you tell me what was happening? Why didn't you tell me what they were threatening you with?"

"That had nothing to do…"

"Then tell me why, damn it! Tell me why you threw us away!"

Harry's chest heaved as he fought some internal battle. His mouth opened and shut, the struggle to speak written on his face.

Becca closed the last distance. Only inches separated them, the scent of him engulfing her. "Please. Tell me."

"This was a mistake. I shouldn't have come." Instead of moving away, he leaned forward resting his forehead against hers.

Becca's hands came up to frame his face, and Harry's eyes blazed back at her. "This is definitely a mistake," she whispered. One hand slid from his jaw to the back of his neck, and she pulled his head down to hers brushing her lips lightly across his. Once. Twice. Testing his resolve. She wanted answers but her body had taken control. "Harry," she whispered against his lips, and like a lit match to dry palms, Harry ignited. In one quick movement, he wrapped his arms around her, crushing her against his body with a groan.

A tiny voice in her brain warned her to stop, reminded her that this was a terrible idea, but she was too far gone. In a mad rush making up for lost time, they pulled at each other's clothing until there was nothing between them but the night air.

18

Harry stayed until the sun was just starting to peek through the curtains of her bedroom. For a few precious minutes, Becca kept her eyes closed. She lay on his outstretched arm, using his bicep as a pillow, and pretended that things were as they had been before. A sharp ache hit her chest, and her throat tightened. Time was running out. With the sunrise came the outside world and reality waiting for them. Becca rolled on her side and pressed her face against the warm skin of his chest.

What happens now?

Harry brushed a kiss on the top of her head, his arm coming across her bare back to hold her closer. Neither said a word.

The bright notes of "Walking on Sunshine" rang out from Becca's phone. Harry's arm tightened almost painfully around her before he removed it and shifted off the bed. Swallowing past the lump in her throat, Becca reached to turn it off.

Harry had buttoned his pants and was slipping his arms into the sleeves of his button-down linen shirt, his eyes fixed determinedly on the floor. Becca's heart sank as she watched him finish dressing.

Finally, he dragged his eyes up to meet hers. "Becca," he began.

"It was great to see you again." Becca's smile was too bright, and his brow furrowed.

He cleared his throat. "Last night I wanted to talk to you about something. Before…"

Becca arched an eyebrow at him. He frowned.

"I heard you were at The Conch House last night." Becca's lips parted. Of all the things he might have said, she hadn't expected this.

"If I asked you to stay away from there, would you at least consider it?"

She tilted her head. "Why?"

"I need you to trust me."

"You're joking, right?" Becca laughed bitterly.

Harry's lips tightened. "It's for your own good. There are people there that are… problematic."

Becca froze. He knew about Olivera. How did he know? The sick feeling returned.

"What people? Cartel people?"

Harry stared at her without answering.

"What people?" Becca repeated.

"Just stay away from the hotel." He grimaced. "And be careful. Don't ask questions; don't investigate anything. Go to work and go home. It will all be over soon."

"All what?" she cried. Harry's face was like stone. "That's it? No explanation just 'trust me.' Great!"

Pain flashed across his face. "I know I don't have the right… but I need you to trust me."

"I don't think I can." The words were barely more than a sigh, but he heard them. He nodded once and was gone.

BECCA WAS USELESS AT WORK FOR THE REST OF THE DAY. She couldn't stop thinking about Harry and what he said. On one hand, he was saying everything she wanted to hear and then asking her to trust him. Was it a trick? What reason could he have to make her believe he still cared about her? Was he just playing games?

Becca turned the argument around and around until she came to a conclusion. There was something more going on with Harry. She was no longer buying the whole 'Harry Brennan is destined to be bad and has chosen to embrace that side of himself' narrative that Rey and Detective Ryan loved. She knew that if she needed to defend her conclusion to someone else, it would be impossible. All evidence pointed to that same old story. But one fact remained—she *knew* him—and she was convinced that there was more going on than he said, and she was going to find out what it was.

If she could figure out the connection between Harry and his father, she was sure it would be the answer. The hardest part of accepting the change in Harry was his renewed relationship with James. He was hiding something; she was convinced of it.

But how could she figure out what it was? Harry wasn't about to tell her, and she had no idea how to get James to reveal the truth.

Amelia!

But would she help? Would her hatred for James outweigh her love for Harry? But since Becca didn't have a better idea, after work she biked to the Salty Oar.

"I'm worried about Harry."

Amelia had been typing on her computer when Becca burst into her office. At Becca's words, her fingers crashed several keys at once. The older woman twisted in her seat to glare at Becca.

"No!"

Becca blinked at the stern tone. "Amelia, I'm serious."

Amelia flipped her long, grey braid back over her shoulder and leaned forward resting her elbows on the table. "Did you sleep with him?"

Becca flushed hot.

"Really?" Amelia scowled, "Are you back together?"

"No! Why would you ask that?"

"Why are you worried about Harry?" her friend countered.

"Just because I'm not with him anymore doesn't mean I don't care about him at all. I was hoping you would feel the same."

"Honey, you keep telling yourself that, but ever since he came back to town you've been different."

"I have not! There's been other stuff going on in case you hadn't noticed," she snapped.

"Well, this is the thing you're here asking me about."

"Do you have any idea how to find Miss Helen's cross?"

Amelia scowled. "No."

"Well, then. This is something I can fix."

Amelia looked closely at Becca. "I agree with you actually."

Becca's shoulders sagged. "You've known him a lot longer than I have, without all the…"

"Sex?"

"I was going to say baggage." Becca's cheeks heated again.

"I don't want to say I told you so, but… I told you so."

"What are you talking about?"

"Last August. You showed me those pictures of Harry you got on your phone. I told you something was off. His whole life he stayed away from the press and suddenly he's acting like a B list celebrity calling the paparazzi."

It was true. Amelia had pointed it out, but Becca had been too hurt at the time to listen.

Becca slid into the seat across the desk from Amelia. The ratty sofa Becca had slept on her first night in Key West was gone, thankfully, replaced with colorful vintage chairs Amelia had found at one of the art markets she had accompanied Becca to.

"There is no way he would suddenly forget about everything his father did. The more I think about it, the less sense it makes. One night he's telling me about his horrific childhood, the next he's taking secret meetings with his father and then he disappears, only to show up all these months later arm in arm with James." Becca leaned forward. "It has to be something with his father, right?"

Amelia stared at the door over Becca's shoulder. A couple of minutes ticked by in silence, and finally Becca couldn't stand it. "Right?"

The older woman's eyes met hers. "It has to have been something big. I watched that boy every day for years try everything to get his father's attention with no success, and then came the day he saw who James really was. Harry is different from his father. A different species. You're right. Something is going on—but that doesn't excuse how he has been behaving."

Becca beamed. With Amelia now on her side, instantly she felt better. "What do you think we should do?"

"James wouldn't have come back to Key West unless he thought he was going to get some cash."

"I don't believe Harry would do something illegal just for money. He has plenty." Becca's voice was firm.

Amelia twirled the end of her braid. "There might be a way to get it out of James. But it won't be easy."

When Amelia didn't continue, Becca raised her eyebrows.

"He's not gonna want to do it. Might be stubborn. He's a bit irrational when it comes to James."

"Dan?"

Amelia nodded. "James loves to think he is superior to everyone else. I was just thinking, if Dan went to him in a 'let's let bygones be bygones' kind of way and they were, say... drinking maybe James might loosen up and let slip what his next big deal is. Dan could indicate that he wants in. Plus, there is the whole jealousy thing about Harry between them. James should bite at the chance to brag about how close they are now. He tried to hide it back then, covered it up with snarky comments, but James hated it that Dan and Harry had a special bond. Part of me believes that their relationship was, at least in part, the reason James set Dan up to take the fall on their disastrous Cuban salvage job."

"Do you think that would work?" Becca's forehead creased.

Amelia shrugged. "Not really, but it's all I got."

"Can you get Dan to agree to even try?"

"Leave that to me. I'll think of something." She winked.

THE NEXT FEW DAYS PASSED TOO SLOWLY FOR BECCA. She repeatedly texted Amelia asking what was happening with James, but the only responses she received were variations of "don't worry about it," and "I'm handling it," and finally "don't make me block you." Which, of course, made Becca simultaneously worry and wonder if she should take it on herself. She was trying to do as Rey and Harry had asked and stay out of it. Sort of. She wasn't asking James questions herself, she rationalized.

Regardless, the wait was killing her. Every time she set her brush to canvas, the colors came out dark and muddied. Finally, Becca realized that her head wasn't in the right place to paint. She rearranged her closet and scrubbed every inch of her house in an effort to keep her itchy fingers from either texting Amelia again, or worse... calling Harry.

The next day, after closing up the gallery, she was surprised to run into Michelle standing outside next to Becca's bike.

"I didn't realize you were still in town. Are you waiting for me? You could have come inside." Becca smiled.

"I didn't want to bother you at work. I don't suppose you are hiring?" Michelle asked with a hopeful smile.

Becca shook her head. "It's just me and Dana and some part-time workers, I'm sorry. Aren't you going back to Sun Coast?" Frankly, Becca had assumed that Michelle and Candice had already returned. The exhibition had been a week ago, and other than seeing Candice at The Conch House bar, she hadn't seen them again.

"I'm not sure." Michelle was subdued. "Candice extended our stay at the rental place. Not that I've seen her. She's off with her new boyfriend. Seems like I'm the only one who comes to Key West and ends up alone and bored."

Becca's eyebrows met over her nose. "Candice has a new boyfriend?" It had to be Olivera's son. Does Candice actively seek out the most unsuitable men? First it was her friend's husband, then a money launderer, and now a cartel member.

"This rich guy she met at your party. She's been staying on his yacht," Michelle pouted. "How do I get a yacht boyfriend? Now you and Candice both have one."

"I don't have a boyfriend," Becca said absently. She had told Rey she would steer clear of the Oliveras, but could she in good conscience not warn Candice?

"I forgot!" Michelle clasped her hands in front of her. "We should do single ladies' stuff tonight!"

Becca was only half listening. "Candice is with him now?"

"She's supposed to meet me later for dinner. First time all week. I've been sitting in that condo alone. But now you and I can hang out!"

Becca hesitated. The situation was tricky. How could she warn Candice who her new boyfriend was without bringing attention to herself? She wouldn't put it past Candice to run to Andréas Olivera with a "Becca said" tirade. The last thing she wanted was for the Oliveras to think she was interfering with their lives again.

Argh!

"Come have a drink with me. Candice can meet you at my friend's bar after."

"Yay! Single girls' night out!"

Michelle chattered the entire way to the Salty Oar, but Becca barely heard. In her head, she was mapping out how she could warn Candice. It wasn't until Becca was waiting for a group of tourists to move in order to lock up her bike that Michelle's monologue penetrated.

"I won't have to stay with you long. Just til I get a job and my own place. Then the boys can come down. Oh my god! They will love it here. My parents won't be…"

"What?"

Michelle's face fell. "Weren't you listening? I was talking about moving here like you did."

Becca's eyes flew wide. "Oh! Um…" She was saved by the door opening and a group of older women spilling out onto the crowded sidewalk.

"This is going to take me a sec." She gestured at the bike. "Go in and try to get us a couple of seats at the bar."

Beaming, Michelle slipped in with the next group, leaving Becca alone on the sidewalk.

She closed her eyes and groaned. Now, not only did she have to deal with Candice, she had to convince Michelle not to move to Key West.

The bar was packed. The crowd had turned over from the daytime tourists into the rowdier groups that planned to party up and down Duval until the early hours of the morning. It took Becca a few minutes to navigate her way through the knots of people who stood in the open floor space. Given the crowd, Becca wasn't surprised to find Amelia behind the bar helping out.

"I got you a white wine," Michelle greeted her.

"Thanks."

"I texted Candice. She'll be here soon." Michelle sipped her own drink, body swaying to an imaginary tune. "This is going to be so great! I can't wait to be a regular like you."

Becca met Amelia's eyes over the bar and gave a tiny shake of her head.

"Moving is a pretty big decision. Your whole life is in Sun Coast. It won't be easy starting over in a new town... with kids."

Michelle's eyes narrowed. "You did."

"It's not the same."

"Why not?"

"First of all, it was just me. You have two kids in school and your parents to help you back in Sun Coast. All your friends... besides, I thought you liked living with Candice."

"I do." Michelle's mouth twisted. "She's acting like she's not going back any time soon though. I can't leave my kids with my parents forever."

"It's really expensive to live here, too, and not a lot of well-paying jobs." Michelle took another sip of wine. "It might seem different from the outside, but it hasn't been easy for me. I was lucky that Amelia found me a place to live right away, and that I had savings from my divorce." Becca felt terrible when Michelle blanched, but it was true. Michelle didn't have the same financial resources Becca had. Michelle's money had been lost when her husband had put all their money in fake investments. "I work all the time, and my love life is abysmal."

Amelia snorted, and Becca glared at her.

"Key West *is* a beautiful place, but if you are going to move here, you need to do it with your eyes open. Your boys need you."

Michelle's shoulders slumped. "But I could start over. Just like you did."

Becca pushed down her feelings of guilt. "Why don't you go back to your parents and discuss it with them. Who knows? They might want to move here, too." Becca mentally crossed her fingers and silently apologized to Michelle's parents for pushing the problem off on them.

It wasn't that Becca minded so much that Michelle might move to Key West. It was that she had the distinct premonition that she would somehow end up responsible for her. In their group of friends, Michelle had been more comfortable following someone's lead, and Becca wasn't in the market for any more complications in her life. Turning from Michelle's dejected expression, Becca ordered another round of drinks from Amelia.

"You haven't even touched the first one," Amelia pointed out.

"Have you and Dan settled on a plan?"

"Pest. I'll get you another glass." Amelia grumbled under her breath as she retrieved the bottle.

A few men shifted away from the bar, and Becca nudged Michelle to claim the seats before any of the other patrons noticed. Sitting with two full glasses of wine in front of her made her feel foolish. She gulped a good portion of one watching Amelia serve the other customers. Becca tamped down her disappointment. She knew she was being unreasonable expecting Amelia to magically have a solution, but she was anxious to learn what was going on with Harry. Anxious to discover if she had been a fool to trust him.

"What happened with your boyfriend?"

Lost in her own thoughts, she startled at Michelle's words. Becca swallowed. "It didn't work out."

"You said that before. Did he cheat on you?"

"Why would you ask that?" Becca exclaimed, and Michelle squirmed in her seat.

"I saw him the other day. With a red head."

Becca's chest clenched. "We broke up after the Bahamas. I have no idea when he met Allison."

"I'm sorry. You seemed really happy… before I mean." Michelle's face darkened.

Time to change the subject.

"Did you and Candice fly down or drive?"

"We drove in my car. Why?"

"I was just thinking if you wanted to go back without her you could. You don't have to wait for her to decide she's tired of this new guy." And, hopefully, the new guy wouldn't be around long, she thought.

"Trying to get my friend to ditch me, Becca?" The noise of the bar, had covered Candice's approach. The blonde put a hand on her hip and surveyed the bar with a smirk aimed at Becca. "Are you *always* here? Alcohol is full of sugar you know. Terrible for weight loss," she added, raking her gaze over Becca. "Bad for the skin, too. Ages you."

"Since I'm not trying to lose any weight, I'm not worried about it."

"Huh?" Candice filled the sound with doubt. "My bad. Michelle, are you ready? Let's go someplace a little less…" Her nose wrinkled.

Amelia had overheard the comment but only rolled her eyes. Becca grit her teeth. Why did Candice have to make it so hard to be nice to her?

"Michelle told me you have a new boyfriend."

Candice was instantly suspicious. "And?"

"Is it the guy you were with the other night at The Conch House?"

Candice's face relaxed, her features rearranging into a smug expression. "Andy? He's hot right? Can't get enough of me either."

"Yeah, Michelle said she hadn't seen much of you this week."

"You said you were cool with it," Candice snapped at her friend.

"I wanted to talk to you." Becca was intensely aware of the

crowd around them and Michelle listening closely. "Do you want to go outside where it's quieter?"

Candice tapped her red nail against the matching lipstick. "Let me think about it." She made a face. "No."

"It's important. I have some information you need."

"I highly doubt that." Candice reached forward and took Michelle's untouched wine glass.

"It's about this new guy."

Candice paused with the wine glass at her lips, and Becca seized her silence. "You just met this guy, and I'm sure you're excited about it, but you don't know anything about him." How do you tell someone they are dating a criminal? Becca thought back to when she came to Key West and people warned her about Harry. She had to use the language Candice valued. She tried again. "Key West is a small town and people say things... some not so nice things about who people are and how they get their money. I was told something about Andréas..."

Uncertainty flit across Candice's face but she waved her hand. "I'm not interested in whatever made-up gossip you have, Becca. God, you are so obvious! Andy isn't even from here."

"I'm just saying you should take it slow, check him out. I mean what do you even know about him?"

"He's hot, he's rich, and he's into me. That's all I need to know." Becca had heard this mantra before. Candice's angry eyes burned into Becca's. "C'mon, Michelle, let's go."

Michelle cast Becca an apologetic smile but stood up.

Dang it!

"I think he could be dangerous, Candice."

That stopped her. "Don't be ridiculous. Of course, he's not dangerous. You don't want me to be happy, and you're jealous. You lost your rich boyfriend and now you want to wreck it for me."

"That's not true. If he were anyone else, I wouldn't care."

"Okay then, Miss Know-it-all. What is it you think you

'know' about him that makes him so dangerous?" Candice's eyebrows rose. Becca looked from Candice's haughty face to Michelle's worried one.

Becca licked her lips. "I don't have specific details. Like I said, I heard some rumors... really bad rumors... Candice, for heaven's sake you just met him!"

A laugh burst from Candice, and then she tapped a manicured finger against her lips again. "Well, if Becca 'heard' a rumor, I better break up with him right away. Because she knows everything about men." Her eyes gleamed. "I saw that ex of yours the other night. You've been replaced with a younger model again, huh?"

"Candice, don't be mean." Michelle's eyes darted between Becca and Candice.

"Shut up, Michelle. You're my friend not hers. Let's go."

Without another word, Candice tossed her hair over her shoulder and worked her way back to the door.

"Sorry," Michelle mouthed before following her friend.

Becca bit her lip. The exchange hadn't gone well, but she had warned Candice. Even if Candice didn't listen to her now, the woman wasn't stupid. Becca could only hope that the blonde would be more on guard.

"What was that all about?" Amelia asked leaning over the bar.

"Drama," Becca said grimly.

Amelia let out one of her belly laughs as she turned away. "What else?"

Becca finished the first glass and debated whether she should have the second. With only the prospect of her empty cottage and brooding thoughts ahead of her, she decided staying in the bar with Amelia and lingering over a second glass was by far the better option.

An hour later, Becca was ready to go home. It was late for her, and she had to work the next day. Becca had just placed enough cash on the bar to cover her bill and was preparing to leave when Amelia gave a little wave to get her attention, followed by a finger pointing at the door with a smile. Becca turned her head, squinting through the crowd to see Dan making his way to the back office.

A grin spread across her face, and she gave Amelia a thumbs up before the older woman followed him.

Finally!

19

The next evening Becca pedaled home, blood boiling. Just before closing, the bell over the newly replaced door jingled, and to Becca's horror, Candice and Andréas Olivera strolled in dressed for an evening out. Becca's heart seized, her mouth suddenly dry. She thought there would be a confrontation of some sort, but after walking around and making derogatory comments about the items for sale, in particular Becca's paintings, they had left. Candice had been snarky but Andréas simply appeared bored. Why had they come to the gallery? Had Candice told him what she had said? Did he hope his appearance would scare her?

After feeding Furball and glaring at her open refrigerator for a full five minutes, she finally couldn't take it anymore.

"Why haven't you arrested Olivera, yet?" she asked when Rey answered his phone.

"Becca." His tone warned. "Tell me you didn't talk to him again."

"Of course not! Not on purpose. I ran into Michelle yesterday, and apparently Andréas is carrying on a whole relationship with Candice. They came into the gallery today. Why hasn't he been arrested? He's in a freaking drug cartel!"

"Are you all right? Did he threaten you?"

"No, but that's not the point. He should be in jail."

"Becca, I've told you before, and this is the last time I'm going to tell you. Stay out of it. I'm dead serious."

"I *am* staying out of it! I didn't say anything to him. I'm asking *you* a question." Becca left out the part that she had already told Candice that Olivera was dangerous. Rey wouldn't appreciate her warning her ex-friend, but she still believed it had been the right thing to do.

"Even asking questions is a bad idea. You have no business asking anything. You know I can't answer them."

"Rey?"

"Damn it, Becca! Stop pushing. It's being handled. You just need to be patient."

Grateful that Rey couldn't see her through the phone, Becca gnawed on her lip. She was risking Rey completely shutting her out, but she couldn't help herself. "The FBI has Olivera and James Brennan under investigation right? Are they watching them?"

Rey grunted. "Becca you know I can't answer that."

"Can you at least tell me if Harry is involved with any of it?" She swallowed. "Rey, I need to know."

Rey's dramatic sigh was louder, and longer than it needed to be. "Becca, I can't discuss ongoing investigations with you. You know that. Stay away from all of them, and you won't have anything to worry about. Don't ask any questions. Don't speculate. Don't get in the way. Paint, go to work, go home… that's what you need to be concentrating on right now."

"But they *are* in business together?" The simple no she was hoping for wasn't forthcoming, and the knot in her stomach twisted tighter.

Much to Becca's alarm, he abruptly changed the subject.

"Why do you care? Any more run-ins with lover boy? Do I need to come put in another appearance as the fake boyfriend?"

Normally, Rey's teasing her, wouldn't have sounded an alarm in her brain. But his tone, combined with the change of topic, made her believe he was actually checking up on her.

"No, I haven't seen him at all." Becca stared at the floor. She didn't like lying to Rey, and wasn't sure why her instincts told her she should. "Why?"

"Just curious."

"That's it?"

"That's it."

He said it innocently enough, but it was obvious he wasn't telling the truth any more than she was. It made her sad that they were at odds on this.

"I'm hanging up now. Things are happening quickly. It'll be over soon." Becca's antenna went up. That was almost word for word what Harry had said. "I'm all too aware standing down isn't your specialty, but keep in mind that if you keep interfering, you might inadvertently screw the whole thing up."

Becca grit her teeth. "Got it."

Rey hung up without saying goodbye. She regretted that he was upset with her because she truly valued their friendship, but this was serious, and even though she wished she didn't... she still wanted to protect Harry.

Minutes ticked by, and Becca paced the small space of her cottage. She jabbed the buttons on the television remote control unable to settle on a program. She only made it another hour before she texted Amelia again.

Becca: Please tell me what you have planned. I'm worried we are running out of time.

Amelia: James agreed to meet Dan tonight to discuss a possible business deal. Dan is picking him up at The Conch House Hotel. It's where he is staying. Hopefully, we'll have answers in the morning.

Argh. Becca let out a frustrated huff. *What is Dan going to say? Did Amelia prep him enough? Oh god, James is going to see straight through him... and then he'll tell Harry.. and then Harry will know it was me... and then...*

A new thought popped out amongst the other racing thoughts, and no matter how many times she told herself it was a bad idea, it wouldn't go away. If James is out of the hotel that meant Harry was alone. Harry said Allison was working in Miami, presumably getting the permanent exhibition at the museum ready.

If I could just talk to him...

She continued to argue with herself even as she did her make-up and hair and pulled out a knee-length floral sundress Harry had always loved.

This is a terrible idea, the voice in her head reminded her when she slipped her keys out of her purse. Whatever is going on, he's not going to tell you.

You just want to see him and this is your excuse, the voice argued back. The other night he was the Harry she had loved.

That thought brought her to a stand-still. One hand on the door handle, she hesitated. Was she secretly hoping for a repeat of that night? Was 'protecting Harry' just an excuse? Becca pressed the hand clutching her house keys against her stomach. Frozen by her thoughts.

It wouldn't be the end of the world would it?

She groaned.

This is pathetic

She shook her head to rid herself of the thoughts. She refused to think any more about why she was really heading toward the hotel.

THE LOBBY WAS MOSTLY EMPTY. GUESTS OF THE BOUTIQUE hotel generally avoided the lobby, instead preferring the seclusion of their bungalows. One desk attendant manned the registration and was helping a family check in, while the concierge helped another group with what sounded like dinner reservations. It was quiet except for the happy sounds emerging from the restaurant or when the doors to the bar swung open as a guest left.

Now that she was here, she wasn't sure how to proceed. It was unlikely the front desk would give her Harry's room number. If they called, would he even agree to meet with her? She wasn't sure she was ready for the humiliation if he said no.

Before she had a chance to make a decision, the bar doors opened again, and an unsteady Robert Clarke emerged. Glancing around, she realized there was no place to hide. He turned his glassy eyes toward her, and his face flushed a deeper red.

Becca struggled to keep a polite smile on her face. When he stumbled closer, the smell of scotch rolled off of him.

"Well, well, look who it is." Robert's lip curled, and he leaned close to her face.

Great! This is the last thing I need.

"How is Miss Helen doing?" Becca hoped her question would head off what she suspected could be an unpleasant conversation.

"She's dying," he barked.

Several heads turned their way, and Becca's smile slipped. "I'm so sorry to hear that."

"Now thanks to you, she's refusing to leave the island! Says she wants to die here." He brought his pointer finger up between them. They were so close he almost brushed her nose. Becca took a step backward, resisting the urge to slap his finger away. It would only escalate the situation, and all she wanted was to get away.

"This has been her home a long time. I'm sure it brings her

comfort to be in familiar surroundings. It was nice to see you," she lied, "but I'm meeting someone." Becca moved to step around him. Robert suddenly grabbed her forearm hard enough to bruise.

"It's your fault," he hissed. Her first instinct was to jerk away, but she could see the redness in his eyes wasn't just from the alcohol. "She's just... given up. She says it's her time, but I know it's the broken heart speeding this up."

Becca winced. "I truly feel awful about what happened." She kept her voice low, and placed her hand over where his was clamped tightly around her forearm. He stared down at where she touched him, then dropped her arm as if he had been burned.

"She thinks she is responsible for losing the family's heirloom, but it's *your* fault. It was in our family through hurricanes, the depression... and because of you, now it's gone forever!" He snarled at her, conveniently forgetting he had planned to sell it. "If it is the last thing I do, you are going to pay for it."

"You're making a scene, Clarke," Harry barked.

Becca hadn't even noticed him walk up. But now she saw that the rest of the room was watching as well, and she flushed bright red.

"Mind your own business, Brennan. This has nothing to do with you."

"That's where you are wrong. You're accosting a woman in a public place. That makes it everyone's business."

Becca looked nervously between the two men. Harry's eyes were laser focused on Robert, and she was worried that in his inebriated state Robert wouldn't notice the implied threat radiating off of Harry. Robert glanced at the room, and for the first time, he seemed to realize they had an audience.

"Remember what I said." With that parting shot to Becca, he stormed somewhat unsteadily to the door.

"I hope they call him a car..." Becca stopped, realizing

Harry had already begun to walk away from her toward the doors of the restaurant.

"Wait!" With a quick step she caught up to him and placed a hand on his back to stop him. She tried to ignore the way her chest ached when he immediately moved out of range. She moved to stand between him and the doors to prevent him from leaving. "I wanted to talk to you."

Dang it! This is not coming out the way I planned!

All the things she had practiced mentally in the car evaporated with Robert's angry words. The moment was all wrong, but she didn't know if she would get another chance. She had to try.

Harry looked over her head for a moment, his lips pressed so tight they almost disappeared. Then as if coming to a decision, he lowered his eyes to meet hers. Their postures were so similar to what they had been in her cottage a few nights ago. Instead of hot eyes meeting hers, as they had before, the ones that stared down at her were flat, emotionless. One of Harry's eyebrows crept up.

"What was it you needed to say?"

"Why are you being like this?"

His voice was cold and his expression disdainful. If she believed in evil twins, that is exactly who she would have thought was in front of her. Not Harry.

"The other night," she began.

His eyes flickered, but before she could decide what it meant, he blinked and the emotion was gone. "I'm sorry if I misled you the other night. If there was a misunderstanding…"

"Misunderstanding," she repeated dumbly. Shame flooded her stomach.

I. Am. An. Idiot.

"I shouldn't have gone to your home. I regret it."

Becca felt like he punched her in the stomach.

He regrets it.

Her cheeks flamed.

"I have a girlfriend now," he continued in that same awful, casual voice. "I've moved on. I thought you had as well with your FBI boyfriend."

A cold sweat formed between Becca's shoulder blades. She wanted to curl up into a little ball and howl at her stupidity.

How do I keep getting this wrong?

"I hope that this mistake won't have any lasting impact on your relationship or that I've made you believe…"

She dragged her eyes from the floor. That's right. He thought she was dating Rey. Grabbing onto her last sliver of pride, she cleared her throat.

"Of course. We should keep this *mistake* between the two of us. It didn't mean anything at all." She lifted her chin. "I'm not here about that. I need to speak with you for a few minutes about something else."

"We have nothing to talk about, Becca."

"I just…" Despite the shame burning through her veins, she needed to warn him about the FBI closing in. But her brain felt like mush, and what came out of her mouth was, "What are you doing here with your father?"

A muscle flexed in his jaw, and he averted his eyes. "That's none of your business."

"I don't know what you think you're doing," she rushed on. "Or, if you're trying to do some sort a good deed to make up for…"

"You don't know me as well as you think you do." The anger in his voice lashed her already raw nerves. He gave a small humorless laugh. "We had a fling. It was fun for a time, but then you got too serious, too clingy." He smirked down at her. "Don't read more into it than it was. You were a hot housewife on the rebound. Why would I pass that up? I told you what you needed to hear. It was fun for a bit. Anything more was entirely in your head."

Becca reared back, her body trembling. She crossed her arms across her body clutching her elbows. "I…"

"There is no reason for us to speak again. I hope you can be an adult about this. I know you're not very experienced, but this is how it works."

Her hand sliced through the air before she realized what was happening. She stared at the angry red mark on his cheek that had, for at least a second, wiped the smug grin off his face.

It's not true!

She wanted to scream, but tears were already clogging her throat, and she needed to leave before she fell apart, humiliating herself further.

Harry's face was tight. "I'm meeting some people for dinner. Goodbye, Becca." Without waiting for her response, he stepped around her to enter the restaurant. She shifted to the side finally registering that everyone in the lobby had witnessed their exchange. Her horrified eyes met Dan's sympathetic ones, where he stood with James just inside the entrance to the restaurant.

It hadn't occurred to her that Dan would have invited them both out, or that they would change their mind and eat at the hotel. That wasn't the plan!

Becca swallowed convulsively not knowing what to do. She was half afraid she was going to burst into tears in the middle of the lobby.

How can I be such a fool? I should know better by now. No one is who they say they are. I can only trust myself.

Becca repeated the phrase to herself, over and over, even as tears streamed down her cheeks on her ride back to the peace of her cottage.

20

A few hours later there was a sharp knock at the door. It was late but Becca hurried to the door, wine glass in hand. If she had been thinking clearly, she would have checked to see who it was before whipping the door open.

"Hey?" Becca said.

Candice reached out and took the wine glass out of Becca's hand. "You don't mind, do you?"

"Uh!" Becca was stunned to find the woman on her doorstep. Even more so when Candice pushed past her into the house. "What the hell, Candice? What do you want?"

Candice screwed up her mouth as she took in Becca's small home. "Cute." Her tone indicated it was anything but. Becca bristled. She didn't want Candice in her space. She didn't belong there!

"What are you doing here, Candice?" Becca repeated. Ignoring her, Candice, walked to where Becca had her current paintings up on easels by the front window.

Becca tapped a hand against her leg. "Look, I'm expecting somebody."

"That hot FBI guy you've been hanging out with?"

"No." Becca's eyebrows came together. "How do you know about Rey?" Becca was certain they hadn't run into Candice during the short time the woman had been in Key West.

The blonde shrugged sipping the wine. "Andy pointed him out."

A chill ran down Becca's spine. That was bad. Really bad.

Candice swiveled away from the art and took a giant gulp of the wine.

Short of physically dragging her out of her home, Becca didn't think Candice was leaving any time soon. Besides, she wanted to know what "Andy" had said about Rey. Becca returned to the kitchen and poured herself a fresh glass. When she turned back, she was greeted by Candice's outstretched arm with a now empty wineglass.

"Refill?" Becca asked sarcastically. Tipping the bottle, she poured Candice another inch. She wasn't interested in Candice staying for another entire glass of wine.

Candice cupped the glass with one hand in front of her, tapping her acrylic nails against it. The noise set Becca's teeth on edge. She had had a horrible night, and all she wanted to do was have a pity party with her bottle of wine.

Out of patience, she snapped, "Candice, what the hell are you doing in my house?"

Candice narrowed her eyes and then the words came out as if they were being pulled painfully from her. "I need your help. I think I've gotten myself in over my head."

Becca's first inclination was to say something like "who cares," but the tight lines around Candice's mouth made Becca bite her tongue. "Why are you coming to me? We're not friends."

"Uh, duh. Trust me, if I had anybody else I thought I could go to, you would be the last person I would ask."

"Yeah, you're not exactly making me want to help you."

"Ugh!" Candice groaned loudly. "I have information you want. If you help me, I'll give it to you."

Candice was nothing if not shrewd, Becca thought. What if there was some threat toward Rey because of the task force? If Andréas Olivera recognized Rey as the former undercover agent, he was very likely in danger.

"Like what?"

"Like that cross you were so upset about."

Becca blinked. "What are you talking about? What about the cross?"

"I think I know…" Candice stopped, her face taking on a hunted expression. She took a deep breath and continued. "I think I know where it is."

Becca gaped at her. "What? How?"

Candice reached for the bottle of wine and poured the remainder into her glass.

"So, Andy, the new guy I'm dating, invited me to his boat. It's a huge yacht." Candice preened for a second before remembering her purpose. "I'm pretty sure I saw your cross thingy sitting on the table in his dad's bedroom."

"His dad?" Becca paled. "Oh my god! Tell me you didn't snoop around Juan Olivera's yacht?"

"You don't understand, Becca!" She threw her hands up in the air, sloshing her wine in the glass. "Things haven't exactly been easy for me."

"I've heard this from you before, Candice," Becca said. "It was your excuse when you hooked up with John, who was defrauding all of your friends."

"I didn't have a clue about what John was doing. I was a victim, too!"

"You're lying…" Becca said. "And I'm not buying that it's just a coincidence you suddenly have enough savings to get a place for you and Michelle. Please! I'm not sure how you did it, but you must have held on to some of John's money. Were you storing one of the suitcases for him?"

Candice gave Becca a death glare. "That's ancient history."

"It was less than a year ago!" Becca exclaimed.

Candice waved her hand. "It's in the past. You know as well as I do, if you don't move on, you'll just flounder. You're not doing too bad for yourself. You got thrown over by one hot boyfriend and picked up another already."

Becca held her glass in front of her face. She wasn't about to admit to Candice that her faux relationship with Rey was just that, fake. It would sound even more pathetic out loud. However, it was a reminder that she needed to find out what Andréas had said.

"Whatever, Candice. I don't want to fight with you. I don't suppose you took a picture of it?"

"Do I look like Michelle with a camera always in my hand?" She tossed her hair. "I totally understand why, but Andy has developed more of an attachment to me than I'd like."

Becca's forehead crinkled. "I have no idea what that even means. I thought that's what you wanted. Remember you said he was 'hot and rich' and that was all that mattered."

Candice rolled her eyes at Becca's mock innocent tone. "It was, but he's moving a little fast for me. He seems to think I should go with him when he goes back to Colombia in a few days whether or not I want to go. Spoiler alert. I don't. Anyway, after being on his boat and seeing the amount of men with guns on it, I finally put together that he might be dangerous. I don't need all that in my life."

"I told you that," Becca muttered, but something else occurred to her. "You didn't know him from before this trip? You never came across him with John?"

It was Candice's turn to look bewildered. "What does he have to do with John?"

Candice was not a great actress, and Becca believed her. "Are you sure it's the Santiago cross?"

"Pretty sure. It's not really the kind of thing you see in a Christian book store, and he seemed very anxious when he saw that I noticed it. I wasn't snooping by the way. I was checking out the boat to help me decide if I should go with him. His dad's bedroom door was open, and it was sitting there in the middle of the dresser. I wasn't opening drawers or anything. Andy saw me and hustled me out of there before his dad saw me." Candice downed half her glass. "He seems kind of scared of his dad."

Becca leaned a hip against the kitchen counter and studied her ex-friend. Candice's face was more drawn than it had been that afternoon, and the shadows under the woman's eyes weren't completely obscured by her makeup. It was clear that, beneath the bravado, Candice was afraid.

"He should be! I tried to warn you. These are scary people."

Candice set her wine glass down and began fidgeting with the hem of her blouse. "Normally, I know how to handle guys like that. Give them what they want, and then I get what I want. He's different... I didn't realize it at first. Must be out of practice."

"What is it you think I can do?"

"You're dating an FBI agent, right? Can't he do something? Arrest him?" Candice picked up her glass again and drained it. "It's in your best interest, too. That night at the bar, when we ran into you, Andy saw your boyfriend." Candice gave Becca a sudden approving smile. "Your ex was there in the lobby with his new chick, and she told Andy that the two of you were dating."

"Allison told him that Rey and I were dating?" Becca was having a hard time following the story. "Why?" But the chill returned along with a sick twisting feeling in her stomach.

"Because they are all doing some business deal together. Duh! Plus, I think she was trying to make some point to your ex, because she was staring at him the whole time she was talking. Wow, I really thought you were smarter than this."

Becca fought against the buzzing in her ears. "Tell me exactly what happened."

"It's not that big of a deal. Andy and I were coming in through the front door of the hotel when we saw your new boyfriend walking away from the bar. Andy turned purple and called out to him but he didn't stop. I explained that he had the wrong guy."

"Wrong guy?" Becca whispered.

"He called him Dr. something. I told Andy I recognized him from the Bahamas, and he's an FBI agent not a doctor. Right about then, your ex and what's her name, Allison?" Becca nodded. "They joined us because originally we were all supposed to go to dinner, but Andy was super mad. I couldn't figure out why he was so upset about it. Allison piped up and said she'd met the guy in Miami and he was dating you. Andy got quiet and pulled your ex aside. They talked, and then Andy said he needed to speak to his dad."

Becca had the oddest feeling that all the bones in her body had dissolved. Candice's oblivious version of how Becca's world imploded came to her through a fog. She needed to call Rey. The Oliveras had discovered who he really was, and about his connection to her.

"When you came into the bar that night, Andréas knew who I was and that I was dating Rey, an FBI agent?" Becca wanted it spelled out.

Candice rolled her eyes. "That's what I said. It's not all about you, Becca. So, are you going to help me or not? I don't want him knowing I'm the one who told the police where it is. So, I was thinking what if the police got the info from your boyfriend. You know since Andy and him already have history and all… Are you okay? You look kinda green."

Becca licked her dry lips, her heart racing. Andréas Olivera had smiled and spoken with her as if he had no idea who she was. His ability to dissemble was chilling. "I'll call Rey. He'll know what to do."

"You would definitely be doing me a favor," Candice admitted.

"How is that?"

"Because I'm not sure I can get away from this guy on my own. He doesn't strike me as the type to take getting dumped well. If he gets arrested for stealing that cross thing, then..." Candice swiped her hands together like she was wiping him away. "It sounds bad, I know. But I tried to leave the boat one night, I made an excuse, and... he wouldn't let me. Just acted like I had said nothing. It was scary." She pursed her lips. "I know you hate me..."

"I don't hate you, Candice," Becca answered automatically, and was surprised to find that it was true. She didn't like Candice or want anything to do with her. However, Becca realized at some point over the last year her hatred for her former friend had mellowed into a strong dislike. There was one bright spot in this nightmare. "I do want that cross."

They knew where the cross was, and Miss Helen would get it back. Surely *this* was enough for Rey to finally arrest the Oliveras.

"Do you think your boyfriend can take care of it?"

Becca's brain quickly catalogued everything she'd just learned. "I suspect he's going to say something about warrants." Becca didn't want to reveal Rey's former undercover position.

"I don't want to wait for all that. What about your ex? He looked pissed when Allison said you were dating the new guy."

The knot in Becca's stomach twisted even tighter. She had a feeling she knew where Candice was going with this, but Becca doubted Harry's expression would have been a jealous one. He knew the danger Allison's revelation put her and Rey in. But... he hadn't said anything to her, or warned Rey. Candice said they were in a business deal together, and he had been so hateful to her tonight. She shook herself. No, regardless what may or may not be between them, she didn't believe he wanted her harmed.

"I don't really talk to him anymore."

Candice waved her hand, "Yeah, yeah, you could probably persuade him though. I mean it's nothing more than a little feminine wiles. Even *you* should be able to pull that off." Candice rolled her eyes. "Don't give me that look. You think you are so much better than me. It's the way we all get what we want."

"Gross. That isn't how women get things done, Candice. Some of us work for it."

"Ha! I've worked for it."

"Besides, I can't ask Harry to do me any favors, and I'm not going to put him in danger asking him to sneak onto the boat to get evidence."

"He wouldn't have to sneak onto the boat." Candice said. "I know for a fact that they have a meeting scheduled. It will probably be there, so your boyfriend is going to be on the boat anyway. He could take a picture for us."

Becca's heart stopped. Meeting with a cartel head on the cartel's private yacht. That was a little too cozy. Was she wrong after all? Was he one of the bad guys?

"If they are in business together, we don't know where his loyalty lies," she improvised. Then added silently, *and I won't put him at risk.*

Out loud she said, "I'll talk to Rey. He might have a way to help us."

"Whatever. Something needs to be done though, and soon. I am not at all interested in traveling to South America with this guy. What would Michelle do without me? I'm like her everything right now."

"Your devotion is truly touching, Candice," Becca drawled sarcastically.

"I know," Candice deadpanned, and examined her nails.

Becca pulled out her phone, dialing Rey's number. "I found the cross! I mean I know where it is anyway," Becca exclaimed for Candice's benefit when he answered. Then sotto voce, "I have a lot I need to tell you about an old friend of ours." Becca heard feminine laughter in the background. "Where are you?"

Rey didn't answer at first, which was odd, until another familiar giggle sounded, and her mouth dropped open. "Is that Dana?" Becca noticed Candice looking at her curiously and realized her mistake. "Oh, that's right, honey. You said you were going to hang out with her."

"What? Of course not." Rey sounded defensive. *Interesting.* If Becca hadn't been so consumed with her worry about the cartel and Harry, she wouldn't let it go but she had bigger problems.

"Anyway," she continued, "I found the Clarke family's cross."

She heard rustling, and then Rey's voice was clearer. "How did you do that? Do I even want to know?"

Becca made a face. "I didn't go looking for it. The information just kind of landed in my lap." She paused. He wasn't going to like this part. "It's on Olivera's yacht. But it's perfect. This will give you grounds to arrest him. You can go get it now that we found where it is."

"Hang on a second." His voice sounded angry. "I'm gonna take this outside." And then in a softer voice, "Hey, babe, I'll be right back." Becca scowled. He could at least pretend to be faithful while he was being her fake boyfriend. "Becca, I'm afraid to even ask this... but how the hell did you find it?"

Becca looked at Candice. "Candice came by tonight." Candice shook her head furiously. Becca widened her eyes at the woman with a what-else-could-I-say face. "She was on his boat for a date. She saw it there."

"Please tell me you are joking. That dingbat is *actually* dating Olivera?"

There were a lot of names she could think of to call Candice. Dingbat wasn't one of them. Realization hit. "Oh! No, not Michelle... her husband was the murderer. Candice is the other one, Raybourn's girlfriend."

"Yeah that makes much more sense."

"Even Candice knows that in this situation she's bit off more than she can chew this time. She needs our help to get away from him. This is good news, right? Now you can go arrest him, and Miss Helen can get her cross back." She spun the story out for Candice's benefit, but what Becca needed was to find a way to warn him that his cover had been blown.

Rey sighed heavily. "Becca what is it going to take to get you to leave this alone?"

"I'm not going to leave this alone. Rey, we know where the cross is... go get it!"

"This is the craziest thing you've suggested yet," he hissed. "I'm not going to talk about this with you. I can't just search someone's private yacht because you 'heard' something. Does she have a photo of it? Something to prove that it's actually there?"

Becca looked at Candice. "No picture."

"Then on what grounds do you think I have to go onboard?"

Becca glared at her phone. "I don't need the tone. Why are you getting so mad at me? Rey, there's something else."

"No! Damn it, Becca, enough. I'll pass the information on to the right people. I can't believe you! I asked you to stay out of it and you didn't."

"Rey, listen to me there is something more important." She was going to have to say it in front of Candice.

"Nothing else. I'm done. I've had a terrible day running down human traffickers, and I need to blow off some steam. Go to bed." It took Becca a second to realize he'd hung up.

"Stupid, stubborn men!" She jabbed at her phone calling him back. The fourth time he sent her to voicemail, she left a message telling him to call her back asap. She swiftly typed out a text.

Becca: I need to see you! Come over it doesn't matter how late.

Her shoulders slumped. *Now what?*

"Oh dear. I guess your feminine wiles aren't very good after all." Candice wiggled her mouth back and forth. She put her shoulders back and lifted her chin. "That settles it. I'll go get Michelle, and we can be on the road in an hour. If I'm out of sight, he'll forget about me."

Becca's mind was whirling. She wanted Helen's cross back. Robert had made it clear that there wasn't much time, and she couldn't bear it if she were to blame for Miss Helen's last moments being any less peaceful than the woman deserved. Plus, if there was irrefutable proof, this 'patience' Rey kept preaching to her wouldn't be necessary. She could almost hear a clock in her head. She was running out of time. She wasn't sure why the Oliveras hadn't come after her or Rey yet, but it was only a matter of time.

"Wait! What if we get the proof Rey needs? We could still sneak out to his boat. What if you went back out there and took a picture…"

Candice's eyes rounded. "I'm not going anywhere near that man again. What is wrong with you?"

"I'm sorry. You're right. It's so close to being over, and he's going to sail away with it."

"You feel free to play super hero. I have packing to do." Candice set her glass on the counter and headed to the door. Her hand on the knob, she looked back at Becca and cocked her head. "Not for nothing, thanks for trying to help." The door opened, and just before it closed, she stuck her head back through the opening. "I really am sorry about… well, everything. I never meant to hurt Evie, or for things to turn out as they did." The door clicked shut, and she was gone.

Becca was shaken after Candice had left. She double checked all the locks on her doors and sent Rey another text that she needed to talk to him. She changed into her pajamas but felt too uneasy to stay in her bedroom. Settling on the sofa, she turned on the TV for company and opened another bottle of wine.

Even after she put on a boring documentary, she couldn't relax. She was half way through the bottle and trying to figure out how to get Amelia to take her to Olivera's yacht when there was another loud knock on her door. It's about time, she thought, as she opened the door expecting to see Rey.

Becca had the quick impression of a dark, hooded figure before pain exploded in her head. She stumbled backward into her house. She heard Furball's angry yowl right before stars exploded in her vision.

21

Her throat burned. Becca tried to wet her lips, but her tongue felt thick and too large for her mouth.

What was that noise? Is someone calling me? Oh god, why does my head hurt so much? Did I finish the bottle?

Becca struggled to remember, but her thoughts were muddled. Her head throbbed with what felt like the worst hangover she'd ever had. Her fingers flexed in front of her, and she felt the jute throw rug scratch beneath her finger tips. Had she passed out on the floor? That didn't seem right. Her name rang out again, urgent and frightened.

"I'm here," she croaked, her voice little more than a whisper. She tried to swallow, but all the moisture in her body seemed to have disappeared.

A painful cough racked her body. She struggled to open her eyes, every nerve screaming at her to move. Someone called her name again, and her eyes finally opened. Thick smoke surrounded her, and her body convulsed in a fit of coughing. *Get out!* She struggled to pull herself to her knees. *I have to get out!*

The panicked voice came again, followed by, "Ow! Damn cat!"

Furball! Becca opened her mouth to call her cat. The acrid smoke burned her mouth and coughing racked her body. Strong arms closed around her.

"I've got you."

The arms dragged her across the room. She tried to help, commanding her legs to move, but her efforts must have frustrated her rescuer. Suddenly, she was swung up and tucked against a familiar, strong chest. Moments later, fresh air surrounded her, and she struggled to bring in air.

Harry lowered her to the ground, and Becca bent over, elbows on knees, coughing. Flames shot from the back door of her cottage.

"Furball!" she whimpered.

"She's safe. She's out here somewhere." Harry coughed roughly again. "I was trying to pick her up when she gave me this." He extended his arm to show bloody scratches down his arm. "And then she ran past me outside."

Becca scanned the yard, anxious for a glimpse of her pet. The animal must be terrified, but up until a year ago Furball had been a stray. She would be all right for a few hours outside.

Sitting on the crushed shell of her back yard, her arms resting on her bent knees, Becca sucked in gulps of fresh air. Gradually her coughing spasms eased. Harry sank to his knees in front of her, his face streaked with soot. Cupping her cheeks, he scanned her face with bloodshot eyes. "Are you all right?" His voice was urgent, and her hand lifted to rest over one of his.

"I'm okay, now."

Shouting echoed around them, and Rey appeared. Fire personnel flooded her yard, yelling instructions to each other, as they directed streams of water toward her home.

Harry stood, pulling her to her feet. She was weak, her throat was raw, but she was alive. Her life was burning in front of her. It was almost too much to take in.

"I need my cat." She turned her eyes to Rey. "Furball is out here somewhere. She'll be scared. What if she runs off..." Becca's body began to shake, and to her surprise, she realized she was sobbing.

"Get her out of here," Harry demanded. "She needs medical attention and then someplace safe."

Becca was shaking violently. "Owen's birth certificate, my paintings... I have to get them." She took a step back toward the house.

Harry's arm pulled her back, tucking her face against his chest. He bent his head until his lips were buried in her hair. "I have you. Everything will be okay. I promise. I won't let anyone hurt you."

His words penetrated the shock. Harry's arms locked tighter around her, and her trembling began to subside, though rational thought was still far on the horizon. At the moment, she would accept that he was here and she felt safe in his arms.

Over her head, Rey's voice was angry. "You shouldn't be here."

Was he saying Harry should leave? Becca's arms tightened around Harry's waist as if to hold him in place. When had she put her arms there?

"I know. I saw the smoke..." Harry's voice broke. "She needs to be checked out." His arms loosened. Becca tilted her head back to object, but pain made her moan. She released Harry, raising a hand to her head. Harry's hand followed her action to where a lump lay hidden under her hair.

"He hit me when I opened the door. I should have checked before I opened it," she explained. Harry and Rey's faces were mirror images of thunderous anger. An unspoken message seemed to pass between the two men.

"Did you recognize who it was?" Rey asked.

Becca shook her head and groaned again. "Sorry, it happened so fast."

"She needs to be somewhere safe. Now!" Harry growled.

Rey nodded. Becca knew she was woozy from the blow to her head, but she was completely bewildered by what was happening. Rey and Harry were talking as if they were allies, not two men who hated each other. Lights flashed around them strangely haloed from the smoke. More people came into the yard. Harry's eyes began scanning each face that arrived.

"It's too open."

Rey nodded. "You have a car?"

"A couple of blocks down."

"I'll have EMS check her out and meet you there."

"I'm fine, really. Just sore." Becca didn't want him to go. She wanted him to put his arms around her again. She should have emotional whiplash from his behavior today, but when he told her it would all be okay, she believed him.

"Don't let her out of your sight." His words were for Rey, but his stormy eyes met hers in the kaleidoscopic haze of smoke and spot lights. Her chest tightened at the intensity reflected back at her.

Before she could say anything else, he was walking away, and Rey was steering her by the elbow to the front of the house where EMS was waiting.

The paramedics took longer than she liked to examine her. She passed their concussion protocol, but they were unhappy at her insistence that she didn't need transport to the hospital for further observation. After promising that she would go to the emergency room if new symptoms appeared, Rey walked her to where Harry waited. Rey gave her a swift kiss on her head.

"I'm sorry."

"For what?" Becca's head still ached, and the adrenaline was beginning to wear off.

"For not listening earlier. If I hadn't been so stubborn, I would have understood the threat, I would have…"

Becca leaned up and pressed a kiss to his cheek.

"It's not your fault. I've cried wolf plenty of times. You were here when it mattered."

Rey cast a glance to the shadowy profile of Harry in the darkened car. "Loverboy was on scene pretty quick."

"You think he was involved?"

"I'm only wondering if you've been seeing him, and keeping it a secret."

Becca wanted to laugh but she couldn't. Overwhelming sadness suddenly swamped her, and a tear splashed down her cheek.

"Damn! I'm sorry. You've had a hell of a night. I shouldn't have said anything."

Becca's throat ached when she swallowed. She didn't want to cry. She was afraid it would just make her feel worse. "He's taking you to my place. It's secure. I'll come as soon as I can. Dana is waiting there for you. I called while you were being examined. She knows what to do."

"So that *was* Dana I heard on the phone." Her friend was going to have some explaining to do.

"I'm not talking about it now." Rey bent to open the door, and she gingerly climbed into the passenger seat. She may not have a concussion, but she felt like someone's punching bag.

Rey leaned in the window to give Harry the address.

"Hey!" Becca called as he straightened to walk away. Rey stuck his head back in. "If you are hanging out here for a bit, keep an eye out for Furball."

Rey nodded. "Your cat is a survivor. Once everyone clears out, I guarantee she's back looking for food."

"I hope so." Becca bit her lip.

Harry pulled away from the curb, the silence heavy.

Becca rested her head against the window as he navigated through the dark residential streets heading for the causeway. The events of the night had caught up with her, and she closed her eyes, as much to block out what happened as from fatigue.

The back of Harry's hand grazed her cheek, his worried expression illuminated by the fluorescent street lights lining the causeway. "You need to stay awake."

"I'm okay. They said I didn't have a concussion and I could sleep if I wanted to." Rey's words came back to her. "Dana will be there. She can wake me up a couple times to check."

"I think we should take you to a hospital. Get a CAT scan. Make sure there isn't something wrong they can't see."

"I'm not really injured. Promise." She closed her eyes again but sensed his gaze return to her over and over.

"Probably should keep your eyes on the road," she joked. "I'm not really interested in a swim tonight."

When he didn't respond, she opened her eyes. Harry's face was tense, and with the causeway streetlights above, she could see dark shadows beneath his eyes. "I should have known this would happen."

His palm slapped the steering wheel, and she winced. "Cool it with the banging. There's nothing you could have done to prevent this."

Harry's knuckles whitened on the steering wheel. His eyes darted to her again. "I should have been there," he ground out. "Realized what they would do. I never should have gone to see you the other night."

Becca's head hurt and she was exhausted. She wasn't in the mood to be reminded that he thought the night they spent together was a mistake. "This had nothing to do with that. Candice told me your new buddy Andréas recognized Rey, and that he was an FBI agent. I think it's more likely that tipped them over the edge. I guess seeing Rey and me together reminded them they hated me? As far as reasons go it's weak, but why else would they suddenly decide to openly attack me?"

"He isn't my friend," he snarled. "I'd like to kill him."

Becca blinked. "I thought you were in business together?"

Harry didn't appear to hear her. He stared at the road, several emotions racing over his face. "I never should have left you." His throat worked. "I wasn't there. I should have been."

Becca sat straighter in her seat. "Harry."

"It was never supposed to…" He suddenly veered off the Overseas Highway onto the thin stretch of sandy terrain between the roadway and the water.

His chest rose and fell rapidly, and his hands clenched the steering wheel over and over. Becca held her breath. She had never seen him this close to losing control.

Harry stilled, staring out into the darkness. His voice was flat when he said, "I never thought I could love someone the way that I love you."

Wait. What?

Becca released her seatbelt and turned to fully face him.

"That a life like the one we had together was possible. That someone could love me," he continued, his voice strained.

His fingers flexed around the steering wheel again. His head tipped forward until his chin was on his chest.

"Tell me what's going on." She tentatively reached out, gingerly placing her hand on his shoulder. "Harry?"

"Do you have any idea how it felt seeing the smoke coming out of your house?" Her ears had to strain to hear him. "And then when you didn't answer…" His voice broke, and his whole body seemed to shudder. "I thought you were gone."

Becca bit her lip. "I'm okay. Everything's okay…"

"It's not okay!" His voice lashed out, his hands reaching up to grip his hair. "I don't know what else to do! What else should I have done?"

Her eyes went wide. *What is he talking about?*

"But you *were* there. You came in time. I'm safe," she repeated, shaking his shoulder in an effort to free him from whatever mental torture he was inflicting on himself.

Harry turned haunted eyes to her then threw open his car door. Spinning in her seat to open her own, she rushed to meet him at the front of the car, conscious of the cars rushing by them just a few feet away.

"Tell me what is going on!" she cried.

Harry paced back and forth, his shoes scuffing the crushed shells. Headlights picked out his legs as he passed in and out of their beams, the rest of him in darkness.

"I need you to trust me."

"Trust you to what? You aren't making any sense! I'm done with vague explanations and half-sentences!" Becca's anger spiked, hot words spilling across the dimly lit space.

"Trust that I love you!" he shouted, abruptly pacing forward until he was within inches of her. "Everything I have done is to keep you and your son safe."

Becca shook her head. "What are you talking about? You left me in the Bahamas!"

Her words hit him and he froze, his entire demeanor changing. His hands fell limply to his sides and his entire body slumped.

Becca felt hot tears slide down her cheeks. "You leave me, then you're back. You tell me I mean nothing, then you ask me to trust you. You act as if your heart has been ripped out. *My heart was the one destroyed!*"

Harry's face crumpled before becoming a hard mask again. He stood silent, watching her across the headlights.

"I *know* you." Her voice was strong even while the tears leaked into her mouth. "You are hiding something. Why are you doing this? Just tell me what is happening!"

For one heartbeat, Becca thought he would tell her. She watched the internal war he fought flash across his eyes before he walked back to the driver's side door.

"I need to get you to Foster's house."

Becca angrily wiped the tears from her cheeks. "Excellent!"

They finished the ride in silence. Becca was at her breaking point; her frustration at his continued deception was swiftly turning to anger. Harry stopped the car on the street. "Becca, I understand this hasn't been easy, but I promise you…"

She didn't wait for him to finish, and she didn't trust herself to speak. Dana was already approaching from the front door preventing any further conversation. Just as the door shut, she thought she heard him whisper "I love you" but wasn't sure if he'd spoken or if it was wishful thinking. Either way, she wasn't sure it was enough anymore.

22

Dana had tried to tuck her into Rey's bed the night before, but Becca had taken one look at the empty wine glasses on the table and eyed her friend.

"No thanks, not until the sheets are changed."

Dana blushed. "You said you weren't interested."

"I'm not. I wish you had told me though. What happened to that girl you were pursuing?"

"It only happened tonight. He was giving off an I-can-be-corrupted vibe, and it was like catnip for me. But more importantly… was that who I think it was dropping you off?"

Becca opened her mouth to make a flip comment but instead burst into tears. "Must be from the hit to the head," she blubbered.

Dana pursed her lips. "Rey said you don't have a concussion."

"Well, he's not a doctor!"

Her eyebrows rose high. "Then we should go get you checked out don't you think?"

"Let's just say I've had a crappy day and leave it at that," Becca grumbled.

Dana smiled and then wrapped her arms around Becca. "Rey said I needed to put you to bed, but you reek of smoke. First shower and then bed. Oh, and don't be mad, but I have been given strict instructions to wake you up every hour or so."

After a long shower, where Becca allowed herself another good cry, she borrowed one of Rey's T-shirts and climbed into the makeshift bed Dana had made on the sofa. Dana turned out the light and kissed the top of her head.

"I'm so glad you got out in time. I don't know what I'd do without you."

AMELIA ARRIVED AT THE CRACK OF DAWN LOADED DOWN WITH herbal tea and arnica cream for Becca's bumps and bruises.

"Here take some of this elderberry syrup. It'll help your lungs." Amelia fluttered around where she rested on the sofa.

Becca shook her head at the bottle her friend thrust toward her, and sipped the chamomile tea. She would have preferred a strong cup of coffee. Physically, she was much better this morning. Dana had woken her as she had warned, but Becca had slept solid in between. Now she was awake and needed a plan. If Harry wouldn't tell the truth, and Rey wouldn't move on the Oliveras, then she would just have to do it herself. However, when she floated the idea past her friends, they stared at her horrified.

"Honey, what is it exactly you think you're going to do? Pull up to that boat, climb aboard, and nobody is going to challenge you?" Amelia peered at her. "How hard did you get hit?"

Becca's mouth set in a mutinous line. That was exactly what she was planning on doing. If Olivera was in town, then nobody should be on the boat. Any security he had would most likely be with him. She would watch for their tender and then sail out with Candice. She could climb up and pretend like she'd left something. If she hadn't left town already, that is. That could be a serious stumbling block. Had Candice really run home, packed up her own and Michelle's things, and already left? Becca doubted it.

"We just need to get a quick picture. Security doesn't know who I am. There's no reason to suspect anything. I'm just Candice's friend."

Amelia's eyes bulged. "They don't 'know' who you are? Someone set your house on fire last night with you in it! Safe to say, they are aware of who you are! Besides, you realize the giant flaw in your plan, right?"

"I think there's more than a few flaws," Dana muttered.

"You're not helping," Becca accused.

"I'm not trying to!" the blonde retorted. Dana sat cross-legged on the floor wearing the same clothes as the day before.

"When did you learn how to drive a boat?"

Becca's teeth snapped shut at Amelia's reasonable tone. "It can't be that hard. I have the basics. I've never taken a boating class, but if I don't have to dock, and I just trawl slowly…" The words coming out of her mouth finally pierced her brain, and she realized that her plan, which she'd been so excited about, didn't have a chance of working.

She fell back with a groan. "The cross is so close; all we need is a picture and then Rey can get…"

"Rey can get what?"

Becca jumped. How the hell had he snuck up on them like that?

His face was stormy, and she gave him a weak smile. "How much of that did you get?"

"Enough to realize that you've lost your mind!"

"Why does everybody keep saying that?"

"Because you're acting like it! We get it. You think you're responsible… but trying to board, a *cartel,*" Dana whispered the word as if someone was listening, "boat is the stupidest thing

I've ever heard you say, and you're not stupid. They tried to kill you!"

"Can you ladies give us a few minutes?" Rey asked.

Amelia gave a quick nod, and grabbing her arm, dragged Dana to the back door. "We'll just go look for fish off Rey's dock."

Rey waited until the French doors had clicked shut before leveling a glare at her. Becca folded her arms tightly across her chest. She realized now how foolish she sounded, but she didn't like it being pointed out by everyone. Rey paced back and forth in front of her, fury evident in every line of his body.

"I told you to stay out of it. Hell! Even Brennan told you to stay out of it!"

"Well, of course he would!" Becca bit her tongue. She'd almost given away that she thought Harry was a part of whatever the cartel leader was doing. Why did she still care about protecting him?

"I would have thought that after what happened last night, it was enough to convince you that these people don't play around. They tried to kill you!" Rey pinched the bridge of his nose. "You were supposed to come back here and rest. Stay safe. Instead, you are plotting some half-baked scheme to storm the Olivera yacht!"

"You think I should just sit here and wait like a sitting duck? If I can solve the theft of the Santiago cross, then it would all be over and we could move on!" Becca threw her hands up in the air and did her best not to wince when the lump on her head objected. "If you don't arrest Juan and Andréas, I'm going to be forced to run for the rest of my life. If you're sure that was Olivera last night, then you know he's not going to stop just because he failed once."

"You're trying to play superwoman again. You have to trust me."

Becca let out a scream of frustration. "If one more man tells me I need to 'trust,' I'm going to murder someone myself!"

"It will all be over by the end of today," he said ignoring her outburst. "I want you to stay here with your friends, out of sight and safe." He poked a finger in her face. "Do you understand? Or do I need to arrest you for interfering with an active law enforcement investigation?"

Becca gasped, "You wouldn't..."

"I absolutely would," he ground out.

"Fine! Go off. Do your thing. Let me know how it turns out."

Rey stalked to the door then suddenly stopped, his shoulders sagging. "Look, I understand this is tough and... because I'm worried that I can't trust you to stay put and not interfere... I'm going to share something with you." He glanced to the doors, reassuring himself that the other two women were out on the dock and not eavesdropping.

Becca forced her face to relax, but inside she was fuming. Part of her suspected it was embarrassment and frustration more than actual anger.

"If I share this information with you, do you promise me you won't go to the boat, or try to find another way to get a picture of the cross?" His eyes sought hers and everything inside of her stilled.

"If I say yes, will you believe me?"

"I will." He sounded sincere, but Becca knew he was lying. They trusted each other but not unconditionally. They both had prior allegiances that had yet to be broken, and that would always stand between them.

Rey had a firm belief between right and wrong, legal and not legal. For most of her life, Becca believed she was the same. Over the last two years, she had learned that her loyalty was solely to those she loved. If sometimes that meant breaking the rules, then she could live with it.

Becca nodded her agreement. By the way Rey scrubbed a hand over his face, he knew she was lying, too.

"There's an undercover operation going down today at the airport. By tonight, they'll all be in jail, and we'll be able to board the boat and get the cross back."

Hope burst through Becca's chest. "That's amazing! What's happening? When? What about Harry?"

Rey pierced her with his dark eyes. "I want your promise not to say anything, or do I need to arrest you?"

"I promise I won't go to the boat," she said, raising up on her tip toes, her excitement growing.

"Keep that Candice Davenport woman under control."

Becca made a face. "That might be harder than you think. She may have already left town."

Rey's expression darkened, and he cursed. For an uncomfortable minute, she thought he would call her bluff—that they would both admit, despite their friendship, there were limits. Instead, he released the doorknob and strode back to her, leaning forward to kiss her on the cheek and squeeze her bicep.

"I'll see you later."

Becca swallowed hard as he walked away, feeling as if she was making a life changing decision.

Less than a minute later, the glass doors cracked open, and Dana stuck her head in.

"Is it safe to come in?"

"Yeah, Rey left."

Amelia snorted, "We saw."

"You look weirdly calm," Dana observed, eyeing Becca warily.

"I am," Becca laughed. "Hard as it is to swallow, I'm going to do as I've been told. I'm not going to the boat."

Amelia humphed and moved to take the cup of tea from Becca. "I'll warm this up while you decide on whatever lie it is you're about to tell us."

Dana sat on the sofa. "What did Rey say? Is he coming back?"

Normally Becca would have teased her friend about her new fling, but Becca's brain was racing through what Rey had just told her. "They'll all be in jail." Who was 'they'? Did he mean Harry, too?

Her heart rate picked up, and she pulled her phone from her pocket to stare at it.

"Hello? Becca?" Dana waved her hand in front of Becca's face.

Her instincts told her to make the call, but could she trust them? She chewed her lip.

What if I'm wrong again? What if I'm being a fool?

"Did you decide yet?" Becca looked up to meet Amelia's eyes, then down again as she punched in the number. There was no answer.

"I need a ride back to my cottage."

"You won't be able to go in. Not until they are done with the investigation," Amelia said.

"I don't need to go in. I want to check on Furball, and get my car," she lied.

"No way! Rey said you needed to stay here. Besides, someone hit you over the head last night. You should be resting." Dana plopped on the couch next to her.

"I'm fine! I'll go to my cottage and then come back here." *Eventually*, but she added the caveat silently.

Amelia and Dana exchanged a look. Becca lifted her chin. "I can always call a rideshare."

Dana sighed, "Whatever. But I'm telling Rey you made us do it. We'll have to go by my house to get your spare keys."

Becca grit her teeth against the urge to yell at Dana to drive faster. They had stopped at Dana's condo to retrieve her extra set of car keys. But instead of the quick in and out Becca anticipated, Dana decided to change her clothes and water her plants. Becca stood by the door tapping her foot, willing her friend to hurry.

"Uh, no offense, but do you want to borrow something?"

Becca looked down at her clothes. Dana had washed the smoke smell out of them while Becca slept the night before, but the soot stains had stayed.

"All of my pants will be too short on you. I'll grab you a dress."

"Great, thanks." Becca didn't care about her clothes, but it would take longer to argue with Dana.

By the time they were back in the car, Becca was ready to scream at the delay. Rey hadn't told her what time the 'undercover operation' would take place, and she was conscious of every minute that passed.

She felt guilty lying to her friends, but Harry's tormented face the previous night played before her over and over. She couldn't let him go to jail. Even if he'd briefly lost his mind... there had to be a reason. She had to find him.

Crime scene tape draped across her front porch, and a police officer stood guard.

"You don't have to wait," Becca blurted, when Dana started to get out of the car. "I won't stay long, and Furball might be scared."

Dana frowned. "Are you sure you are good to drive?"

"Absolutely! See you back at Rey's."

Dana hesitated. "You aren't going to do anything dumb are you?"

"I'm going to search for my cat."

Not bothering to hide her unhappiness, Dana climbed back

into her car. Becca called the cat and looked around the yard that wasn't cordoned off with no success.

"Is it an orange tabby?" the officer asked her. "It was around here earlier."

Relief flowed through Becca. Furball had made it out. She didn't realize how worried she had been until she teared up. "Thank goodness!"

The young man smiled. "I wouldn't worry. Pets are pretty skittish after an incident. She's still hanging around which is a good sign. Give me your contact info. I'll text you when she shows up."

"Thank you. Can I leave her some water?"

The police officer agreed, and Becca used the hose to fill a drip pan from under one of her plants. With one last sad look at her burned cottage, she headed toward The Conch House.

23

The concierge wouldn't give her the room number, and the phone went unanswered in his room. Becca loitered hoping he would come back, but after an hour, Harry still hadn't answered any of her messages or texts. She didn't want to risk telling Harry about the FBI over text in case someone saw his phone, but she thought the seven "call me asap" messages would have gotten a response. She was running out of time. Her only other option was to intercept him at the airport before the FBI got there.

At each red traffic light, Becca let out a stream of expletives fueled by thoughts she couldn't escape. She was betraying Rey. She suspected there was a very real chance their friendship would never recover. Rey bent the rules a few times for her, and his sense of right and wrong might not be quite as rigid as when they first met, but this was different. This was Becca giving a heads-up about an impending arrest to a man Rey believed was a criminal. He might understand her need to save Harry, but he would never agree with what she was about to do.

Everything pointed to Harry being involved with the cartel.

Logically, there was no other explanation, but her heart couldn't accept it.

Why? Just to prove to myself that I'm not the absolute worst judge of character?

Her foot eased off the pedal. Was she being stupid? It was entirely possible Harry was deceiving her, and it was her love for him that made her see things differently.

Becca mashed the gas pedal. She knew him! Something else was going on, there had to be. If he had gone into business with his father—okay, that was bad—but she could deal with it later. There was absolutely no way he would have gotten involved with the cartel and drugs. Maybe he hadn't realized who they were to begin with? Becca hadn't. Hope rose inside her. His father could have made the introductions, and it's possible Harry didn't find out who they actually were until it was too late.

That must have been what happened, she assured herself. It completely explained Harry's behavior over the past weeks, too. Becca's shoulders relaxed, and her death grip on the steering wheel eased. He said it wasn't what it seemed and warned her that it was dangerous.

Was he trying to protect me?

Becca remembered Celine gleefully telling her that the cartel found Becca's constant presence a little too coincidental. She frowned. So why was Harry doing business with them now? Wasn't that drawing her closer to it? There were too many loose ends that didn't fit.

Becca hit redial on her phone.

Come on! Answer!

THE CARS IN FRONT OF HER SLOWED. A CAR WITH SOUTH Carolina plates, at the front of the line of traffic, started to turn into a condo complex before abruptly pulling back out, blocking the other cars again.

Argh! Stupid tourists!

"Come on! Move!" Becca slammed her palm against the steering wheel.

She was almost to the airport, and it felt as if the universe was conspiring against her. The long line of cars stretched in front of her, tapping their brakes every time one approached a driveway to one of the various hotels or warehouses adjacent to the airport. Her heart raced as she toyed with the idea of passing them despite the double yellow line.

She blew a heavy sigh of relief when the last car appeared to have found the right hotel. She stomped on the gas pedal, nearly clipping the bumper of the car in front of her as it completed its turn. Pulling into the airport behind a minivan, Becca snatched the ticket from the machine almost ripping it, but she didn't care. She almost had a complete breakdown when there were no spaces in the short-term parking.

"Screw it!"

She cut off a car also looking for a spot, and zoomed up the ramp of the parking garage. The car had barely rocked to a stop on the top level before she had thrown the door open and was running toward the elevator. Out of the corner of her eye, she caught the colorful stream of tourists as they exited the main terminal below her, posing and taking pictures.

Wait! Something's not right.

Becca squinted, taking in the scene, and wracking her brain for what it was that felt out of place.

They wouldn't do this out in the open, right? It didn't make sense. The FBI isn't going to try to take down a cartel head, a huge international criminal, in the middle of a crowded airport. There's too much risk that innocent people could be hurt.

She stabbed at her phone. "Damn it, Harry! Answer!" Becca

held the phone to her ear, groaning out loud when Harry's voicemail picked up again. She stared out at the Atlantic Ocean in despair. "Now what?"

Almost as if in answer, a long line of black SUVs roared up A1A, approaching the airport. "Oh my god! This is it." She jabbed the elevator call button again.

From her raised vantage point, she watched in horror as the vehicles turned onto one of the side roads, before the airport's main entrance, that led to a large warehouse. Two skidded to a stop blocking the road while the others parked closer to the building. *Oh, no!* Her heart sunk. When Rey had said 'airport,' he hadn't meant the literal airport. Spinning, she sprinted back to her car. Even as she yanked the door open, she realized that in all likelihood he had deliberately misled her.

Racing down the ramp, she had no idea what it was she thought she was going to do… her rational brain was screaming at her to stop, that she was only going to make the situation worse, but she was acting on pure instinct at this point. She needed to get to Harry.

She slammed on the brakes at the electronic arm, fighting the temptation to ram it. Instead, she rolled her window down to insert the ticket and heard the unmistakable sounds of gunfire.

Becca stopped breathing.

"NO! Please, please, please!"

The two SUVs that had stopped a hundred yards up the access road, essentially blocked the entrance and prevented her from pulling closer to the warehouse. Her air came in short, shallow pants, as Becca jumped from the car and attempted to run around the agents standing there, oblivious to the fact they were reaching for their weapons. "I'm with Agent Foster!" she cried, "I need to…"

"Becca!" A bulletproof vest strapped over his button down shirt, Rey stormed toward her, nostrils flared and veins visibly pulsing in his neck.

"Are you all right? I heard gunfire..."

"What the hell are you doing here?" he thundered.

"I... I..." There was no point in lying. "I had to try," she finished miserably.

"Get. In. Your. Car," he said through his teeth. She wasn't sure his lips had moved.

"Is Harry..."

"Becca," he growled.

"Is Harry all right? The gunfire..." Her throat tightened painfully. "Is he hurt or..."

An ambulance, lights flashing, raced past them, swerving around both Becca's parked car and the two SUVs. She became aware of voices nearby directing the ambulance and the words "two subjects" and "gunshots."

Becca's heart thudded. "Harry?"

Rey rolled his lips in so tightly that the edges of his mouth whitened, and for a moment she thought he wouldn't answer. His eyes bored into hers, then he shook his head. "Brennan is unharmed. But from the look of him, I don't think Juan Olivera is going to make it."

"Oh!" The breathy sound was all she could manage. Overwhelming relief made her light-headed. Past Rey, she saw several men coming out of the warehouse. Most were clearly agents, wearing bullet-proof vests identical to Rey's. But in handcuffs and flanked by agents, James and Andréas came into view.

Becca frantically scanned the group searching for Harry. Rey gripped both her shoulders and spun her around, pushing her back toward her car.

"Rey, I don't..."

"You can't be here right now." His grip tightened when she tried to turn around again.

"But..."

"You need to go home right now." His voice was low in her

ear as they passed the two agents she had pushed past. "You made a wrong turn, were curious about the activity, and were worried when you saw me." His voice was louder now, clearly for the other men's benefit. The two agents exchanged a look before one glared first at Rey and then lowered his eyes to her. She swallowed hard. Had she gotten Rey fired? Was she about to be arrested?

"Ma'am, you really should be more careful." The agent's droll tone made it clear what he thought of the ridiculous story. "Even if you do have a *friend* in the FBI."

Rey opened her car door and not so gently pushed her in.

"I don't want to leave until…"

"You may have already gotten me tossed. Don't make this worse. If I don't arrest you for obstruction, they might." He jerked his thumb at the two agents.

Becca opened her mouth to argue but saw he was serious. His face was still a dull red, and with a sinking sensation, Becca feared she had gone too far this time.

"I'm sorry," she said quietly through the open window, when he slammed the door.

Rey stared at her for a moment, conflicting emotions on his face.

"I know," he sighed. "Part of me actually gets it." He threw his arm out, gesturing for her to leave. With no other choice, Becca put the car in reverse, carefully inching back toward A1A. She glanced briefly through the windshield and abruptly hit the brakes. Alerted by her movement, Rey pivoted back to the warehouse.

Emerging from the warehouse's front door were the unmistakable figures of Harry and Allison, followed by two more FBI agents. Harry tipped his head toward Allison, as if to listen closely to what she was saying. When they reached the SUV's door, Allison reached up and placed her hands on Harry's jaw pressing a quick kiss on his cheek. One of the agents got in beside her and another opened the driver's side door.

Becca watched, her chest aching, as Harry ran his hand back through his hair. He turned to enter another nearby SUV, and only then did Becca tear her eyes away. Rey scowled at her through the windshield, then shook his head and waved a hand indicating she should go.

She had no choice. The SUVs containing James and Andréas were moving toward her, and she was blocking the exit. Unable to trust that she wouldn't give in to the temptation to look at Harry again, Becca turned her entire body in order to see out the back window. Luck was with her for the first time that day, and there was a large gap in the traffic making it possible for her to back out onto the normally busy road.

BECCA FOUND IT IMPOSSIBLE TO FOCUS ON ANYTHING. SHE drove blindly, forbidding herself from raising her eyes to the rearview mirror to check if the vehicles were still behind her. Five minutes later, she realized she had mindlessly driven toward her ruined cottage. Turning onto the next street, she pulled to the side and rested her forehead on the steering wheel. Where could she even go? Her house was ruined, and she didn't think it was appropriate to go to Rey's. Out of habit, she pulled out her phone to call Amelia and saw to her dismay she had several missed calls and texts from Dana. By the increasingly terse messages, her friend was pissed. She'll understand, Becca assured herself. Not wanting to face another lecture, she dialed Amelia's number.

"Hey, honey!" For once, Amelia's cheerful voice didn't help Becca's mood. "Dana's looking for you."

Becca skipped any preamble and asked, "Can I come stay with you on your boat tonight. It suddenly occurred to me that I don't have anywhere to go."

"Of course you can, but I thought you were staying at Rey's place."

"Thanks." Becca ignored the question. "I'll head there now."

"I'm actually at Dan's for the night, but I'll come back if you need to talk."

Becca grimaced. The last thing she wanted to do was explain to her friend what a mess she had made.

"No, stay there. I've just had a really long day, well forty-eight hours," she chuckled darkly. "Hell, I've had a really long year and a half. I think I need some peace and quiet to figure some things out."

There was silence from Amelia's side and then muffled voices as if Amelia had covered the phone.

"This wouldn't have anything to do with all the commotion at the airport would it?"

Becca was stunned though she shouldn't have been. She had ceased wondering how Amelia seemed to know everything that happened in Key West. "It's only it seems to be if there is a police action somewhere on the island, you're somehow involved."

"I'll tell you more about it tomorrow. I'm not up to a debrief right now."

"Is there anything I should be worried about?" Amelia's tone was suddenly serious.

"I honestly don't know, but I don't think there's anything we can do about it tonight."

"Well, the key is in its normal hiding spot. I'll come back with donuts in the morning. Try to get some sleep. Whatever it is, we'll figure it out together."

Those words were a balm to Becca's spirit. At least she still had Amelia. Becca struggled to process what had just happened. Her brain was mush, and she couldn't hold on to any thought long enough to make a plan. She'd tried to save Harry and probably lost one of her best friends in the process. And, it had all been for nothing because she had been too late in the end. On top of that, she felt stupid. Despite what had happened between her and Harry over the last week, he was with Allison. And now they both were going to jail. Had it all been wishful thinking on her part? A self-delusion she created in order to have her happy ending—at least in her imagination?

By the time she made the short drive to the marina, she was completely exhausted. Habit carried her to Amelia's boat, and after fishing the key from its hiding spot under the dock, she sank into one of the cabin chairs. She pressed her fingers against her eyes. The adrenaline had evaporated, leaving behind limbs that were simultaneously heavy and shivery.

Keep breathing Becca, she told herself. She inhaled through her nose, and held the air for a moment before blowing it out again hoping it would help her calm down. Harry was alive. That's what mattered. Her brain replayed the moment the gun shots rang out, and her stomach turned. She pressed harder against her eyes as if it could block out the memory. He was alive but going to jail. The events of the last hour continued to play, and she saw again Allison's handcuffed hands cupping his face. Harry resting his hands on her shoulders in comfort.

A weight landed on her chest. In the excitement, she had let herself forget that they were a couple now. Becca rose from the chair and proceeded to the kitchen. A pan of brownies was sitting covered on the counter. *Don't they say sugar is good for shock?* Becca took the entire pan with a glass of water back to the chair.

As she pinched off bites and put them in her mouth, she told herself that she was okay. In fact, she might be better than okay. If Rey was correct and Olivera was dead, his last son in custody, then she and Owen were safe. The thought should have cheered her. Instead, it was the memory of Allison's expression when she looked up at Harry that relentlessly tortured her. The next bite of brownie was accompanied by a hot tear.

Stupid. Stupid. Stupid!

Her stomach was suddenly queasy, and she put the brownies away. Amelia's boat only had the one berth, and it didn't feel right taking it. It was still light out, but Becca didn't care. She retrieved a pillow and blanket and curled up on the sofa, her hands tucked under her head. She sniffed hard when the tears threatened again.

Her eyes popped open. *Hang on!* She called back the vision of Harry and Allison together. Allison's hands cupped Harry's jaw because they were handcuffed, but Harry's hands were free when he touched her. He had even put them on his head.

What did that mean? Allison was under arrest but Harry wasn't? Why not?

Swinging her legs out, she retrieved her phone from her purse. She saw that she had missed two calls from Amelia. She ignored those and called Rey. Her eyes narrowed and her mouth pinched when she was sent immediately to his voicemail. She called again with the same result.

Her temper rose as she put more pieces together. Why had Rey even been there today? He had told her he wasn't working on any drug cases. He told her he was off the task force. How did he know to tell her the undercover operation was happening? He claimed he only handled small cases and background stuff now. It's why he had been able to take so much time off and hang out with her.

Liar!

The whole time, he was still working on the Olivera case! Becca felt like she was boiling inside. She stormed around the boat, growing even more furious because there wasn't a decent amount of room to pace. He made her feel so guilty with his 'you have to trust other people' line. She caught a glimpse of herself in the mirror and realized she had screwed up her face mimicking him.

"You know what! That's it! I'm done with all of them. I'm going to move to my own island away from everyone. I'll send a boat for Owen, and Amelia can bring Dana, but that's all!" she muttered.

"I can help with that." The deep voice so close behind her made her screech in surprise.

Seriously?

24

Harry was smiling, but his eyes were wary, clearly unsure of his reception.

Yeah, well, he should be.

"No thanks!" She glared at him. "I want you to leave."

"Becca…"

"Get out," she seethed. "Go back to your girlfriend. Back to whatever it is you've been up to." She gave a humorless laugh and shook her head. "The airport, whatever that was… that's what you've been doing? Well, great! Looks like it was successful since you are standing here, the only one of your friends not arrested."

"They aren't my friends. Becca…"

"True. One is your father, one is your girlfriend, and two are freaking cartel!" Her voice had raised so that she was shouting. "What is wrong with me?"

Harry looked confused and opened his mouth to speak, but Becca was lost in her emotions now.

It felt like everything in her life had coalesced into this one moment.

"Seriously! What is it about me? Because it must be something fundamental. Something in my very nature that makes me not worthy." Tears flooded Becca's eyes and slid down her face. She couldn't have stopped them if she'd tried. "It's the story of my life. My parents couldn't be bothered to take the time to care about or support me. Their lives, their careers, were always more important. 'She's fed and with the nanny.' That's where their interest in me stopped. They were my *parents*! Surely they knew me best of all, so if they didn't think I was important enough... then I met Jake, and got pregnant, and I thought okay there's my value."

Harry took a step forward, his expression stricken, but Becca held up her palms to stop him. These feelings had churned in her for so long, and it felt like an eruption out of her control. All the pain she had been holding onto poured out of her. "Jake valued me, at least for a little while, because he wanted to be a family with me. For a few years, it was great because I shaped myself to be what he wanted, but eventually even fake me wasn't enough. Again and again, throughout our marriage, he made choices that proved I wasn't enough for him to sacrifice anything for... and then there's you. The second things became even the least bit complicated, you left. And to be honest, that hurt me more than Jake ever did." Her voice broke on a sob. "Because I *trusted* you! I was myself with you, and you made me believe that I was enough. You *said* I was enough. But then not only did you leave during one of the hardest times of my life, you teamed up with people who most likely wanted me dead!"

Becca swiped at her nose that had begun to run. She didn't care anymore. "So, you tell me. What is it about me that makes it so hard for people to love?" Becca wrapped her arms around her middle, her shoulders shaking.

Harry's jaw fell open. He swiftly closed the distance between them, pulling her hard against his chest. "Becca you can't truly believe that."

His breath was hot against her hair. For a split second, she allowed herself to forget and take comfort in his embrace. But it was fleeting. She brought her hands up between them and pushed hard. Taking a step back, she wiped her cheeks.

Her voice was matter of fact. "Why shouldn't I believe it? Other than a few friendships here and there, I've never had anyone put me first, and I'm sick of it! I'm sick of always being the one to pick up the pieces for everyone else. I'm sick of trying to prove that I am worth it."

"I had no idea you felt that way." He shook his head bemused. "Becca *everything* was for you. You're amazing, and I'm so sorry you have been hurt by so many people in your life. You deserve everything good this world provides." When he slowly reached out and cradled the back of her head and neck, she let him. His eyes burned into hers. "You taught me that there was more value to me than what I could give people. That I could rise above the terrible things I saw and experienced growing up... that I was worthy of love."

"And yet you left," she whispered, but made no move to pull away. "You left me when I needed you... I wasn't enough for you to stay and..."

"That's not true!" he interrupted fiercely, his hands tightening on the back of her head. "You don't understand. When I say it has all been for you, I mean it. Everything I've done since August... leaving the Bahamas that day, letting my father back into my life, meeting with Olivera, risking my best chance at happiness in this life by driving you away..." He stopped, pressed his forehead to hers, and said against her lips, "It was always for you."

His lips slowly slid against hers, and Becca closed her eyes against the sensation. It was so tempting to believe. But she had trusted before...

Becca pulled back putting a slight space between them. "I don't think having sex with Allison was for me."

Harry's lips quirked. "I've never had sex with Allison. In fact, I haven't been with anyone since I was last with you."

Becca made a face and put more space between them. "Riiight," she dragged out the word. "You've been dating a beautiful young woman for months, and you've never slept with her. And I'm sure all the women you dated around the Caribbean last September were equally chaste."

"What women?"

Becca couldn't believe he had the nerve to pretend to be confused. Did he think she was an idiot? She shook her head. Would she never learn?

"I saw the pictures, Harry. The women you took out in St. Lucia and the Caymans." She continued when he still looked lost. "Oh my god. Have there actually been so many you don't remember? Celine sent me the pictures of you that had been posted in the society pages."

Harry's face cleared. "Oh, those pictures. Celine didn't send those to you. I did."

Becca's mouth fell open. "What kind of cruel…"

Harry caught the hand she reflexively raised. "They weren't real dates. They were staged." Becca tried to yank her hand free, but he held tight. "Becca, listen to me for a second. Ow!" He jerked his leg back but didn't let go. "Don't kick me. Just listen."

"Fine, I'll listen, but then you have to leave, and I never want to see you again." She kept her voice even, in direct contrast to the hurt and anger whirling inside her.

Harry's face fell. "It was a calculated risk. This whole thing has been one calculated risk after another. I didn't have much choice. I could tell by the messages that you kept leaving me you weren't going to give up on us. Even though I hurt you, even though I abandoned you, you still reached out." His face softened. "One of the things I love most about you is that when you love it's with your whole being. I had betrayed you, let you down when you needed me, and you still were going to give me a chance to explain. I had to find a way to make you let go, and it had to be public to help with the plan."

He loved her?

"You aren't making any sense. You sent me pictures of yourself with other women so I'd leave you alone?" At the time that thought had actually occurred to her, but she had dismissed it as ludicrous. "If you wanted me to stop, you could have answered one of those phone calls and told me it was over. The bizarre subterfuge wasn't necessary."

"If I had called you, heard your voice, I wouldn't have been able to go through with it. I would have taken you away and hidden you, to keep you safe... but you would have hated it. Trust me, that was my first response. When Sean told me the cartel was turning its attention to you, I made plans for you to go into hiding. But then as everything transpired with the murder, and your son, I knew it would be selfish. I could kidnap you, keep you isolated and safe, and I'd be happy, but you would be miserable. I couldn't be selfish. I realized I had to come up with a way to get the cartel out of your life for good. As long as Olivera and his son were still at large, you and your son would always be in danger."

Becca's head was spinning. "What are you talking about... Sean? But Rey said the cartel wasn't interested in me, that they were essentially hamstrung and broke after the money laundering scheme blew up?"

This time when she tugged on her hand, he let go. Becca slowly paced the length of the lounge trying to make sense of everything he was saying. "I need you to spell this out like I'm a child." She gave him a meaningful stare. "From the beginning, and don't leave anything out. One lie and we are done... forever."

Becca's words echoed his from the day Harry found out the truth about who Rey really was, and she could tell by his expression that he remembered.

"Can we sit down? Have a glass of wine? It's kind of been a stressful day."

Becca glared at him, but she rummaged in Amelia's cabinets bringing out two glasses and an unopened bottle of wine.

Harry took the bottle from her, and as he twisted the corkscrew, he asked, "Do you remember the night we had dinner with Sean at the Royal, and he started to act weird once he realized that Jake was your ex-husband and that you knew all the key players in his wealth management firm?"

"Celine explained it to me." Becca's voice was cold. "About the money Sean and James had lost and that they thought I was there because of it."

"Celine told you? Why?" Harry's brows knit together.

"It's not important. Keep going."

"Did she tell you that Sean had already expressed his concern to my father?" Becca shook her head. "That was a red flag for him. That, and the fact that I was ready to make a deal with my father to gain information simply to benefit you."

Becca kept her face blank, willing herself not to react. She knew he was referring to the flash drive implicating Owen, but Harry didn't know she already had that piece of the puzzle. "Turns out they didn't have the information I wanted but... I had already spoken to Foster."

It took Becca a beat to realize he meant Rey. "You talked to Rey about the information?" This was news to her! If Rey had known about the flash drive then...

"No, of course not. It... it would have been damaging..."

"For Owen, you mean?"

"How do you know about all this?"

Becca waved a hand. "Long story."

"You'll tell it later," he demanded.

"Maybe."

When Harry's eyes narrowed, she couldn't help the little smile that tugged at her lips.

"I went to Foster's room to find out," he grimaced, "if you were telling the truth."

Becca blinked, but stayed silent. She wasn't surprised. The secret she had kept from him had been a pretty big one, and she didn't blame him for wanting to double check.

"Go on."

"He and his partner told me that when we showed up at the Royal at the same time as the Premier Wealth Management people, it sent alarm bells ringing in Olivera's organization. Where Celine thought you were working *with* them, Olivera was concerned that you were there to cause problems. Sean told me the night he and I met alone... the night of the murder... that Olivera had contacted him and asked a lot of questions about you. When I shared that with Foster, the discussion shifted. They thought your life might be in danger. Initially, they wanted to take you into protective custody but they didn't have grounds. Despite all the coincidental encounters, you hadn't witnessed anything. But the bad guys were suspicious of you. That's when I first thought about whisking you away into hiding, but Foster had a better idea."

Becca frowned, foreboding sending icy tingles down her spine. She wasn't going to like this. "What did Rey say?"

"He suggested that since his cover was blown, and it was too late to embed someone new, that I could help them in kind of... I guess you'd call it an undercover operation."

Becca's jaw hit the floor. "What?"

"As long as the cartel was out there, you and Owen were never going to be safe." Harry had said that before, and Becca knew it was true. "They needed someone to lure Olivera to the States so that they could arrest him. After his daughter Katie disappeared, he went into hiding allowing his sons to be the faces of their business out in the world. He rarely left their compound. The idea was for me to distance myself from you.

Play up my history as a playboy in order to create a cover so that it was believable I'd gone back to my old ways."

Becca arched her brows. "Speaking of 'things' we'll discuss later. I'd like to hear about what *all* of these 'old ways' were. What?"

A grin split Harry's face. "You said 'later'."

"Hmph. Well, that still remains to be seen." But the longer he spoke, the calmer she became. What he said *felt* true—felt like the Harry she had fallen in love with. She relaxed a bit against the banquette before sitting forward abruptly. "Rey is the one that told you to stay away from me? To break up with me?"

Hurt, was quickly followed by anger. At the rate her emotions were going today, she was convinced she would end up with permanent nervous system damage.

"That was my idea," he murmured, and then hurriedly added, "but he was all for it. It was his idea to have me rebound quickly and publicly, so that it looked like we had just been a fling."

"Then you sent me the pictures." Becca thought back to the evening she had told Amelia about them. Amelia was convinced something was out of place, and she'd been right. "You stopped talking to Amelia, too. She didn't have anything to do with your cover."

Harry looked sad. "Deceiving her was almost as hard as lying to you. But she was connected... not just through you, but through her relationship with Dan. I had to make it appear like the new life that I had created with you... a normal life... was gone. These people don't trust anyone. Even less after the smuggling route disappeared and they lost all their bank accounts in the money laundering bust. The only thing we had going for us was that they were desperate for cash. They couldn't move product because they had no way of paying to set up new operations. Plus, the world thought Katie Olivera was in witness protection so nobody wanted to do business with them."

"You're losing me. What does that have to do with you?"

Harry took a large swallow of the wine. "When I left the hotel in the Bahamas, the agreement between me and the Feds was that I would make a concerted effort to do all the things I had in my twenties. I was supposed to keep it up until an opportunity presented itself where the FBI could use me. The deal was they would set up a team, with new leads." His mouth twisted. "They told me that, after the days at the Royal, Foster was too close to the situation. Everyone agreed it would be best if he weren't involved. He promised that while we waited for the opportunity, he would keep an eye on you. He's definitely done that." Harry's lip curled.

It was ironic to hear Harry use words like 'we' in reference to the FBI. When she first met Harry, he had an extreme aversion to law enforcement, and now he was working undercover with them. But what brought the smile to her face was how jealous he sounded.

Harry's story also meant that while Rey hadn't been lying to her the whole time, he certainly left a lot of important things out. Rey might not have been aware *specifically* what Harry was doing in Key West, but once he saw him with his father, he must have figured it out. That explained the odd camaraderie between Harry and Rey the night she was attacked.

"But you couldn't have known something would come along, or how long it would take."

He gave her a sad smile. "It was a risk I had to take. At the very least, my hope was that the cartel would see the break from me... I hoped once they saw you resume your normal life, they wouldn't see you as a threat. You and I showing up at the Royal was the final straw with them. One coincidence too far."

"So, if whatever this was today," she waved her hand, "hadn't happened, you would have stayed away forever?" Becca's chest clenched.

"I'd like to say I'm that noble, but when I saw you in Miami, my resolve flew out the window. I knew I should stay away...

had to stay away... for your own safety, but I was too selfish. I just couldn't."

That shouldn't make her tingle but it did, and then she remembered. "What about Allison?"

Harry set his wine glass down and turned his body to fully face her. "There was nothing between us."

"I saw you together! There were definitely feelings there."

He grimaced. "She did develop feelings. It made things extremely awkward at times, but it was part of the cover. She hoped it would become something more. In a way, I felt terrible for having to pretend with her even though she knew it was fake." His face hardened. "And then I remembered that she was helping a drug cartel, and my qualms disappeared. I could have strangled her when she told Andréas that you and Rey were dating. She knew what she was doing, the threat she was creating, but I couldn't react and give it all away. I called my contact at the FBI as soon as possible—I hoped they would give you protection—that's why I came to your cottage that night and again the night of the fire... but I was too late."

"Allison? No way!" Becca pictured the vivacious woman. "What could she possibly do for them?"

"She served as their art buyer at auctions. They could be blind buyers that way." Becca's confusion must have shown because he continued, "Let me back up a little. After the money laundering was exposed last August, the cartel had serious cash flow problems. Without access to the majority of their accounts, they were desperate. Wealthy individuals, and even some corporations who are looking to hold investments without paying taxes, buy art. They keep what they buy... paintings, sculptures, etc... in a freeport zone. They get cash off their books and buy items that could appreciate in value. If it's never taken out of these freeport zones, they never have to pay duties or taxes on them. There are tons of them around, seven in Florida alone. Essentially they are warehouses, but they have this special tax designation." Harry shrugged. "Who knows? Possibly, at some point, Olivera would have taken the art out and paid the taxes. Allison said he would email her which auctions to go to, and that he particularly preferred religious themes. However, once his other assets were gone, the art investment was all he had left. He needed to liquidate it."

"Did Allison know whom she was buying for?"

"She claims she didn't at first. But the Feds think it's a lie. She definitely knew who it was at some point and kept working for them."

Becca learned during her ex-husband's court case that even if Allison wasn't part of the cartel's regular business, the fact that she used criminally acquired funds made her guilty.

"So why did you have to date her? If it wasn't a real relationship, then she must have known you were working against the cartel."

Harry's face relaxed, and he gave her a little smile. Probably because she no longer looked like she wanted to murder him. "Luck was actually with us. About a month after I last saw you, Allison was pulled over in Miami for a DUI. When they searched her car, they found a large quantity of cocaine, enough that they believe she was selling not just using. Allison may present as sweet and innocent. Trust me, she's not. The cartel most likely found her through her supplier. When she found out she was facing a hefty sentence, she realized she might have something of worth she could use as a bargaining chip."

"Flipping on the cartel is a pretty big risk to take."

"It was," he agreed. "But rather than face decades in a federal prison, she got a deal. She will go into custody under a new name and just serve a handful of years."

Becca nodded. That was essentially what Jake had negotiated, too. "So…"

"I had been spending a lot of time with my father."

"I noticed." She hadn't intended it to sound so bitter.

"I had to. He was my best option for establishing this disreputable persona. Plus, he had the connections I originally thought might lead to Olivera. I needed to put myself back into that shadow world my father lives in. He rarely gets his hands directly dirty, but they aren't clean either. I learned from Sean that my father had done business with Olivera before, setting them up with Sean. But after the fiasco in the Bahamas, they weren't eager to use him again. I had to be close by to find an opportunity."

Harry ran a hand over his face, and for the first time during the conversation, Becca recognized what a toll the whole experience had taken on him. She thought about what his newfound camaraderie with James must have cost him. Harry had shared his belief that his father was responsible for his mother's death.

Becca reached for his hand and gave it a gentle squeeze. The corner of his eye twitched, and suddenly he was squeezing her hand almost too tight. She met his eyes and couldn't look away. The air heated between them.

"I missed you." His words were quiet and full of emotion.

Her chest ached. "I missed you, too."

She hadn't wanted to admit it. The words spilled out before she could stop them. He shifted slightly closer, and as much as she longed to lose herself in his arms, forgetting everything else, she knew it was important they finish this conversation. There had to be honesty between them.

"Tell me about James."

Her words worked like cold water, breaking the connection between them. Harry's gaze fell to his wine glass, and he fiddled with the stem. "It was even worse than I imagined it would be. I don't know if it's because so much time had passed since I had seen him, or if it was because I finally glimpsed what life could have been like. But the more time I spent with him, the more determined I became that when Olivera was arrested, I would be sure James was, too." His voice was hard. "He's slick. He acts behind the scenes directing everything. He sets up the meetings, makes the introductions, takes his cut, and slips away. Not this time."

Ahh. Now it makes sense.

"When the FBI notified me that they had a plan, I knew instantly how I could use him. The FBI prepped Allison for her role... to everyone, including my father, we were a couple. I had to pretend to be with her for a few months to make my father believe it was real before I could approach him about brokering a deal. I was worried that if it was too soon there was no way he would buy that I wanted to act as a go between, with his help of course, to broker a sale of the Olivera art. It must be his narcissism, because he never even questioned it. Of course his son would come to him."

"It's just... probably I'm reading more into it than I should, but..."

"But what?"

"The day Allison came to the gallery with her boss, Hathaway... oh my god! Is he really an FBI agent?"

"No, he's her boss at the museum. For the plan to work, they sealed her arrest record, and she kept living her normal life. Why?"

"That day... you came to pick her up at the gallery..." Even knowing that it had been fake, the memory still left a sour taste in her mouth. "Later, James came by. He... he had a lot of weird questions, or... not even really questions, more insinuations." Becca tried to remember what James had said. "I don't remember his exact words, but the feeling I got was he was checking up on you. Trying to see if we were still together or how I felt about you."

Harry's face paled and then flushed red. "He came to the gallery that day to question you? Did he frighten you?"

She shook her head, even though James had left her very unsettled that day. It must have shown in her expression.

"Becca, I'm so sorry. I never should have gone there that day. The whole point was to get you off everyone's radar, and I almost ruined it." He grasped her hands tightly again. "I saw him that day... walking on Duval. He was cagey about what he was doing. The tourist scene around Duval isn't his thing. I assumed it was about the deal. That he was suspicious of me. Up to that point, he wouldn't give me any information about when the Oliveras were coming to Key West to finalize the sale."

"It's all right, really. He seemed to like my answers."

Harry looked thoughtful. "Yeah, he must have. That night he told me the meet had been set and Olivera was coming in on his boat. He said it was time for me to let the buyer know."

"How did you find a buyer? You don't exactly have a background in art... oh, Allison."

"Exactly. I told James that she had another buyer she worked for who was looking for a deal and a quick one. I presented it as Allison thought she could make two customers happy and therefore twice her commission. The other buyer was another undercover FBI agent. The deal was contingent on the seller being present at the sale. It was an unusual request, and we weren't sure Olivera would go for it. Ironically, it was the advertisements for your exhibition that did it."

"The Santiago cross?"

"Contrary to everything else he does, Juan Olivera fancies himself a religious man. In addition to his investment art, he ordered Allison to procure religious objets d'art in the past, for his personal collection. Your timing couldn't have been better if we planned it." His face darkened. "Except, once again you were in the cross hairs. James reminded them that you worked at the gallery. He's a big fan of yours, well your looks anyway."

Becca grunted, remembering how he had touched her hair, "Gross!"

"I'm not going to lie, there were a couple of times I wanted to punch him in the face, but I had to keep up the façade that you meant nothing to me. After what you've just told me, I'm wondering if it was a test."

"Why did Olivera steal the cross? He could have just bought it at auction. Seems like a stupid thing to do. It brought the FBI to Key West."

Harry reached forward and tucked one of her curls behind her ear. She couldn't help the shiver that skated down her body.

Pay attention, Becca!

"For one thing, even with the sale of the art they had stored in the freeport, Olivera wasn't going to have enough to cover the projected price the cross was supposed to bring. He needed the bulk of his money to get his drug routes back up and running." Harry shrugged. "But, part of it might just have been he wanted it, and it was an expedient way of getting it. Find a petty criminal then kill him to cover his tracks. That's minor compared to some of the stuff he's suspected of doing."

"He would have gotten away with it, too. Candice spotted it on the boat when Andréas took her there. Rey said there was nothing… wait! Was he lying?"

Harry grimaced. "I don't know anything about that. Foster and I didn't have a lot of interaction, but yeah, if they thought it might endanger their ability to arrest him on U.S. soil. With boats, there's always the question of international waters. I'm sure if Olivera's captain saw the Coast Guard coming, they would have beelined it the three miles."

Harry might not talk to Rey, but Becca did. They were definitely going to have words about it later!

"So, that's what today was? The transfer of the art collection at that warehouse?"

"That warehouse is the freeport. They substituted all the workers with agents."

Suddenly, Harry's intense stare was back. "Why were you there today, Becca? Were you looking for Foster?"

"Rey? Why would I be looking for Rey?" Her mouth formed

an O. "Rey and I aren't dating. I never intended to pretend. It came out when Allison assumed… and then with everything that was happening between us…" She felt her cheeks heat. "I was embarrassed and maybe a little glad you were jealous."

Harry's eyes blazed hot, and he pressed a fierce, quick kiss against her lips. "Then why were you there?"

The time for prevarication was over. If they were to have a future, they had to be honest. "I wanted to warn you."

"Warn me? Why?"

Becca could see in his face he knew the answer to the question, and she also understood he needed to hear the words out loud. "Because, you jerk, even though you broke my heart, and it looked like you had become a criminal," she said as she scooted closer to him. His finger reached out to stroke down her cheek. "I still love you and couldn't bear the thought of you going to jail."

"I love you, Becca. I'm so sorry I lied but…"

"Shh," she said, pressing fully against him. "The rest of the story can wait."

25

"Becca?"

She paused in the middle of pulling her dress over her head. "Oh, no," Becca moaned. Amelia said she would be back for breakfast, but Becca hadn't thought it would be this early.

"Harry," Becca hissed, shaking his foot. "Wake up!" She shook his leg harder when he mumbled grumpily, his eyes still closed. "Get up! Amelia's back."

His eye cracked open. "I'm pretty sure she's not going to be shocked."

Becca glared at him for a minute, her hands on her hips, before ripping the sheet off him.

"You aren't her favorite person in the world right now. So, yeah, she's going to have something to say about finding you here."

Harry scrubbed a hand down his face, but didn't make any move to get up. She didn't have time for his normal, slow wake-up routine. "I'll go up and stall her while you get dressed."

"Becca?" Amelia's voice approached the door. "Are you still in bed? I brought donuts. We have a lot to talk about. The whole island is buzzing with the bust at the airport."

"Just getting dressed. I'll be right up." Becca winced. She meant her voice to sound carefree but the shrill tone hurt her own ears. Harry covered his mouth to hold in a laugh.

"Take your time, honey. I'll start the coffee." The sympathetic tone in her friend's voice made Becca feel guilty. Amelia must have assumed it was all the stress finally getting to her, not that she'd just passed a rather fantastic night.

Harry widened his eyes at her and pantomimed drinking. Becca rolled hers in return but obligingly called out, "Could you make some extra coffee... I could use it."

"Sure thing."

Becca waited till she heard the sound of Amelia climbing the steps back to the main level of her boat before she pinned Harry with a stare. "You are going to have a lot of explaining to do."

Harry looked up from where he was doing the clasp of his belt. "How mad has she been?"

"Well, let's see. The man she thinks of like family disappeared on her and then showed back up acting like an ass, all while helping his father who had screwed over many of her friends. Oh, yeah, and broke her best friend's heart."

Becca now understood why he had done it, but there was still the echo of pain in her voice. Harry's face grew concerned, and he took the step that closed the distance between them, folding her in his arms and holding her tight against him.

"I'm so sorry it had to be that way."

"I know." She gave a weak smile. "Really, I do. It's just..."

"Going to take time before you trust me again?" His eyes were sad. "I understand. I'm going to make it up to you."

"You don't have to make anything up. You did what you had to do to keep me and my family safe." She lay her cheek against his chest.

When they were together like this, her body trusted him. Her inner self-doubts, however, were trying to throw up roadblocks. Not until she had final confirmation from Rey could she allow herself to give her heart again completely. She smiled realizing that she didn't doubt Rey would confirm everything Harry had said, and that meant she was already well on her way to trusting him again.

"What are you smiling at?"

"Just you. Oh, and imagining the uncomfortable breakfast you have ahead of you." She laughed as she pulled away. "See you up top."

The galley kitchen and lounge were empty when Becca reached the top of the stairs which surprised her. Despite what she said to Harry about being on his own, she planned to lay the groundwork with Amelia.

The box of donuts was open on the counter. So, after pouring her coffee, she grabbed one and went on deck to look for Amelia. Sure enough, her friend was seated in her favorite chair, her face tipped back to the sun. Becca tugged her gray braid playfully to get her attention.

"You are in a suspiciously good mood." Amelia squinted at her and then gestured to her mug. "Just coffee in there?"

Becca choked a little on her bite of donut. "Yes."

"No Irish in it?"

"I gave up alcohol for breakfast a couple of years ago. It led to some rash decisions."

Amelia grinned at her. "Good decisions though. I'm getting a refill and another donut, do you…"

Amelia stopped abruptly, her face going bright red. Angry eyes landed on Becca.

"Just what the hell is going on here?"

Harry offered her a half-grimace, half-smile.

"Morning, Amelia."

Amelia glowered at Becca, refusing to look in Harry's direction for several uncomfortable seconds. Animosity radiated off her friend, and Becca was worried the older woman would actually throw Harry overboard. She suspected the extreme anger was fueled by much of the same hurt Becca had experienced.

"There were reasons," Harry began.

"No!" Amelia's hand cut through the air. "I don't want to hear it." Harry moved out of the way as Amelia barreled past him.

Becca sent Harry an I-told-you-so look. He sighed, his shoulders slumped, and followed the older woman back into the boat. Becca took another bite of her donut, trying to decide if she should go mediate. The sound of glass breaking made up her mind.

"Everyone okay in here?" Becca asked, half-joking. Shards of glass were on the floor next to where Harry stood. He looked calm; however, Amelia's chest heaved as if she had just finished a marathon.

She turned to Becca, stabbing her finger in the air. "What is wrong with you? After everything that has happened, you couldn't keep your clothes on? Dan told me what he overheard at The Conch House the other night." Becca opened her mouth to explain but stopped when she realized Amelia's eyes were full of tears. "Why?" she cried, and then faced Harry repeating herself, "Why?"

Becca and Harry exchanged a glance. Becca had known Amelia would be angry, but the woman was more upset than Becca had seen her. Amelia was so cavalier about her own love affairs it had never occurred to Becca that this would be her reaction. Amelia paced toward the door to leave, frenetically stroking her long gray braid, muttering. "This is ridiculous. I can't even believe... I just... I can't believe it."

When she drew level with Becca at the door, she stopped. "You might find it easy to forgive and forget, but don't expect me to go down that path with you."

"Amelia?" Becca reached out a gentle hand to stop her friend. "Let him explain. Please."

Harry's voice was low behind them. "I know I have explaining to do, and I'll do it. I only need you to give me the chance."

Amelia finally broke her stare with Becca. She pursed her lips, stomped to the banquette, and sat down. She clasped her hands and rested them on the table. "Let's hear it then."

Becca nodded to Harry before joining her friend at the table.

"Last summer..." he began.

"I haven't seen you but once in passing since last August! Last conversation I have with you is when you were off on your trip with this one," Amelia interrupted. "I genuinely thought the two of you might come back engaged. Instead, you ditched her in the Bahamas. *And,* I find out you've been lying about James being alive." She curled her lip. "You show up back here, acting like you're a happy little family, as if nothing over the last twenty years had happened." Amelia's breathing had picked up pace again. "And just what the hell is this?" She waved her hand toward Becca.

In spite of the tension, Becca couldn't help the warmth that spread through her. She'd never had anyone defend her before, and in the span of twelve hours, she had found out that she really did have people in her life willing to fight for her. She refocused on Amelia's words. "I've seen that young girl you're here in town with. Flaunting it in front of Becca, like you didn't break her heart." Amelia shook her head and directed her next words to Becca. "I really thought you had more sense than that, girl."

Becca flushed a little, even though she knew the truth, she was aware what her friend was thinking. "It's not what it looks like."

Amelia snorted.

"Seriously," Becca persisted. "Do you remember last August when I came back from the Bahamas, and got those pictures on my phone... you kept saying that it was completely out of character for Harry. That something else must be going on... you said that even in his," she made a face at Harry, "days of running around, he never wanted his picture in the paper? Suddenly, within two weeks there are multiple pictures. You wanted me to investigate it, find out who sent them to me, because you *knew* something was off. Just a week ago you agreed with me!"

Amelia's face lost a little of its angry color but she stayed quiet.

"Is it my turn yet?" Harry asked when Amelia didn't speak. She lifted her chin as if she didn't care, but her expression was much more relaxed than when she first sat down. Harry leaned his shoulders back against the wall and arched a brow at her, waiting.

"Are you going to talk or not?" Amelia challenged.

Harry hid a grin. "Can I at least get a donut first?"

"Don't push your luck, boy. Now start talking."

It took a while for Harry to recount the story. Amelia stopped him often, peppering him with questions that Becca should have asked the night before. She had been too caught up in emotion to think clearly. The more Harry spoke, the clearer the whole undercover operation became. It also became painfully clear that Rey had known all along that Harry hadn't betrayed her. That hurt.

"What now?" Amelia asked when he was done.

"Now it's over." Harry shrugged.

Amelia glanced between him and Becca "What about the two of you?"

"Amelia!" Becca cried.

Harry crossed the small kitchen to pull Becca to her feet. Out of the corner of her eye, Becca could see Amelia's satisfied smile. Harry pressed a kiss against her lips before saying, "Now, I never let her out of my sight again."

LATER THAT AFTERNOON, BECCA HAD AN APPOINTMENT TO MEET the fire department's arson investigator and retrieve some of her belongings from the cottage. When she exited onto the porch, she squeezed her eyes tight, more to stop the tears that had formed than in reaction to the bright sun. She had been lucky. The damage was primarily limited to the kitchen and the front room. Her paintings were ruined by smoke and water, but the plastic bins she kept in her closet with her important papers had been mostly spared. *I'm lucky*, she repeated to herself when sadness threatened again. She had survived. Harry had saved her… still, the home she had built for herself was ruined. She squared her shoulders.

I'll be all right. It can be fixed.

"Since the FBI is fairly certain who is responsible, we will be closing the investigation soon," the fire department official was saying. Becca nodded not really listening. She knew who was to blame, but adding arson charges wasn't going to make any difference to Juan Olivera now. The man handed her a folder full of papers and began explaining the steps she needed to take to file her insurance, but she had stopped listening. Rey stood at the entrance to her garden taking in the damage, hands shoved in his pocket.

"What a mess," he said when she joined him.

Becca looked at the broken glass from the windows littering the porch and the hole covered by a tarp on the roof. "Yeah, it could have been worse. They said there isn't any structural damage, but I'm going to have to find somewhere to stay while I sort out the insurance and repairs."

Rey gave a terse nod and then walked around to the rear of the house. Becca frowned at his back. If anyone had the right to be mad, it was her. Why was he acting like the injured party?

Her eyes narrowed. He had stopped by the boxes the fire marshal had helped her carry out. "I had an interesting conversation last night." Rey ignored her, continuing to inspect her belongings. "Rey!"

He looked up; his expression was blank.

Becca arched an eyebrow. "Don't give me that face. I'm really mad at you. With good reason! You lied to me!"

"You couldn't stay out of it! You put the entire operation in jeopardy. You didn't trust me and took off half-cocked. You almost got yourself killed in the process!" He exploded waving his arm at her ruined home. "Even after they attacked you in your home, you kept going, putting yourself in danger."

"I didn't put myself..."

"Did you or did you not drive toward where gunshots had just been fired? Push past two armed agents? It was reckless and stupid." Rey's jaw clenched.

Okay, well put like that, it sounded bad.

"I know it was... now. I really do. But I wasn't thinking about that at the time. I needed to..."

"You were going to Brennan." There was no point in denying it. "You are a smart woman, Becca. You created a life for yourself, but you have a blind spot when it comes to him. Look at that life now."

"Wait a minute! That's not fair. My instincts about him were correct. Didn't he just help you take down the Olivera cartel? Not to mention his own father."

"That's true," he conceded. "But you have to ask yourself, how was it he slotted so easily into the criminal world. Was able to convince them that he was one of them? You always say that you can't trust anyone. What has he done but lie? How can you build a life with someone like that?"

Becca's memory flashed to Harry's eyes when he told her his reasons for why he had done all the things he had over the last ten months. Becca didn't know how to describe why she trusted Harry the way she did, in words Rey would understand. There had been months when she doubted her instincts, her judgment. Now, she knew she hadn't been wrong.

"He lied to protect me." Becca felt the last bit of her heart, the part she had kept back, afraid to truly trust, expand as she realized her words were true. "He put his own happiness at stake, to make sure that I was protected. Even to the point of making me hate him."

Becca could tell by the way Rey shook his head, he didn't approve. She didn't need or expect him to. If it had been one of her friends telling her this, she would have had her placed on a mental health hold. But Becca couldn't deny what she knew in her heart.

Rey's responses confirmed everything Harry had said, which meant she'd been right all along about Harry. He was exactly who she thought he was. "I know you don't understand, Rey. I hope someday you will, that you will find someone that you would do anything for. Maybe even bend *all* the rules for?" She poked him teasingly trying to lighten the mood. His face eased a little. "Did I get you fired?"

"No, the FBI was happy enough with the bust. Fortunately, I was able to smooth things over."

"I'm glad. I never wanted to hurt you. I truly care about you."

Rey's lips twisted sadly for a second, and he looked away. After a few beats, his face cleared, and he rolled his eyes dramatically. "I've said it before, and I'm sure I'll say it again, you will be the death of me one day. Brennan deserves you."

Becca smiled at his teasing, but she still wanted an explanation.

"Why didn't you tell me he was working with the FBI? That you'd placed him undercover with James? You let me believe he had given up on me."

"I couldn't tell you. It was important that you look," he hesitated, "heartbroken. It had to appear genuine. I'm sorry you had to go through that. I really am, but I honestly believe your life is better without Brennan in it. The reason you didn't tell him the truth about me is the same reason I couldn't tell you what was going on. We were both protecting people we cared about. And the fact of the matter is, I didn't know for sure. After I handed him off to the agents in the Bahamas, I was no longer read in on what they were doing."

"Really? You thought it was a coincidence he was suddenly back with his father." Becca accepted the explanation, but she wasn't letting him off the hook completely.

Rey rubbed a hand along his jaw. "Okay, that's fair. When I saw him with his father here in Key West, I figured it was most likely part of his assignment, but I didn't know anything about the museum girl. I genuinely thought they were an item."

Becca stared at him. Rey wasn't stupid. He had to have known the relationship with Allison was fake if Harry's whole reason for being undercover was for Becca. She sighed. After all his years undercover, Rey was an excellent liar, and she would most likely never know the whole story. She tilted her head to the side considering him. In all fairness, how could she stay mad at him for his omissions when he seemed to forgive her interference?

"So, friends?"

He stared at her for several long seconds, and Becca's stomach clenched. She meant it when she said she cared about him and didn't want to lose his friendship. Was he going to say no?

Finally, he grinned. "Friends." He stuck out his hand, at the last second pulling it back. "I'm still not a hundred percent about Brennan."

"You will be." Becca smiled back. "Give it time. However, there is one more thing I wanted to ask you."

Rey looked at her warily.

"Hey, it hasn't all been completely one sided. You've gotten a lot of wings out of this relationship," she laughed.

"True, very true."

"And," Becca said archly, "if you play your cards right, there's a certain blonde that I think you are going to need help managing."

Rey smirked, "I've got that covered."

"If you say so." Rey had no idea what he was getting himself into with Dana.

"What is it you want, Becca?"

"The Santiago cross. What's going to happen with it? Have they retrieved it from Olivera's boat yet?"

"They seized the boat last night, and the cross is going into evidence. Without his father, Andréas fell apart once he was in custody. He's trying to make a deal for himself, trading what he knows about the Columbian drug trade for leniency. He won't get much." Rey put his hands on his hips. "Olivera, for all of his evil, thought of himself as a religious man. When he saw the press about the cross, he convinced himself it was a sign from God that he should, in fact, go to Key West and be present at the deal Brennan had put together. Apparently, up to that point, he hadn't been sure it wasn't a trap."

Becca nodded. "Harry told me about that. It's mind-boggling though that someone like him could be so self-deluded he thought God wanted him to have it." Becca remembered how passionate Juan Olivera had been when he had spoken to her at the exhibition. "It's insane."

"Well, yeah, he was. He'd have to be to do all the things he has. Anyway, he saw it and had to have it. Andréas wasn't happy about it. One of the investigators I talked to said he's now convinced that his father's death was divine retribution." Rey grimaced.

"Did they…" Becca hesitated, not sure if she wanted the

answer. "Did he mention me? Did they realize I was still here in Key West?"

"It doesn't seem that way. Olivera didn't even realize who you were at the exhibition. It wasn't until later when you showed up at the hotel with Dana. That Davenport woman spotted me and revealed my identity to Andréas, who in turn informed his father. Combine that with the fact you suddenly showed up at his hotel... he suspected you knew about his plans. And since you have a history of blundering in and ruining them... let's just say he was deeply unhappy." Rey gave her a speaking glance. He had told her to stay away from the investigation, and she hadn't. But how could she have known they would all come together at the same time and place?

Becca grimaced. "I guess I wasn't as discreet as I'd meant to be."

"Somehow it got back to him, probably through James Brennan, that you and I were an item. Most likely after he saw us at the restaurant. Anyway, Brennan Sr. and Olivera started to think that it was highly likely that you were working with the FBI. That's why they attacked your house the other night. They wanted to get rid of you for good."

Becca closed her eyes briefly and blew out a stream of air. "Candice recognized you, but it was Allison that told him we were a thing. It doesn't matter now. I'm glad it's over." Her eyes popped open. "It *is* over, right?"

"With Juan dead, and his remaining son in prison, their organization has been broken. It looks like you and Owen will be in the clear."

"What about Harry? Won't they know he double-crossed them?"

"On that, James Brennan is more an issue. He's not talking at all. I have no idea what the final charges will be against him, or how much time he will get. Interpol wants a crack at him, too, so I wouldn't worry too much."

Becca nodded satisfied. "When will the Clarkes get their cross back?"

"You are like a dog with a bone." Rey shook his head, laughing. "I'm not sure. I'm trying to expedite it because the guilty party is dead, but it's not going to be as quick as you want."

"Rude. Don't love your dog analogy, but I'll let it pass this once. I'd love to be able to give the cross back to Miss Helen before she…"

"Dies?"

"I was trying to say it nicely," she scolded.

"I'll see what I can do. If nothing else, maybe we can get an agent to go with you, and you can show it to her."

"That would be wonderful, Rey, thank you!"

Rey shrugged and hoisted up two of her boxes. "I'll help you carry these to your car."

With Rey's help, it only took a couple of trips to load her remaining belongings into the car.

"That's pretty much all I arrived here with." Becca's joke fell flat as she looked again at what remained of her cottage.

Rey followed her gaze and then looked down at her. "Do you know what you are going to do?"

"Start over. I'm getting good at it."

"And lover boy? I'm assuming after his grand gesture you're giving him another shot?"

Becca only smiled.

Rey rolled his eyes.

"Harry and I are meeting Amelia and Dana at the Tiki Bar by the marina later. I'd love it if you'd join us."

Rey shook his head. "I've got to head back to work. Ton of paperwork."

Becca chewed her lip. "See you soon?"

Rey pulled her into a hug. "You aren't getting rid of me that easily. I hate to admit it, but I've gotten attached to you and that kid of yours."

"Good." Becca gave her tiny garden, littered with debris, one last look, only to see a streak of orange dart under the steps.

"Furball!"

It took a lot of coaxing before Becca finally secured her pet. She cuddled the cat under her chin and was rewarded with a strong purr when she scratched her ears. Furball was unhappy about the carrier Rey retrieved from the house, but finally acquiesced with minimal yowling. With a last wave to Rey, she placed the carrier on the front seat and drove back to where Harry was waiting.

THE SUN WAS SETTING IN ITS INTENSE SHADES OF GOLD AND lavender when Becca parked her car in the lot of the marina. She paused, her hand resting on the top of the car, as she took in the view. It was hard to believe that less than two years ago she had stepped away from her cruise ship, her friends, her entire life… and met Amelia only steps away from where she now stood.

She couldn't help the smile that spread across her face as she gathered Furball and a bag with all she needed for the night. A chance meeting over breakfast rum runners had led to a whole new life, and she would forever be grateful.

Her smile only grew when she saw her group of friends waiting for her at the tiny bar, and happiness suffused her. The last two years hadn't always been easy, but in many ways, she had found everything she had been looking for… people who cared about and believed in her and that she loved in return.

Harry stepped away from the group to meet her, taking the cat carrier, and putting a rum runner in her hand. Becca shifted her bag to the other shoulder and took a long sip of the sweet drink.

"How did it go?" Harry's free arm wrapped around her waist,

and he kissed the top of her head. She leaned against his side careful not to bump Furball.

"It was fine. The house is a bit of a mess, but it can be fixed."

"You can share with me," Dana piped up. "If you start returning my phone calls, that is."

The arm around her waist tightened, eliciting another smile. "It's okay. I have a place."

Harry bent his head to whisper in her ear, "Always."

ABOUT THE AUTHOR

Kate Breitfeller writes character driven mysteries full of romance and adventure—perfect for an escape from reality! The Caribbean Series is Kate's first foray into fiction, as she has previously written nonfiction as well as several published articles dedicated to the antics of her family.

Kate currently lives on the Space Coast of Florida with her husband, two sons, and rescue dog, Charlie. Whenever she gets a chance, Kate escapes to the beach with a good book and a fruity cocktail… because everything's better at the beach!

Kate loves talking to her readers! Sign up for her newsletter Katebreitfeller.com for updates and subscriber only content or you can find her at all of these places:

ALSO BY KATE BREITFELLER

The Caribbean Series

Becca Jumps Ship

Becca Dives In

Made in United States
Orlando, FL
05 September 2023